Madness and Insanity

Anthony Squiers

Irish Eye Publishing
Grand Rapids, MI

Irish Eye Publications
801 Broadway Ave. NW #450
Grand Rapids, MI 49504

Squiers, Anthony, 1978—
Madness and Insanity

LCCN: 2009932242

ISBN: 978-0-615-30220-1

Printed in the United States of American

To Rich and Teri Frantz,

for making poets out of philistines.

If it wasn't for you, I would have never given two shits about
literature.

I was supposed to go to the University of Michigan, but I managed to fuck that up pretty good. My father is on the alumni committee and was pulling some strings to get me into the PhD program in Political Science. All I had to do was fill out the application and go to the interview. The application was no problem at all. It was the interview that was tricky. I got there forty-five minutes late and was slightly intoxicated. Actually, to be fair, I was an hour late and really drunk. Fortunately though, I was only a little bit stoned, or things might have really gotten ugly. I don't want to bog you down in details, but I really did make an ass of myself. But, at least I tried; a lesser person would have never shown up under those circumstances.

Recollections of that day were crowding my thoughts as I was speeding across the Atlantic in an Airbus A310 headed for the United Kingdom. I was steadily draining a bottle of Beefeaters that I bought at the duty free shop in Detroit. I could feel the warm spike of the alcohol sailing its way up into my shoulders and the back of my neck, gracefully washing away the stress and tension that had accumulated there.

I knew that my father would be pissed when he found out what happened in that interview. I had a delicate situation on my hands. I needed to think hard about how to explain myself. That's precisely what I was doing on the way home, when I got arrested for drunk driving. Actually, the drunk driving arrest may have been a good thing because it made my father completely forget about the interview fiasco. I was happy about that, but he still had plenty to say about the arrest. Although, I don't know what the big deal was; it wasn't as if it were the first time I'd been arrested or anything.

It's a long flight to the UK from Michigan, a little over seven hours. I had a window seat; but, I kept the blind pulled shut, blocking out the seemingly endless stretches of sky and water on the other side of the window. It was sunny that day, gorgeous in fact. But, the bright light formed a murderous combination with the gin and the five or six sleeping pills I washed down with it. I hadn't planned on drinking so much or taking so many sleeping pills for that matter, but I didn't have much of a choice. These were stressful times and I had to get some sleep and put these memories behind me. To make matters worse, the asshole in the seat next to me kept trying to talk to me about pig futures and industrial light fixtures or something. He was one of those big, fat, boisterous Texans that wear gigantic belt buckles, drink whisky straight and always refer to people as 'sonsabitches.' He was long winded and

1

talked like he was some kind of a big shot who knew everything. I couldn't stand listening to him. He reminded me of my father.

After the drunk driving arrest, my father gave me a two-hour monologue that pretty much centered on how I was selfish and ruining his political aspirations, which meant his running for the Michigan Supreme Court. Ever since he was a kid, he has always been driven by a string of self-serving aspirations like that. It was like he was trying to prove something, but I could never understand what. It wasn't like he was short or anything. I never really got a good look at his penis, so that might have been the problem, but whatever it was it was absolute bullshit and I didn't give a shit about any of it.

I hated listening to my father's lectures. I wanted to get up and leave. I wanted to tell him to go fuck himself. But, I never did. Don't get me wrong. It wasn't out of respect that I stayed. I sat there and took it like a dummy because, as crass as it was, I wanted his money. If I didn't need his money, I wouldn't have listened to a word he said. But, I was broke and not at all interested in getting a job. My father made our relationship very clear, if I wanted his money I had to do what he wanted me to.

But what did all that matter to me, then, while I was being propelled through space at thirty-eight thousand feet above the world. Actually it mattered a lot. It was the reason I was on the plane in the first place. Since the University of Michigan thing didn't work out, I had to go to school in Britain. My father 'talked' me into it. Well basically, I didn't have much of a choice. Like I said, he was footing the bill and that's what he thought was best. So I went. He probably wanted me so far away because he felt I was a liability to his political career. I guess I didn't care that much though. Getting away from him seemed like a good idea from where I was standing too. I didn't mind going to the University of Manchester. I had some friends who went on exchange there a few years earlier and they said the nightlife was great and they had gotten laid a bunch of times. That's why I applied there in the first place. Besides, from what I heard my program was supposed to be pretty good anyway.

My father bought me a plane ticket three days after I pled guilty. Three weeks later, at the end of August he and my mother took me to the airport. My mother was nervous for me. She didn't say that she was, but she told me several times to be careful. She's like that. My father really didn't say much. He just gave me a firm handshake and nodded his head. I don't even know why he came. He probably just wanted to make sure I got on the plane.

The last thing I remember before the alcohol and pills forced my eyes shut and the familiar darkness of a stupor robbed me of my consciousness were these thoughts…these thoughts and a fuzzy glimpse of that loudmouth Texan's big, bulbous, inebriated, red nose as he was trying to talk to me again.

Simplicity, Simplicity, Simplicity

When I got off the plane I was weaving all over the place.

"I got to straighten up," I said to myself.

I stumbled down the tunnel that led from the airplane, down a ramp and followed the lethargic mob that trickled from the plane to the luggage carousels. I needed to get my duffle bag and suit case. That's all I had, two parcels and a carry-on. They couldn't have possibly contained everything I owned, but there inside those three bags was everything material that I needed: clothes, some toiletries and a few books. Everything else I owned had somehow become superfluous. Packing those bags was an actualizing life moment. Looking down at them I could hear the words of Thoreau resonate gently through my mind, "Simplicity, simplicity, simplicity."

What a fucking crock that is.

I hated simplicity. Simplicity is for amebas. Complexity, chaos and bedlam are for humankind. If I could have taken twenty bags, I would have done it. I would have shoved them full of porno magazines, CDs and drug paraphernalia.

Once I had my bags it was on to passport control and customs. After customs, the only thing separating me from my inevitable future was an automatic, sliding-glass door. I could see it there waiting for me. It was no more than five or six steps away. I had arrived. I walked on toward it, not confidently, but not reluctantly either. The doors parted and I passed through stopping a few feet beyond the threshold. I needed a moment to adjust.

Everything looked so foreign, which of course makes sense since I was actually in a foreign country. I guess I knew that it would be different, but I hadn't really thought about that much before I arrived. There was rain coming down in a persistent drizzle. Strange accents drifted past me while I stood watching tiny clown cars of unfamiliar makes and models and double-decker buses speeding off on the wrong side of the road. It was all new and strange to me, but I really liked being there despite the fact I didn't have a clue what I was doing or where I had to go.

Before I left, I had signed up to attend an orientation course for international students and received a letter from the University confirming my reservation. However, I was never given its location. I tried several times by phone and email to get the address, but no one I talked to seemed to know it.

I decided to go to the only University of Manchester address I had, the accommodation office. It was a Sunday and I figured that no one would be there, but it was my only starting point. I took my bags down to the row of taxis parked near the curb and hopped in a traditional English, black cab. There was an old timer in a flannel sport coat and tweed cap behind the wheel. He had a soft, grandfatherly look about him but his hands and eyes had a hardened ruggedness, molded, no doubt, from the horrors of war and a lifetime of manual labor. I handed him a business card with the address on it.

"Alright, mate," he said reassuringly, "come on den."

For forty-five minutes we drove, through the high streets of the small towns surrounding Manchester at first and then as we got closer to the city, neighborhoods began to appear with their corner chip shops, local pubs, and infinite rows of two-story brick townhouses stained black and dark green with mildew.

When we finally stopped, we were near an overpass built for pedestrians to cross the street. On it, spanning the entire width of the road, were big, red, block letters that said, "The University of Manchester."

I paid the fare and stepped out of the car. I was still a little groggy from the booze and sleeping pills, so I drew a slow, deep breath allowing my chest to expand its fullest before I exhaled. The air was by no means fresh, but it was new and exciting. It made me feel reborn, energetic and optimistic. It was nice to be away from Michigan and from my dad.

The cab pulled away and I was left standing on the sidewalk of a busy four-lane street that was completely bare of trees or vegetation of any kind. Lining the street was an eclectic mix of buildings. Some were tall, modern buildings that were the dull office block style with little character or distinguishing features. Others, however, were sprawling, ornate Victorian Gothics that looked like fairytale castles. The whole place had an urban atmosphere that was dirty and raw like Detroit or Cleveland or the cities of the Midwest that I was familiar with, but it also had a melancholy enchantment that I never knew existed. It was completely different from the suburban scenery I was accustomed to and I liked it. This was going to be home. This was my new city.

The accommodation office was in one of the modern square buildings. A small red sign above a door on the outside of the building marked the entrance for it. Although, like I had guessed, it was in fact closed. There was, however, a hand written note taped to the inside of the door that said if anyone had come there looking for the orientation they were in the wrong place. It gave directions to another campus about two miles down the road. Normally, this wouldn't have been a big deal, but I spent all my Sterling on the taxi ride over and was forced to walk. I wasn't at all happy about hauling my bags that far.

"What a bunch of jackasses!" I said to myself and smacked the window with the palm of my hand out of spite. The window shuttered from the impact and I could do nothing as the orientation note drifted down, silently to the floor, like a leaf. If any poor bastard went there looking for the orientation course after I did they must've been fucked.

***

I found the registration in the athletic center. In the middle of the basketball court were several collapsible tables set up. On top of the tables were poster board placards with a different section of the alphabet designated to it. I headed over to the one that said H-K. There was only one person ahead of me in line, a tall African man. He was asking the pasty-complexioned British girl sitting on the other side of the table about staying at the student accommodations during the orientation course. She told him how much it was and he took out his wallet and paid her some money.

"Just tell the warden you paid me and he'll give you the key," she said and the African man walked away.

I stepped forward and took his place. The registration only took a few minutes, but before I left, I was asked if I wanted to stay in the student accommodations during the course as well. I politely declined saying that I had already made arrangements. I thanked the girl and left.

The truth was I hadn't actually made any arrangements at all. That is, until I heard what was said to the guy in front of me.

Fucking idiots, how can they reasonably expect a person like me not to abuse this?

I followed a group of students leaving the registration to the residence halls nearby. I went up to the warden's office with the group and got a key. He didn't even question me about paying. He gave me a friendly smile and said, "Enjoy your stay." And that was that, up to my free room I went.

I followed a narrow, stuffy corridor until I saw my room number. Someone was coming out of the room next to it. I just caught a glimpse

6

of him and saw that he had a red sweatshirt with what appeared to say "Only Losers Use Drugs."

Ahhh, I hope this ass hole doesn't try to talk to me.

I was tired and in no mood to be harassed by some anti-drug freak. I don't know how it's possible to tell I use drugs but they always can. I had numerous encounters with these people before and you can't make those fuckers listen, let alone understand anything. The first thing that they always ask is why I do drugs. "Because of people like you." I usually said, to which they would reply that I was killing myself or frying my brain or some other bullshit. After that they would try to make me admit I have a problem with drugs. "I don't have a problem with drugs!" Was my answer to this nonsense, "You're the one that has a problem with them!" Only their problem isn't abusing drugs, it's abusing the harmless, fun-loving individuals like me, who do.

I quickly fumbled with the key to get it in the lock. I wanted to get in the room and shut the door before this freak had a chance to bother me. But it was too late.

"Let me help you with those bags," he said.

His accent sounded British, but had a hint of Indian.

Maybe if I'm pleasant he'll skip the 'just say no' lecture, I reasoned.

"Alright man…thanks," I said, getting a better look at him. He was a tall, muscular man in his early twenties with a light brown complexion. He wore a goatee and had jet-black hair that was spiked up on the top and cropped short on the sides.

While getting a closer look at him, I noticed his sweatshirt again. Only I had read it wrong the first time. It really said, "Only Users Lose Drugs."

Maybe I was a little hasty to judge.

He grabbed the backpack off my shoulder and I opened the door.

"Hey man, that's a pretty cool sweatshirt you got there," I said.

"Thanks…I'm Akal, but everyone calls me Kal?" He said extending his hand for me to shake.

"Akal…What's that man, that Indian?"

"Yeah, it's Punjabi, but I'm not from India, I'm from Singapore. My grandparents moved there from India."

"Singapore? Alright."

"And you, where are you from?"

"Michigan, you know where that's at?"

"In America."

"Yeah man, you know where all the really big lakes are, by Canada?"

"Yeah, Okay."

"Well, that's where I'm from."

"Do they have cannabis in Michigan?" Kal asked out of the blue.

"Of course they do. What kind of question is that? They have cars and electricity there too!"

"No, mate, I was just asking because…we could have a smoke if you like."

"Yeah…you got some?"

"Yup. But, I have to get some skins?"

Skins? I had no idea what he was talking about, but I put my bags inside the door and walked with him to a convenience store across the street.

"What did you mean skins?" I asked.

"You must not be familiar with the slang. Skins are Rizzlas."

"What the fuck is a Rizzla?" I replied.

Kal gave me a look but didn't answer. We entered the tiny cluttered store and went up to the clerk.

"Give me some blue Rizzlas please." Kal said.

The clerk turned around and handed him a small blue package.

"Let me see those," I said, snatching the package from his hand. It was a package of rolling papers.

"Ah man, they're Zig-Zags," I said.

"What's a Zig-Zag?"

"Never mind."

We went back to the student accommodations, to Kal's room. He had a half bottle of cheap whisky and some warm Coke which he offered me. I took two glasses off the desk and poured us each a strong one. Kal slammed his down, in one drink, and asked for another. Then he rolled a joint that was half tobacco and half pot. I had heard that people in Europe smoked like that, but had never seen it before.

"What do you call that?" I asked pointing to the joint.

"It's called a spliff."

He lit the spliff and blew huge puffs of gray smoke in the air.

"You think it's okay to smoke in here?" I asked.

"You're not supposed to, but no one will know," he replied, passing me the joint.

We smoked the spliff and Kal quickly rolled another. Smoke started gradually accumulating above our heads like an early morning, midsummer fog. We were completely unaware of this, however because we were too busy talking and getting high. It wasn't until we heard the piercing shrill of a smoke detector that it was brought to our attention. The noise was a tremendous, high-pitched wail. I cupped my hands over my ears to protect them from the horrible, unholy noise. It sounded like impending doom, bouncing off the concrete walls of Akal's room and slamming into my head.

"Fuck, man! We better split!" I shouted.

"No, no I'll sort it!" Kal replied animatedly.

He jolted out of his seat and dragged the chair under the smoke detector. Without pause, he jumped onto it and began to flail his arms franticly like a castaway trying to flag down an airplane in a hopeless, futile attempt to fan the smoke away.

"What the fuck are you doing?" I yelled with my hands still covering my ears. "Just pull it down!"

He extended one arm above him trying to reach it, but it was too high.

"Hurry, shut it off!" I yelled again. "Just jump up there!"

Hearing my plea, Kal jumped up at the smoke detector, flapping one arm like he was swatting at flies. The chair began rocking side to side from his leaps and landings. He tried three or four times but missing, just barely, each time. Finally, he let out a rather effeminate grunt, something to the effect of UHHAAAHH and gave it all the effort he could muster. He bounded into the air and swatted his hand powerfully over his head, like a volleyball player making a serve. He struck the smoke detector and sent it smashing into the cinderblock wall. The chair teetered under him and one of his feet hit the edge of the seat on his way down. His balance was lost and Kal fell with a crash of dinging metal, clothes ripping and wood cracking. When the dust settled, so to speak, the chair and smoke detector were in pieces and Kal was sitting inside the armoire. Behind him was the broken door that he had gone through on his way there.

"Fuck man! Are you alright?" I shouted, despite the ensuing silence.

He didn't say anything at first. He slowly pulled himself out of the armoire, checked himself over and briefly assessed the damage to the room. After a moment of what appeared to be silent reflection he poured himself another drink.

"I'm alright..." he said absorbing the entirety of the moment. "At least we won't have to worry about the smoke detector anymore," he continued, cracking a cheeky smile.

9

A few minutes latter as we were laughing about the accident and just about to clean it up, there was a loud, authoritative knock on the door. Kal and I looked at each other briefly as panic started to set in. We both knew that knock. We scampered around the room hiding the drug paraphernalia. When it was out of sight, Kal open the door. Outside were two men in uniform. They were wearing florescent, yellow coats that looked like the kind police wear in Britain, but the patch on their arms said 'Public Safety.'

"We got an alarm from this room," one of the officers said as his eyes roved across Kal's room, observing the damage.

"I didn't hear anything." Kal told the officer, "Did you?" he said, directing the question to me.

I answered with a façade of idiocy that was no doubt transparent. "Ahhh…Nope…I didn't hear anything and we've been here all day."

The officer looked at me contemptuously and then turned back to Kal. "Why is your smoke detector in bits and lying on the floor, then?"

"It was like that when I got here," he responded with genuine composer.

"It was like that?" The officer replied unbelievingly.

"Yeah, look at this place, everything is falling apart. Look, the chair and the armoire are broken too," he said gesturing around the room with open hands.

The officer looked into Kal's red, blood shot, completely dilated eyes suspiciously for a few seconds and then said, "Alright you two wankers clean this flat up and have maintenance fix that first thing."

The officers left and Kal shut and locked the door behind them.

"We almost got busted for pot up here," I said with relief.

"Who cares, those wankers won't do anything. They have better things to do…besides they probably smoke too."

Kal was right. There is a tendency in Manchester for people to just let other people be. I hadn't been there long enough to fully appreciate it at the time, but there was a certain and unique permissiveness in Manchester. I have a theory that this has something to do with a historic proletarian consciousness in the city. Regardless of the cause there's no denying its existence. The public safety officers were a perfect example. If we were in America we would have been fucked. There's no way any cops or security guards or whatever would have just told us to just pick up the mess. We would have been carted off to jail as soon as they smelled the smoke. But, it wasn't just the authorities that let things slide. As I would later discover, it was the people as well. The

10

authorities' actions were simply a reflection of the people's wishes. What a truly spectacular exercise in practical democracy this was. Give the fucking people what they want. Give them freedom, not nominal freedom, but real liberty and let them flourish. Not only will they blossom individually, but socially too. Exceptional ideas can be thought of and great movements started under this system. That's why Manchester was the birthplace of rave culture and not Goshen, Indiana or Davenport, Iowa. The environment means everything. New Order, The Smiths, The Happy Mondays, The Stone Roses, they're all products of this social laissez-faire attitude and the environment it created. And I would be soon as well. I just needed time to absorb it.

I might not have absorb Manchester to its fullest when Kal made that comment, but by the time I found myself listening to the wail of an alarm with my heart pounding and my knee bleeding as I raced from Sunniva's laboratory to that little piece of shit getaway car I did. I was way passed simply being influenced by whatever was going on in Manchester. I was living it. I was the embodiment of it and so were my friends Miguel, Mikko and Solis. They were right there with me.

Moving in

The first time I met Miguel was between two sessions of the orientation course at the beginning of the year. The organizers of it invited us to leave the auditorium where the presentations were being held and have refreshments in the lobby.

I was looking around the room and noticed nearly everyone else but me huddled together in small groups sipping their little cups of fruit punch and chatting. I could see no discernable connection between the people in these cliques, other than they were all foreign, of varying nationalities and trying to make friends.

I considered joining one of the groups but decided not to. They all seemed too eager to want to talk, and meet and befriend each other.

There must be something wrong with them. I mused. *Something they're hiding.* They seemed like they all might be freaks.

Then, I saw a guy standing by himself, in much the same manner as I was. He stood at the edge of the lobby, looking at everybody else. He was wearing a light-blue denim jacket and aviator sunglasses. He had a slender, athletic build and stood three or four inches taller than me. He had a classic Latino appearance and bore a slight resemblance to a young Eric Estrada.

I watched as he reached into the chest pocket of his jacket and pulled out a pack of Marlboro Reds and a lighter. He held the cigarettes in his left hand and the lighter in his right. Slowly, he opened the box, using his thumb. Almost as if it were the same motion, he pushed a cigarette up with his thumb. It stood solitarily out of the box about an inch above the rest. He lifted the box leisurely to his mouth and grasped the cigarette with his lips, not relinquishing his gaze at the crowd. He pulled the cigarette out and bent his head down slightly, cupping both hands around the cigarette to block the flame from the breeze of the overhead fans. His motions were calm and he had a self-assured, calculated nature. An easiness surrounded him like he was a character in a movie, like he was a real-life Steve McQueen or something.

This was a guy that I wanted to talk to. This was a guy I wanted to befriend. He didn't seem like the others.

I walked up to him and introduced myself, "I'm David…David Keller."

"Miguel." He replied, with a light Spanish accent as we shook hands.

"So man...where're you from?" I asked.

"Puerto Rico!" he replied, beaming. "You know where is Puerto Rico?"

"Yeah man, of course. It's in the Caribbean, near Cuba. It's a territory of the United States."

"Ahh! You do know...Wha about you. Where are you from?"

"Michigan."

"Ah. Okay...Hey, it looks like the break is over now. We should go back."

The crowd had begun to trickle back into the auditorium. I thought about the prospects of sitting through another boring lecture on the proper use of computer facilities or whatever they had in store for us then and it didn't seem at all appealing.

"Hey man, you want to skip this bullshit and go smoke a joint?" I asked.

He looked at me with surprise.

"Yes! It would be better than this."

We went outside and found a secluded place behind some athletic field bleachers to smoke. I pulled out a joint Kal had given me and sparked it up. I passed it over to Miguel and exhaled, feeling relaxed as I did. I could already tell that Miguel and I were going to get along.

"So what do you think about the orientation so far?" I asked trying to make conversation.

He looked at me with a hint of agitation. "Man! I did not think that I will ever find this place. I go everywhere looking. I go to the Residence Halls, The International Society, even the accommodation office. When I get here they say there was a sign at the accommodation office...I did not see no fuck'en sign!"

***

The day orientation ended the International Society provided buses to take all the participants to their new accommodations. The room that I had been staying in during the orientation was really nice. It was big and well furnished. It had two dressers, an armoire, a big bookcase, a comfortable bed and a massive desk with plenty of drawers. It even had its own bathroom. I was impressed by that room. It was ten times nicer than any I had seen in the States. If I would have had a choice, I would have just stayed there, but I didn't. So, I put my bags in the undercarriage of the bus and climbed aboard. I was happy to see that

Kal was on my bus. As it turned out he was an orientation leader and had volunteered to help people take their bags to their new rooms.

The bus drove around for an hour or so, stopping at several other dormitories before it got to mine. As I made my way off the bus, I was a little excited about seeing my new room and settling in for my first year of graduate school, my first year in Manchester. I carried my bags down the sidewalk toward my home, nearly shaking with anticipation.

My building was located near where the cab driver dropped me off when I was coming from the airport after I first arrived. It was on Oxford Road, which cut through the heart of the university. My building was part of a larger grouping of about twelve student accommodations known as Witworth Park, being so named because of its close proximity to the municipal park of the same name. Witworth Park, the student accommodations that is, was a gated community. This meant that there was a big black iron fence that surrounded it. It was indeed, an imposing structure, tall and prohibitive looking. There were only two places where you could enter Witworth Park, both located on Oxford Road. On this day, outside the main entrance, two rectangular tables were set up with a large banner hanging down in front of them. It proclaimed "WELCOME" in black, square letters.

Welcome, Indeed!

I hauled my bags and myself up to the tables to check in. I was greeted warmly by a nice looking, soft spoken, older lady. With a smile and pleasantness in her voice, she told me about the different facilities Witworth Park had to offer, a laundry room, squash court, computer lab and other amenities. It even had a bar. She asked my name and after I told her, she procured a white envelope from a cardboard box that was next to her. Inside, I found the keys to my room.

The lady gave me some quick directions to the building and I walked through the gate. I followed a concrete path that snaked its way through yellowish grass and past a few unhealthy looking trees toward Acomb House, my new place of residence. On the way, a large blue circular sign hanging on another building caught my attention. It stated, "On this sight once stood the house of Fredrick Engles."

Communists! I thought, before proceeding.

Acomb House and all the other dormitories in Witworth Park were large institutional looking red brick structures. The bricks didn't look old, but were covered with dark green mildew. This was no doubt due to the heavy rain and lack of sunshine Manchester was famous for. The mildew gave the buildings a gloomy appearance that was somehow a

14

little comforting and romantic to me, in an odd way. Although I had never been there before, I felt home. Everything felt good to me. I took in a deep breath and waited as the air slowly exited my lungs before continuing.

As I got closer to Acomb House, I noticed an excessive number of doors leading into it. However, none of them looked like a main entrance. They were all painted a dull reddish-orange and were pretty much indistinguishable from each other, except for a small black number attached to the upper left corners. I wasn't expecting to see a building like this. I had imagined that it would be more like American dormitories. This didn't look like an American dormitory at all. With all the doors, it looked like something out of Alice in Wonderland. ·

I looked at my envelope to see what door to go in. It said, "Acomb House flat seven, room seven."

Two sevens. How about that, for luck?

I spotted a door with the seven on it and approached. I took out my key to unlock it and was surprised to see it opened for me. There holding the door was a short, slim Asian guy who I took to be Chinese. He appeared to be in his mid-twenties and although there was nothing specific I could put my finger on, he had a comical appearance sort of like an Asian Charley Chaplin or Nipsey Russell.

As I entered I found myself in a dim, dingy hallway. There was a peculiar smell hanging around in the air probably stuck to the grimy yellow walls. It smelled like a combination of stale Oriental spices and faint body odor. It was unpleasant but not especially offensive.

The Chinese guy helped me pull my bags through the door and said with a toothy smile, "Herro I ham Dang. Ou mus bhe ore neu frat mate."

What the fuck did he say?

"What?" I said.

"Oh! Er rue riving here?"

"What?"

"Oh! Er rue riving here?"

"Ummmm, I am arriving here?"

"Umhum."

"Ahhh…I guess so…I'm David Keller. I'm in room seven."

"Kerra?"

"Keller."

"Umhum."

"Ohhhkay."

15

"Oh! Etis nice ta me rue."

"Rue what?"

"Yes!"

"What?"

"Rut?"

"Alright Dang, okay, it's good to meet you...I'm ah, I'm going to go to my room now. I'll see you later," I said and continued down the hallway to my new abode.

About halfway down the hall I saw a door painted the same dull yellow as the corridor walls. It had a metal placket that said, "Kitchen." I set my bags down and opened it to take a peek. Inside the door was a large white kitchen with a stove, two refrigerators, a freezer, a microwave, and plenty of cupboards. It looked fairly clean and squared away.

Pretty nice.

By the stove was a group of Chinese guys standing around talking to each other in Chinese. When they saw me they stopped talking. They looked at me and everyone smiled. "Herro, Herro, ha ra rue?" I heard from the crowd. I just smiled back and gave them a quick wave. It was evident that I wasn't going to get much in the way of a conversation from that group.

I exited the kitchen, took my things down the hall and stopped outside my door.

"This is it!" I said to myself, enthusiastically.

I took my key and opened the door.

***

The hallway was dark; but, when I opened the door sunlight flooded my vision from a window in the room, blinding me. It took a couple of seconds for my eyes to adjust. And then, I saw my room. I scanned it, eying each and every detail like a mother would a newborn child.

"AH, WHAT THE MOTHER FUCK!!! WHAT IS THIS SHIT? YOU GOT TO BE FUCKING KIDDING ME." I screamed.

As you can see, I wasn't at all happy with the room. It looked like it should have been a closet not a room. It couldn't have been much more than seven feet wide and ten long. All the furniture had to be shoved together end to end so that it could fit. There was a small armoire that couldn't begin to hold all my clothes, a tiny desk, a bookcase with only three shelves and a bed. There wasn't even a dresser. It was smaller

16

than the holding cell I had been confined in for my recent drunk driving arrest, or for that matter any of the other jail cells I had spent time in for various other alleged, petty crimes.

I was confused, at first. *This can't be the right room!* I looked at the envelope again. It said room seven. Then, I looked at the door; it said seven. I looked at the envelope one more time and it still said seven. The envelope and the door seemed to agree; but, as far as I was concerned one of them was mistaken.

I was crushed. I just stood in the doorway looking over the room again and again as if I had overlooked an expanse of space somewhere. After all, it was only a fraction of the size of the room I had just vacated. But, I searched to no avail. It was what it was.

Initially, I was crushed; but, when I thought about it more, I realized that I wasn't simply crushed. I was insulted. I was outraged. How could they do this to me?

I threw my bags into the room, slammed the door shut and set out for the accommodation office. I was going to set those bastards straight.

***

I marched out of the building, right passed the Chinese guys, up the path and out through the black iron gate that surround Witworth Park. The accommodation office was about a half mile up Oxford Road, toward the city center from where my so called "room" was.

I made it about halfway there when I saw Kal walking down the sidewalk toward me. When he got closer he stopped and waited.

"What's wrong?" He asked, obviously aware I was upset.

"I just saw my fuck'en room, that's what's wrong!" I replied animatedly.

"You don't like it?"

"I hate it. It's no bigger than a jail cell."

"What are you going to do about it?"

"I'm going down to the accommodation office and set those bastards straight. That's what I'm going to do about it... You know something, they got that whole goddamn building filled with Chinamen. You know why? Because Chinamen don't realize how much of a piece of shit that fucking place is. They don't know any better. Shit, that place is probably like the Hilton to a Chinamen and the accommodation office can get away with that shit, with them. But if those bastards think they

17

can put ME in a room like that, THEY'RE OUTTA THEIR FUCK'EN MINDS! They might be getting away with this scam when they're dealing with Godless Communists, but I'm from the U.S.A. And we don't put up with shit like that, GODDAMNIT! There is no way they're getting me to stay in that piece of shit, Stalinesque housing block. Do I look like I'm a Chinamen to you?"

I paused and waited for Kal's reply.

After deciding that the question wasn't rhetorical he answered meekly, "No. I guess not."

"That's fuck'en eh right I'm not!"

I had managed to work myself into quite a frenzy. My palms were sweating, my heart was racing, and my head pounded like a jackhammer was going off inside it. I knew I needed to calm down.

"You want to get a drink before I go?" I asked Kal.

He responded, not entirely sure what to say, "The accommodation office closes in an hour."

"That's okay, we'll just get a quick drink, you know for my nerves. Then I'll go set those bastards straight."

"There's a good place just across the street, we could go there."

***

We walked across Oxford Road and stopped in front of a two-story, rectangular building with a white stucco face that had grown gray from the pollution of the cars and the frequent rains. There was a small patio in the front that had a half dozen picnic tables with umbrellas sticking out from the middles of them. On the edge of the patio near the sidewalk, about ten feet in the air, was a sign which read "Krö Bar." We walked up a few stone steps and entered the pub through a tall, heavy oaken door with white frosted windows. Inside there was some modern looking square, metal tables and matching chairs. Against the far wall was the bar. It wasn't at all ornate but had a contemporary sleekness that embodied the motif of the establishment.

Kal and I moved over to the bar. I ordered a pint of Boddingtons and Kal got a whisky and Coke. We took our drinks through a doorway into another room, with skinny rectangular, cafeteria-style tables lined in rows from wall to wall. We continued through that room out onto a lanai that overlooked a courtyard that contained even more picnic tables and a few struggling plants poking out of the ground. We choose a table on the

18

patio and sat down facing the tall, crumbling brick wall that enclosed the courtyard.

I looked at my watch. I only had one hour before the accommodation office closed. I understood that it was a risk to stop for a drink when I had important business to attend to because I rarely had just one. But, I also felt it would be better to calm down a bit. I didn't want to get flustered and not clearly articulate my point to those fucks. I wanted to be on my 'A' game so I could give them a caustic tongue lashing, something I inherited from my father, the big shot trial lawyer. Regardless, I needed to hurry. I picked up my beer and drank the creamy, bitter ale quickly, not setting the glass down until it was empty. When it was, I looked at my watch again. I still had fifty-three minutes and twelve seconds until closing time. I took a moment to re-access my mental condition. I still felt pretty unsettled.

Ah, fuck it!

"Kal, I'm getting another drink. You want one?"

"What about the accommodation office?"

"I just need one more. Then, I'm gunna go down there."

I went back to the bar and got another pint. When I came back to the table, there was another guy sitting there, talking with Kal. He was quite a bit shorter than Kal and had short black hair that looked erratic, yet it was obviously styled that way. His clothes were slim fitting, dark colored and hugged tightly to his body. He sported thick, brown, tortoise shell eyeglasses. He seemed intellectual and somehow detached. He was sipping a beer with a self-assured but friendly demeanor. I sat down and Kal introduced me.

"David, Mikko. Mikko, David."

"It's nice to meet you." I said.

"Likewise." He responded with an accent that I couldn't place.

Kal, Mikko and I made small talk about the weather and our courses while I finished my second beer. When it was gone I told them that I had to go.

"So soon?" Mikko inquired, "Why's that?"

"Ahh...I have to take care of some business." I told him, then said goodbye again and left. I actually felt pretty calm by that time.

I started again for the accommodation office. On my way, I noticed Dang, the Chinese guy who had opened the door for me earlier, crossing the road. This triggered an unpleasant flashback of the events that led me on the path I was currently taking. I had nearly forgotten the reason I was pissed off in the first place. In just a short period of time, the problem had become somewhat abstract to me, but seeing Dang brought it all back, in a flash of anger. With every second of that short walk, my anger grew exponentially. Every step I took brought with it new ideas of biting and explicit things to say to those bastards. By the time I reached the office, my rage was causing my teeth to grind together and I was perspiring like a hog. The reaction may have been excessive but I couldn't help it. I was pissed.

I marched up to the accommodation office door, the same one I went to when I first arrived and…*GODDAMNIT!* All the lights were off and the door was locked tighter than a drum. I looked at my watch. It was only four-thirty. In the window next to where the orientation note had been was a sign with the office hours. They were nine to five.

"LAZY FUCK'EN PIECES OF COMMUNIST SHIT!" I screamed at the door.

"Dats rite mate, fucken com-me-nists, alum. Canya spare sum change mate?"

I turned to see where the voice had come from. Sitting on a wooden bench behind me was a shabby derelict carrying an empty McDonald's cup. He was wearing filthy, torn clothes and had defeated eyes. I felt sorry for him. I jammed my hand in my pocket, and fished out some loose change to give to him.

"Dhay do it owl da thime, dhay do." He continued.

"What's that mate…leave early?" I replied softly, as not to take my anger out on him.

"Lheve hurly? Dhay don even com en ta work. Nunna dem."

"You mean the accommodation office?"

"Eye, an en da whole univer-city alsa…Da shops too allofit…Jus lazy I recon."

"I guess so." I said and walked away, not entirely sure what he was going on about.

I was hotter than ever. It was possibly the angriest I have ever been at foreign people which is saying a lot given the existence of French-Canadians.

Now I have to wait and take care of this fucking thing in the morning. That's just what I fucking need.

Then a bright idea exploded in my head.

Maybe I can meet back up with Kal and have a few more drinks!

It was a small consolation at the time but I figured I could forget about the whole ordeal, just for the night and then get pissed off again in the morning.

I checked my watch once more to see what time it was. When I did, I noticed something that I hadn't the other times I had looked at it previously that day.

"AH, fuck, it's Saturday!" I said aloud.

This should have eased my anger because it gave the accommodation bastards a legitimate reason for not being at work, but sometimes I'm a glass-half-empty kind of person and it pissed me off more.

Now I have to spend the whole weekend in that shit hole!

***

Kal wasn't at Krö Bar when I got back, but Mikko was still there. He was sitting at the table by himself, smoking a cigarette and reading the *Guardian*.

"Where's Kal?" I asked.

"He went to get this guy, Solis."

"Who's Solis?"

"I don't really know. I think that it's his new flat mate, from Costa Rica."

I sat down across from Mikko and struck up a conversation while we waited for Kal to get back. "So man…Where you from?"

"Finland."

"Oh yeah? You're the first person I've ever met from Finland."

"That doesn't surprise me. There are not a lot of us."

"That's because no one wants to live where; it's so fucking cold all the time." I replied, jokingly.

Mikko laughed and suddenly our conversation became comfortable and unforced. I could tell Mikko was a good guy and from our discussion we had a lot in common. A half an hour or so later Kal showed back up with a Hispanic guy.

"This is Solis." He said as they sat down. Mikko and I introduced ourselves.

Solis was a well-built Latino with fair skin. He was about average height, but his arms and shoulders were square and burly. He had an intimidating presence in his physical appearance, yet he seemed somehow cordial nonetheless. His pupils were dilated to the size of dimes and he had a slight smile on his face. His hair was without a doubt his most distinguishing feature. It was jet black and formed a perfect circle around his head, in an orb of wild, un-kept curls. It reminded me of an afro I

21

saw once on a homeless man in Flint, Michigan. The shapes and sizes where nearly identical and they both had bits of debris trapped in the snare-like tangles of their bushy heads. It was a bizarre look for sure but Solis pulled it off. He had a nonchalant manner and seemed like the kind of person who wouldn't let anything bother him, especially something like his hair.

Solis sat next to me and I offered to buy him a beer. He declined saying that he didn't drink.

"How about an ice-cold Coca-Cola, then?" I asked.

"No tank you, mate. I don take no caffeine."

"You don't drink and you don't have caffeine?"

"Dats right. I donna like it...I only smoke a cannabis, mate...cause it come from da eart."

"Yeah...but, caffeine comes from the earth, as well man. It's in the cola bean."

"AHH FUCK! It do. Dats right. I forgot dat. Okay, get me a Coca-Cola den, please mate."

This fucking guy's odd.

He was odd but he had an energy about him that easily wore off on me and I liked him instantly. There wasn't anybody like him in Michigan, not that I met anyway. His speech was loud and direct and he had difficulty sitting still. He looked like a coke head or speak freak. He kept bobbing his head to the beat of the background music and allowed his eyes to dart around the room, like a cornered animal.

Later, Kal and I went up to the bar for some more drinks and I enquired about Solis.

"Is Solis always like that?" I asked.

"Like what?"

"You know...like...all hyper or whatever."

Kal shook his head and laughed. "You think he's bad now, you should see him when he hasn't smoked marijuana. He's out of control."

"I can imagine."

"Last night he and I went out to this club. We didn't have a smoke beforehand though. We just took a couple ecstasy pills and left. By the time we got inside the club, he was so hyper he looked like he was having a seizure on the dance floor. Then he tried to chat up every girl there. At some point I lost track of him. He just disappeared."

"What happened?"

"I figured he pulled some bird. I asked him about it this morning, but he didn't. He said he couldn't pull any birds at the club so he went

22

home and tried to shag this fat, ugly flat mate of ours called Jill. And she wasn't up for it. So that crazy tosser went to his room and wanked for like six straight hours."

"You're kidding me?"

"That's what he said and I don't doubt it. He's got an uncontrollable sex drive. I'm telling you he'll shag anything!"

***

Miguel joined us a little later and we all stayed at Krö Bar until it closed. Afterwards, we got some cans of beer and went to Kal and Solis's flat for a smoke. As it turned out they lived in Witworth Park too, not far from Acomb House.

We went up to Solis's room and another of his flat mates joined us, a Japanese guy named Haruki. I was surprised to see that Solis's room was the same size as the one I was so worked up about. I started to think that perhaps it wasn't the insult I had believed it to be.

Someone rolled a spliff and it went around the room while another was made and cans of beer popped open. Solis put some Credence Clearwater Revival in the CD player. I could feel the grass starting to kick in. It seemed so much more potent than what I typically scored in Michigan.

Everyone was having a good time. The whole mood was pleasant. I looked over at Miguel. It wasn't hard to tell he was really stoned. He had mentioned earlier that he'd been smoking all day. His eyes were all glassed over, which wasn't an entirely uncommon look for him, I gathered already, from the few days I had known him. He was bobbing his head up and down to the beat of the music and tapping his foot.

Mikko was lying on the bed and looking up pensively at the ceiling. Suddenly, Miguel jumped to his feet and started pretending he was playing the drums. He nailed a few beats then he looked over at Mikko and said in an authoritarian voice, "Play the fuck-ing bass!" Mikko turned his head slowly, almost labouringly, and said in a languid voice, "I can't be bothered."

Miguel replied, more eagerly, "Come on, play the fuck-ing bass!"

Mikko, realizing that there was no use in arguing, gave in and starting pretending to play the bass. This seemed to make Miguel content for about half of "Travelin' Band," Then he looked over at me and said pleadingly, "Come on we need a singer." I had no choice his logic was too sound; they did, in fact, need a singer. I started singing and playing

23

the air guitar and Solis, Kal and Haruki joined in too.

There we were the six of us, stoned out of our minds, a whole fucking air band. We just pretended to play the music at first, but it didn't take long for us to start dancing around Solis's room which was as I said no bigger than mine. We barely all fit in the room, let alone had the space to dance. We were bouncing off each other and the walls like pinballs, so much so that the floor shook and debris fell from the ceiling. The desk chair got kicked over and books, papers and pencils were knocked off the desk. We were all jumping up and down screaming "HEY, LIL' TRAVELEN' BAND!" with the music turned up all the way. Solis put his arm around my shoulder and starting jumping around with me.

"MATE! ARE YOU HAV'EN A GOOD TIME?" he shouted over the music.

"YEAH MAN! THIS IS GOOD!"

"IS GOOD, MATE! IS GOOD! IS MADNESS AN' INSANITY!"

"IT'S WHAT?"

"MAD-NESS AN' IN-SAN-I-TY!!!"

Madness and insanity, indeed.

Just then, there was a pounding at the door. We all looked at each other and started laughing. Our noise was outrageous and we knew it could only be someone complaining about it.

"COME IN!"

The door was opened by a generously proportioned girl who looked like the kind who's always angry because they're fat. I found out later that she was Jill, the one Solis tried to shag the day before. She had a scowl on her face which, I am sure if looks could kill Solis would have been dead. When she opened the door, smoke rolled out of the room like a thick white blanket and completely engulfed her head. She fanned the smoke away from her face and scowled even more angrily.

"COULD YOU PLEASE KEEP IT DOWN!" she asked, obviously irate.

She stood at the door waiting for his reply, but Solis refused to even acknowledge her. He stared out the window and kept dancing. She looked contemptuously at him for a few seconds then stormed out, slamming the door behind her. After she left, we all looked at Solis to see what he would say.

"ROLL ANOTHER SPLIFF!" was all he said.

We partied like that until the sun came up. While I walked back to my room, I decided that I wasn't going to move after all. After a night of partying with that crazy motherfucker, Solis, I didn't mind living in Witworth Park so much. I wanted to be as close to that guy as I could. I liked his style and knew he would a good friend.

As the weeks wore on my initial impressions of him wouldn't be proven wrong. He and I became close and shared a profound understanding. There were moments of frankness and intimacy where his humanity, which was both beautiful and flawed, was revealed to me. Moments like the one that happened about a month after my classes began.

***

I was studying alone in a hidden corner of the library, when Solis called me. He wanted to know if I was up for a smoke, which of course, I was. I packed my books away and walked over to his room. When I got inside Witworth Park, closer to his building, I could hear music blaring out of a second story window. I recognized it as a band called Manu Chao and I knew right away it was coming from Solis's room. I also knew that meant he hadn't waited for me to start getting high.

Inside his flat, Solis's bedroom door was open. I walked in to find him dancing with a towel wrapped around his waist. His bushy hair had beads of water dripping from it. He had a lighter in one hand and a hash pipe in the other.

Solis rarely smoked spliffs. He hated the taste of tobacco which was why he preferred to smoke out of the pipe. I had gone with him when he bought it. It wasn't even a month old, but the manner in which he used it border-lined on abuse, both drug abuse and physical abuse to the pipe.

Solis really liked smoking dope. This may seem like an overly concise and simplistic explanation of his habit; however it is the only way to describe Solis's relationship with the drug. For him, it ameliorated every situation. It was perfect to smoke when shagging a girl; it was the perfect thing to enhance listening to music, or riding his bike, sleeping, waking up, walking to class, being in class, doing homework, studying, watching TV, masturbating, etc., etc.

Now obviously, saying that he just liked marijuana seems like a lame, pothead justification to mask addiction. But for Solis it wasn't. He would be the first to admit his addiction. He wasn't trying to hide anything. It went well beyond an addiction for Solis; it was somehow spiritual. True, he may have been mentally addicted to the drug, but, it in no consequential way affected his life. What, in fact, marijuana did was allow Solis to excel to greater heights. It actually made him a better person. When Solis smoked grass, his mind entered some type of transcendental realm or something. He tried to explain it to me once, but to be honest I didn't really get what he was saying. Regardless, when he was high, he had a certain spirituality and everyone and everything fit into it somehow.

However, I will concede that this state of mind (although flawless in the theoretical, intangible corridors of his conscience) was at times deficient in actual real-world applications. It had the tendency to create a disregard for many of society's norms and present a hazy interpretation of his surroundings. It was also responsible for countless, although inadvertent acts of mischief, acts not entirely unlike the one I discovered on that particular day.

"Que Tal?" I said as I walked through the door.

Solis's eyes exploded with delight.

"Mother-fucka! How are ya, mate?" he said with a big smile and embraced me with a hug.

Solis typically greeted his friends like this. It didn't matter if the last time he saw them was three weeks ago or three hours.

"Here, mate! Smoka dis motherfucka!" he said with an animated laugh.

He extended the pipe and lighter to me and I took them. I lit the lighter and slowly brought it down toward the pipe so that the flame was just above it. I drew in a long expansive breath and watched as the fire heated the volcanic embers and spun in a clockwise rotation. I could see the flame sear the bowl with orange light and felt the smoke fill my lungs. I drew heavily, taking in several deep tokes, until I was unable to stoke anything up.

"It's cashed." I said.

"Mate, get more!" Solis replied, as if it were a command.

I sat down at his desk and repacked the pipe with some marijuana that was lying out. That's when I noticed a curious sight. Standing on edge, with their spines facing me, was a row of over twenty travel guide books which weren't there the day before. I glanced through the titles, Singapore, Malaysia, France, Costa Rica, Mexico, Spain— the list went on.

Solis was a geography buff. Indeed, he knew more about geography than anyone I had every known. However, an acquisition like this was odd. He rarely had money to spend and when he did, it went toward his life necessities: food, marijuana and pornography.

I picked up one of the books and flashed it at Solis. "Where did you get all these books?"

"AH mate! Dhey were giv'n dem for free, en de travel agent."

"Which one?"

"En da cidy centre...Thomas Cook."

"What?" I inquired, "What the fuck do you mean they were giving them out?"
I had been there a few days earlier to exchange some money and I didn't see any free travel guides.

Solis proceeded to tell me that he had gone down to the travel agent and saw a rack of these books. Thinking they were giveaways, like the brochures in the rack next to them, he loaded his entire backpack full. He did this in plain sight of the entire office staff. However, they didn't say anything to him. They probably felt it would be best to just let this bushy-headed freak steal the books and leave before he hurt somebody. It must have seemed obvious to them Solis was an uncontrollable, desperate junky who needed money to fuel his drug habit.

"Dhey jus give dem to me," he said.

"They gave them to you or you took them."

"I took dem. But, dhey were giv'en."

"What the fuck are you talking about?" I exclaimed in a bemused way. "Look, you fuck!"

I showed him the prices on the back of the books. They totaled well over three hundred pounds.

"They aren't giving these fucking books away, they're selling them."

"What le'me see dat shit!" Solis replied unbelievingly.

He snatched the book out of my hand and looked at the price tag.

"Dhey aren't giv'en dese books away?" He questioned.

"No man! What the fuck made you think they would give these books away for free? They're expensive."

He gazed at me perplexed.

"Ah mate, I don' know...but when I wen back to dat fuck'en place dhere was one motherfucka who look at me, like what the fuck is your problem—"

"What the fuck do you mean when you went back?" I interjected.

"Ah mate, I wen to dat fucking place and I see all dose books and so I fill my backpack. An...den...when I get home, I start ta tink, would be nice ta have some more. So, I go back and fill it again, mate!" Solis said laughing.

I shook my head in disbelief and offered him the pipe. When he was done laughing, he took a quick, deep toke. He held the smoke briefly and forcefully expelled it from his lungs.

"So mate, I stole des books," he asked, already knowing the answer.

I nodded my head yes.

"I did no mean ta steal dem, but I DON'T GIVE A FUCK!" he shouted, laughingly.

He turned up the music and passed the pipe to me.

"I DON'T GIVE A FUCK!"

This event made me realize how truly special, extraordinary Solis' character was. Despite the circumstances, he had a complete satisfaction, an absolute contentment with himself and his actions. I'd never seen anyone like that before. He had a mental or spiritual enlightenment. He really didn't give a fuck.

I think it must have been this kind of understanding I was looking for nearly a year later when I stood over that map of Europe, stoned, with my eyes gleaming and bag packed as I circled distant, exotic locations with just a slight inkling of what I was about to do. I was going to go in search of Madness and Insanity; not that I really understood what that meant. I was sort of like Justice Potter Stewart, who said he couldn't define pornography, but knew it when he saw it. With me it was Madness and Insanity. I was unable to give it any real explanation but recognized it nonetheless. It was present in Kal's room, my first day in Manchester and also that night after Krö Bar in Solis' flat. However, that certainly would not be the extent of it. My encounters continued to progress in frequency, duration and intensity that entire year. Really, for all practical purposes it all began midway through the first semester when I took a fall break excursion to Rhodes. Things might have started on a remote Grecian island; but, they managed to balloon exponentially from there on, sparking my curiosity and driving me toward being so fucked up I could finally be well.

Fall Break

The middle of October is a very dreary time in Manchester, although admittedly it's always dreary in Manchester. So, when Kal and Miguel suggested we get out of Manchester for the midterm break of my first semester and head to the sunny beaches of Greece, I was game.

In all, there were six of us: Kal, Miguel, me, a friend of Kal's named Jai and two girls Jai supposedly knew from one of his classes. Miguel and I got a room together, as did the two girls and Kal and Jai. Kal had mentioned Jai to me a few times before the trip; but, I never met him. He was also from Singapore and had known Kal there for several years before they went to Manchester together. Jai was the one who found us the package deals to Greece. He was tall and lean and had an awkward manner about him that was easily overshadowed by his handsome face and dark complexion. He was an older student about twenty-eight or so and his age was apparent in the way he spoke with a calm, mature demeanor. He seemed responsible but not a total square. All in all I felt he would be good person to travel with.

The trip was for five days and five nights. I knew that there would be plenty of Ouzo and other alcohol to drink on the island. I was however, concerned about the availability of drugs. I knew several Greeks, in Manchester and they all told me that drugs are pretty difficult to get in Greece because of draconian drug laws. My only choice, then, was to bring some with me. So, I bought ten really good ecstasy tablets especially for the occasion. However, as the trip got closer I became a little anxious about taking them with me. The risk of getting caught with them in an airport, I assumed, was high. Don't get me wrong. It wasn't a matter of being scared so much as it was a matter of risk management. I knew that I would take those pills; I just wasn't sure how I could minimize my personal liability. For this I needed the consul of my close friend and confidant, Miguel, who of course was Puerto Rican and therefore more versed in the ways of international drug smuggling than I. I knew that he would prove, which he ultimately did, an invaluable resource.

"Is simple, man!" He told me, "Jus put de pills in someone else's bag."

Fucking brilliant!

It was so straightforward, yet so ingenious. However, I still needed to figure out whose bag to use and how to do it. I obviously wasn't going to put them in Miguel's or Kal's bag because they were my friends and Jai was a good friend of Kal's so he was out of the question too. That only left the girls.

I met the girls the morning we were leaving for Greece. All six of us rendezvoused on Oxford Road just down from the BBC. The plan was to meet up there and share the two taxis we ordered to the airport. One of the girls, Annika was going to ride with Miguel and me. She was a sleepy-eyed, blond, Swedish girl. Although she was wearing a sweat suit and a baseball cap, I could tell she had a nice body by the way the clothes hung to her breasts and slender thighs. The other girl was short, quiet, and quite frankly pretty unremarkable. Her name was Lidia. She was an undergraduate of Singaporean-Indian descent. She was going to ride with Kal and Jai.

Miguel and I each brought a duffle bag and set them down on the sidewalk while we waited for the cab. Annika had two bags, a big rucksack and a smaller backpack. She put the rucksack down on the ground next to my and Miguel's bags; but, she kept the backpack over one shoulder. I was particularly interested in the backpack. It had pouches with zippers all over the front of it. It was a perfect spot to stash my pills. When our taxi came the cab driver opened the trunk and I threw the large bags in it, conveniently neglecting to ask Annika for her backpack. Then, we piled in the black cab and headed for the airport.

Miguel and I made small talk with Annika on the way to the airport. It didn't take long to figure out that she would be an easy patsy. To begin she didn't seem especially astute. Moreover, she was dozy from staying up late the previous night.

"Why don't you sleep a little? It's a least half an hour to the airport," I told her.

"Yeah, sounds like not a bad idea," she said with a yawn cracking through a heavy Scandinavian accent.

In a few minutes she was out and so was the Tylenol bottle that I hid the ecstasy in. I looked at Miguel and he nodded at me. I quietly opened the front pouch of her backpack and dropped the pills in. I zipped it up just as quietly as I opened it, not disturbing her in the least. When it was done, I looked at Miguel and smiled mischievously. He gave me an approving nod of the head. That was that.

The plane left Manchester early in the morning and arrived on the Island of Rhodes before mid-day. It was a small charter jet that the travel agency lined up especially for the package deal. There were only about forty people on the plane so disembarking didn't take long. In ten

30

minutes we were standing in front of a big shiny aluminum carousel waiting for our luggage.

After our bags arrived it was show time. We headed for customs. I wasn't at all worried about getting caught, because after all the drugs weren't in my bag. I was, however, a little concerned that Annika would. I didn't want to see my drugs get confiscated. Although, I must admit, it was well worth the risk. Ten pills versus ten months in a Greek prison. That wasn't really a choice. I couldn't even imagine spending time in an American prison and in there you would only be surrounded by your run of the mill sodomites. A Greek prison, no doubt would have a much more sinister brand of sodomite due to the historic nature of buggery in their culture.

When we approached customs there was only one guard on duty. I use the word "duty" in a very loose context. All he did was open a gate and smile at us as we went through. This, I felt, was an added bonus. I had my pills and I wasn't responsible for sending a completely innocent stranger to jail. In retrospect, I think that I would have felt badly if she got caught, not as bad as if I got caught, but badly nonetheless.

Getting the pills back from Annika was a breeze. After we left the airport we boarded a tour bus which took us to our motel, in the city of Faliraki. I sat next to Annika. After a minute or two I leaned over to her and said, "Hey when we were in the taxi this morning, I put a bottle of Tylenol in your bag, remind me to get it back; will you?"

As soon as we were unpacked, showered and settled in Annika brought the pills down to my room. She never suspected a thing.

***

It didn't take long for us to get into the vacation mood. Miguel and I walked to a small shop across the street from where we were staying. The shop was actually tiny; but, somehow they managed to carry practically every item someone on vacation might need: toothbrushes and toothpaste, razors and shaving lotion, Band-Aids, condoms, beach balls, soft-drinks, sun tan lotion, naked lady playing cards, feminine-hygiene products and of course alcohol. They had every nook and cranny of that store displaying goods. There were bins in the middle of the aisles and beach towels and t-shirts hanging from the ceiling. We winded our way through a maze of inflatable rafts and candy bins to the back of the store where the shelves of booze were. Miguel picked up a cheap liter bottle of ouzo and headed toward the register.

31

"Wait," I said before he got too far, "we better get two."

"Yeah?"

"Yeah, man. We better start this thing off right." I said eagerly.

"Should we get something to mix it with?" he asked as he took another bottle.

"Probably, but I've never had this stuff before. What would we mix it with?"

"I don't know, I'll ask."

Miguel and I approached the counter. Standing behind an ancient cash register was an old lady with bifocals and a hairnet.

"Excuse me Miss, what do you mix ouzo with?" Miguel asked.

The old lady looked at Miguel for several seconds as if she was in deep concentration then finally said in a harsh accent, "U'ra Ama'ican…Ama'ican bouz?"

"Yes," we replied after her words sunk in.

"Ah." She said shaking her head in the negative. "Yha no mitx ouzo with nut'ting. Ya jusa dre-kin't."

"Ah, okay," Replied Miguel. He turned to me as if I hadn't heard the lady and said, "They don't mix it with anything. So we don't need anything."

"Ah I don't know. If you don't want to mix it with anything, that's up to you. I'm going to get soda or juice."

I found some orange juice and cola next to the Styrofoam coolers and plastic pails and shovels. I grabbed two liters of juice and a liter of cola, then paid for the beverages.

Miguel and I went back to our motel room to start drinking. I mixed my ouzo with cola and poured one straight for Miguel. I put his cup close to my nose to smell the liquor before I handed it to him. It had an overpowering scent like mineral spirits.

"You better drink that fast," I said teasingly "before it melts the cup."

Miguel took a sip and let out a hoarse cough as the booze cleared his throat.

"Put some juice in dis for me," he said extending the cup back to me.

"You said you didn't want any."

"I know, but I wan some now."

"There's not enough." I said pretending to be serious. I knew he would want a mixer, that's why I got some much. I just wanted to rattle his cage a little.

"What you mean, dhere's not enough?"

"Look, there's not enough. You can't have any."

"Are you serious? Dhere's tree liters!" He responded peevishly.

"Sorry." I said raising my palms in the air like the matter was out of my control.

"Man, dat's not right!" he said dejectedly.

I started laughing and handed him the carton of juice. "I'm just kidding man; you can have some."

After a few minutes we called upstairs to Kal's room and he, Jai and the girls came down to our room to party some before we went out for the evening. The girls played Kal and Jai in euchre. Miguel put some Bob Marley on the CD player and I mixed some strong drinks. Everyone was talking and laughing and having a good time. Everyone was also drinking heavily; Jai especially seemed to be in good cheer. After it got dark we decided to make a move and find the nightlife Rhodes was famous for.

Before we left, Miguel and I pulled Kal aside and showed him the pills. He was thoroughly impressed not only in the presence of the pills themselves, but also in the creativity we had used in smuggling them onto the island.

"Nice one," He said as he assayed the pills, "but, you're not going to take them now, are you?"

"Why not?" I asked.

"We should wait. If we take them now we could end up in a shit place and then they would be wasted. We should find the best club tonight and eat them there another night."

"That's fucking wise," I replied and Miguel agreed. There was no use in taking them now. It was best to wait for the right place and the right moment. After all, we had almost a whole week.

***

Pretty much all the night life in Faliraki was located on one stretch of road that started at the beach and worked its way up to a residential crossroad. On this street there were ten or so open-air style clubs. They were nothing fancy, but they were all crowded and you could enter and go between them freely. Outside, dozens of people staggered around drunkenly. They all had glasses and bottles in their hands and no one seemed to mind. It looked like a complete free-for-all, a haven for binge drinking and a launching pad for fornication. There was a teenager

33

wearing an Ipswich jersey passed out on the sidewalk. He looked like a corpse so I quickly checked for a pulse before I stepped over him. He was still alive and still holding on to a can of beer.

The street had a busy fairground feel to it. Colored lights, strobes, and disco balls cast their rays on it from the clubs while music blasted from every direction with dissonance and disorder. There was drum and bass, techno, rock and dance music all mixing together and rumbling on top of each other creating a garbled roar like the sound of a large waterfall. The buildings on both sides of the street trapped the music between them causing it to echo like a cavern. It was festive, intense, and loud. There was mayhem within it; there was Madness and Insanity throughout. It was, I noticed immediately, a good place to be.

The six of us went into a club we had picked at random called The Colossus. Other than some renderings of the famed statue from antiquity on the walls, the place didn't really have much character. But, that didn't really matter to me. I wasn't really in the mood for character. I was in the mood for alcohol. I cut through the mob of people that seemed to fill every crevice of the place and went up to the bar with Kal and Miguel.

***

We stayed where we were for a few solid hours of drinking then decided to look for Jai and the girls. It was almost four in the morning by then and we were ready to get back to the motel. We found them in a bar similar to The Colossus across the street. The girls were talking to each other but Jai was just staring straight ahead with his hands cupped under his chin to prop his head up. There were at least a dozen empty glasses piled on the table next to him.

"You drink all these?" Kal asked him.

"I ded. Etis tu drins for'de prys of one drink." He replied with a strong Indian accent. It was evident that all the alcohol had made him careless in his speech.

"We're ready to make a move. Do you want to go back with us?" Miguel said.

Everyone agreed that they had had enough for the night. We walked out of the club and started back to our motel. After only a few steps, however, it became evident that Jai wouldn't be able to make the walk. He was weaving too much and had to be helped walking. We decided to get a cab. Miguel flagged one down and we all piled in. The fit was a little tight, admittedly, but none of us was too bothered except the driver. He refused to go because there were too many people. He told us that only four were allowed at a time. So, Miguel and I got out and hoofed it back to the motel.

Near the midway point in the walk, Miguel and I passed a large construction site that was enclosed by a tall chain-link fence. Inside the fence was a dusty span of graded land that had been flattened for the building of whatever it was they were building. It was difficult to say what the massive steal frame that was being erected there would ultimately be. Miguel and I were speculating on what it was when I noticed something past the steal frame, past all the large building equipment and through the fence way at the far end of the site. It was our motel there in the distance. After consulting with Miguel we decide to take the shortcut. We jumped the fence and landed on the other side.

Although, admittedly we were trespassing, it actually started off innocently enough. Things didn't start going wrong until Miguel decided that we should take a bulldozer for a ride. I'm not sure at what point during our trip through the construction site he brought it up or even why he thought of it. But, he did.

I was immediately under the impression that it was a bad idea. However, Miguel had never led me astray, and I could easily think of a dozen times when my own conscience had. So, it didn't take long for Miguel to convince me that in actuality, his idea was good.

Miguel and I climbed up the iron ladder of a big, blocky, yellow bulldozer with an enormous plow in the front. We sat down inside the open cab and Miguel took the wheel.

"What do I do now?" Miguel asked as he looked at the numerous levers, buttons and other controls in front of him.

"What to you mean, what do I do? Turn the fucking key."

"There is no key."

"Are you sure you're looking in the right place?"

"No. Where's it supposed to be?"

"How the fuck should I know? Here, let me look."

I made Miguel switch me spots, but I didn't see a key anywhere either. We searched all the usually hiding spots, under the seats, in the visors, etc. but couldn't find it.

Finally, I said "Fuck it!" and got down to go home.

Miguel climbed off after me, but on the way down his pant leg got stuck on the ladder and he fell. He landed flat on his back, surprisingly hard given the short distance of the fall and knocked up a cloud of dust. He got up, dusted himself off and then gave the machine a fierce kick in an act of retribution. The bulldozer however, was more solid than his foot and he let out a moan of pain. The kick may have hurt his foot, but surprisingly it didn't curb his desire for revenge. He picked up a walnut sized rock and slammed a split finger into the side of the bulldozer. The rock bounced off it harmlessly and came to a stop at his feet.

Teasingly, I said, "That's why you never see a fucking Puerto Rican on the mound."

He looked at me, an insulted man. "What the fuck are you talking about? Ed Figueroa was Puerto Rican!"

"What? Who the fuck, is Ed Figueroa?"

"He played for the Yankees in the seventies. He—"

"Man, fuck Ed Figueroa!" I interrupted, "This is how you throw a fucking baseball!"

I found a rock of my own and took a few steps back from the bulldozer. I set myself in the stretch, pretending I was facing a batter. I shook off the imaginary catcher's request for a curve, shook off the braking ball, and nodded to the heater. I cocked back and fired the rock straight for the windshield. It struck it with a sharp cracking sound that echoed throughout the quiet night. The glass shattered into a giant spider web. Miguel and I broke out into hysterical, drunken laughter. But, then we heard some shouts which were probably directed toward us. We didn't stick around to find out if they were. We ran through the rest of the construction site, hopped the fence on the other side and went back to our motel.

***

Miguel and I were surprised to see Kal and the others just pulling up when we were getting back to the motel ourselves.

"Where the fuck were you guys?" I asked Kal.

"This wanker threw up in the cab," he said gesturing toward Jai. "So the driver kicked us out. It took ages to get another."

"You alright?" I asked Jai.

"Yeas, Ihm fine." He replied.

He did seem a little livelier than the last time I saw him. The vomiting must have helped sober him up. He wasn't staggering and his speech had improved.

"Why were you guys running?" Kal asked.

36

Miguel answered quickly, "Because, Keller broke de windows of a bull-dozer."

"What?" said Kal. "Why did you do that?"

"It was only one window," I mumbled under my breath.

"What?" Kal asked unable to hear me.

"Don't worry about it...Hey, let's go swimming!" I exclaimed trying to change the conversation.

"But the pool is closed." Annika protested.

"I don't give a fuck!" I shouted, not so much that she understood my position on the matter, but so that the entire island did.

The rest of the guys apparently didn't give a fuck either and we went to the pool. The girls didn't however, they said they were too tired and went to bed. They didn't really seem all that tired to me, though. I could tell they wanted no part of what was going to happen at that pool. I was a little disappointed that they didn't want to play in our reindeer games; but, I understood. The four of us were in quite a state and they were probably worried our brand of knavery and tomfoolery might be trouble. Which, it turned out to be almost immediately upon our arrival at the pool.

The pool was next to the parking lot, in front of the motel so it took no time to get there. However, once Jai took a look at the water he decided that he was in no condition to swim and sat down on a chair next to the pool. Miguel, Kal and I stripped down to our underwear and did running cannonballs into the water. The noise of our impact with the water was tremendous. It sounded like a bomb going off. It reverberated off our motel, the neighboring motels and the nearby bare, rocky mountains. The whole stillness and tranquility of the night was shattered from mountain to shore. And, as if our thunderous splash wasn't earsplitting enough, Kal followed it up with a deafening, high pitched, effeminate shrill.

"AHH, AHH. It's cold! AHH, it's cold!!!" He shrieked.

Miguel, Jai and I started laughing at him.

"Shut up you wankers. It's freezing." Kal said defensively.

He had his arms crossed over each other and was rubbing his biceps to generate warmth. Miguel and I looked at each other and started laughing again. Then Jai started mimicking Kal's outburst.

"AHH, AHH, AHH, I'm cold! I'm cold! AHH, AHH!"

"Shut up you wanker! You didn't even get in the water." Kal responded even more defensively.

"AHH! AHH! It's cold!" Jai continued.

Miguel and I laughed harder.

"It's cold...It's cold!" Jai persisted, mockingly.

Then out of nowhere, Kal reached his arm out of the pool, grabbed Jai by the sleeve and pulled him in, clothes, shoes and all.

Miguel and I laughed even harder. It was great slapstick. Jai was speechless. He scampered out of the pool and took off all his wet clothes. He stood there naked and shivering in the night air. This, in and of itself, was a humorous sight, but when Kal began taunting our now nude companion it became nothing less than comical brilliance. Miguel thought so as well. We just stood there busting with uncontrollable laughter until tears rolled down our cheeks. Although, I must admit, we didn't understand a word of what Kal was saying. He was shouting in Punjabi but the verbosity, intonation and passion was fantastic.

When Kal finished, Jai just stood there, still speechless, looking at him intently. Then, he went calmly to the ladder and climbed down back into the water, with a menacing look in his eye. Kal, sensing danger backed carefully away from Jai. Jai lunged toward him, trying to grab his arm. He missed and Kal retreated outside of the pool. Jai started to climb out as well and Kal ran toward their room. Jai set chase, pausing momentarily to retrieve his shirt. He threw his shirt over his head and slipped both arms through the sleeves without missing a stride. It would have been a rather difficult feat for anyone, but given Jai's level of intoxication, I felt it was a marvelous display of athleticism.

Miguel and I remarked momentarily about the pursuit then decided that Kal and Jai probably weren't coming back to the pool. We got out, collected our stuff and the things that Jai and Kal left behind and went to our room.

As Miguel was digging through his pant's pocket looking for our key, we heard shouting coming from the floor above us. It sounded like there was a fight and I could make out Kal's voice, Jai's voice and another voice that was unfamiliar.

"Fuck! That's Kal!" I yelled at Miguel, dropping everything from my arms, "Let's go!"

Miguel dropped his things and we ran full speed up the stairs, still in our underwear. It took about ten seconds to get there. It took me about three of those seconds to mentally ready myself for a fight. I had already imagined the scenario. Some racist or fascist or equally worthless fuck had probably made a drunken comment to Kal and Jai and they made one back and then viola.

When we got to the top of the stairs Miguel kicked the crash bar on the door like he was Jackie Chan. It flew wide open causing it to smack into the wall with a huge bang that echoed down the hall. Miguel and I ran through it and down the hall full speed. I was prepared for just about anything, a big rumble, a one-on-one fight, people with weapons or whatever and I sensed that Miguel was as well. However, I believe nothing could have ever prepared us for what we saw when we rounded the corner and laid eyes on the scene.

Kal was separating a small, middle-aged man from Jai who was lying on the floor. The stranger kept shouting, "ya fuc'en pervert, ya lit'l fuck…" while Jai repeated in broken English "Peas sir, ihem sar-re, bery sar-re. Peas sir…"

I had no idea why Jai was apologizing, however I am fairly confident that his pleas for forgiveness were overshadowed by the fact his cock and balls were hanging out from under his shirt.

The stranger kept shouting at Jai and Jai tried to give an explanation. The noise was outrageous and other motel guest started coming out of their rooms to see what all the commotion was about. Several of them started yelling themselves because they were pissed off about being woken up. This added to the noise and confusion of the situation and things looked like they might get out of hand at any moment. Miguel, Kal and I tried to get Jai to go to his room but he wouldn't go. Then, a woman who I took to be the middle-aged man's wife tried to get her husband into their room but he refused. He kept screaming at Jai and Jai kept babbling and the spectators shouted even louder. Lights started to come on in the rooms of the motel next door and people threatened to call the police. Things were quickly getting out of control. Finally, we managed to half convince, half force Jai to his room.

With Jai safely inside, Kal shut the door and locked it, leaving Miguel and me outside. Then, just like that, everything was quiet again. The irate man went back to his room. The bystanders shuffled back into theirs and Miguel and I walked back down to our room, although, we didn't have a clue about what had just transpired. We picked up our things from where we had dropped them unlocked the door and went in. I poured some ouzo and handed one to Miguel. We sat on our beds drinking in silence while we reflected on the events of the night. I ended up passing out before I finished half of my drink. It wasn't until the next morning I found out what all the fuss was about.

I got the story from Kal and I'm sure there must be a moral to it…somewhere. There was a knock at our door early the next morning. I heard the rapping and hoped that Miguel would get it, but then I heard Miguel in the shower and realized that I was going to have to answer it myself. I was hung over so I gingerly slid my feet out of the covers, set them on the cool tile floor and sat up straight. I rubbed the sleep from my eyes and shuffled to the door, still half asleep. I opened it slowly and had to squint as the sun shone in my face. Kal was standing there with three cups of coffee.

"What's going on?" I asked sleepily.

He handed me a cup of coffee and walked in. "I came to get you and Miguel because the manager said we had to go see her."

"What?" I said, sitting back down on my bed.

Kal put down one of the coffees and sat on Miguel's bed. He let out a sigh and said, "Yeah, she came round this morning and said that she needs to talk to all of us."

"Are you serious?" I asked becoming more awake.

"Yeah."

"Why?"

"Because of that wanker, Jai. Don't you remember him running around with his bullocks hanging out?"

I did in fact remember seeing his gonads. An event like that is difficult to forget.

"Ah, fuck!" I said dropping my head in despair. "Did you talk to her?"

"No Annika did. She said that the manager was well pissed and that we'll probably have to leave."

"Shit…What the fuck even happened last night anyway?"

"Remember Jai was chasing me, yeah?"

"Yeah."

"Well I headed up to the room, but I realized I didn't have the key, so I hide round the corner and waited for Jai to come. He's the one who had our key."

"Alright."

"I was around the corner like and I heard Jai trying to turn the knob only the door was locked so he started knocking. He was knocking softly at first but there was no answer, so the stupid bugger started pounding on the door. When that didn't work he let into kicking it! In

40

the mean while, I was just listening to Jai making a fuss and having a good laugh. I was just about to put an end to the whole thing when I heard a door open and someone start shouting at Jai. I hurried back round the corner and was horrified to see that tosser standing two doors over from ours."

"He was at the wrong door?"

"Yeah, he was at the wrong door and he woke that guy up."

"Ah fuck." I said laughing. We might have been in a grave situation with the manager because of it; but, I still found the absurdity of the whole matter humorous.

"You mean this guy was asleep and Jai just started kicking his door? Imagine that was you. You're having a nice dream about sunning yourself on the beach or better yet banging a couple chicks and BOOM BOOM BOOM. Someone's at your fucking door waking you up. And not only that, but when you open it there's a drunk, naked, Indian boy with his wiener hanging out...Fucking hell. No wonder he was so irate. Wouldn't you be?"

"For sure."

"So, what did Jai do when the guy came to the door?"

"He wasn't expecting it. He got startled to see this bloke. He took a couple quick steps back and fell flat on his ass."

I shook my head in silent disbelief.

"That's not even the worst of it." Kal continued, "That guy's whole family came out to see what all the ruckus was about and saw Jai on the floor with his bullocks sticking out. His wife made this gasp like "uhhhh" and put her palm to her chest like she was going to have a coronary and his kids started crying. I'm telling you mate, it was bad."

"Come on mate; you're making that up."

"No, it's true."

I sat silently for a moment contemplating the whole matter when I was struck with a thought. "If you didn't have the key and Jai didn't have the key, who had it?"

"Did you pick up our clothes last night?"

"Yeah, they're over there," I said pointing to a pile on the floor.

"You must have it then. Jai's said it's in his pant's pocket."

"How did you get in your room then?"

"We must have forgotten to lock the door when we left. It was unlocked."

After Miguel got out of the shower, all six of us went to see the manager. Annika talked to her because she knew Greek. I don't know

41

what was said but I know the manager was really pissed off. She kept raising her voice and making wide sweeping gestures with her hands. I was getting a little nervous there for a while; but, at the end of it all she let us stay on the condition that she didn't hear another sound from any of us. We really dodged a bullet on that one. We would have been fucked if she put us on the street. None of us had the money to pay for another room.

It was only our first night on the island and already we made quite an impression. But as large as the impression was we made that night, the night had made a bigger one on me. It had showed me that Madness and Insanity was much more powerful than I had anticipated. That night demonstrated to me that Madness and Insanity had no geographical boundaries. It was mobile and quite willing to travel. We were a long way from Manchester and it had still followed us. Or more accurately, it seems, it was already there, waiting for us when we arrived. Bigger than life it welcomed us just like the famed, colossus of antiquity that once straddled the island's harbor.

As the six of us filed out of the manager's office and strolled down to the pool for some early morning sunbathing, I wondered what else this towering colossus had in store for me and not just in the immediate future. Even then I realized it had significance and therefore began to seriously consider the subject as a scientist would, using observation and experimentation. I knew then that I had to know more about this thing.

***

We took it easy for the next few days after the scare of nearly getting kicked out. We didn't want to chance anything and get booted out of the hotel. For me, things were quiet on Rhodes, that is, until I met a girl named Xia.

I was shuffling through the cool midmorning sands of the beach, recovering from the drinking I did the night before. Further down the shore, I saw a girl sitting by herself. It seemed a rather chance encounter because the entire beach was empty except for the two of us. As I got closer, I noticed she was wearing a one piece bathing suit. She had a beautifully gaunt, Asian body, with dark brown skin. She looked Chinese, but her bathing suit appeared to be of a European design. She was reading a paperback novel through a pair of Jackie Kennedy, sixties style sunglasses and kept brushing her straight, black hair from her delicate, lovely face. I found her sexy and fashionable and couldn't resist smiling and giving her a simple "hello" as I approached.

She gave me an innocent, girlish smile back. "Hi...it's a nice day; don't you think?" She said looking past me, out at the openness of the Aegean. She spoke English with a hint of an Asian accent that made me even more intrigued by her.

"What's that you're reading?" I asked trying to start up a conversation.

She glanced down at the book that was still in her hand. "The Stranger...by Albert Camus...Do you know it...It's about a guy who shoots an Arab."

Standing on the beach...With a gun in my hand...Staring at the sea...Staring at the sand.

"And he's indifferent," I replied, "about the murder. He refuses or is unable to commit to a socially imposed sense of morality and thus becomes an outsider from society, a stranger to it...It's a classic. It's one of my favorites."

She flashed a small, flirtatious smile at me and scooted to one side of the towel she was sitting on.

"You want to sit down?" she invited.

"Sure," I said and sat next to her close enough to smell the coconut scent of her tanning oil.

"I'm Xia."

"David."

"So, why are you here in Faliraki?" she asked engagingly.

"I'm on vacation. It's our fall break."

"And you came all the way here from America...I assume you're American."

"Yeah. No...well, I'm American; but, I'm studying in the UK, in Manchester."

"Oh...okay."

"What about you? What brings you to Faliraki?"

"I live here."

"You do? What do you do here?"

"I'm supposed to be learning Greek. But, I don't try very hard."

"So what do you do instead?"

"I sit on the beach and talk to strange boys."

***

Before we left the beach, Xia told me she was having a party later that night. She invited me and the rest of my companions to attend. She also said that she was well known in the "émigré" community, on the island and that lots of interesting people, from all over the world were going to be there. It sounded good to me and everyone else was up for it as well.

I took two of the smuggled pills before we left, for the party. Miguel and Kal took two as well. I kept two to give to Xia and gave the last couple to Annika. I felt that I should give her some because after all, if it wasn't for her I wouldn't have gotten them there in the first place. She seemed quite happy about it. Of course, I didn't tell her where they came from.

When we arrived at the party, I could feel the pills starting to work. My body was just beginning to experience the first waves of the drug and I was ready to party. I rang the bell and Xia answered the door. She looked really sexy. She was wearing a skimpy, red summer dress that accentuated the thin curves of her body. She smiled when she saw it was me at the door and greeted me with a kiss on the cheek, holding it there, slightly longer, more intimately than I expected. She had a slight smell of alcohol but didn't appear to be very drunk.

I introduced her to my friends, and she looped her arm through mine to lead me into the party. I turned around and flashed Miguel and Akal a smile to boast the fortunate position I found myself in. Xia seemed really lively and I became slightly aroused by the prospects of the night.

Chaos, that's the only way to describe it. Xia's apartment was filled with people all pushed together. The crowd stood like liquid stalks of wheat, flowing and waving from side to side with each collective breath taken by the living mass. They were all dancing like maniacs to the German techno music that pounded the air from the numerous speakers spread across the room. The house was a buzz, a cacophony of talking and dancing and laughter and music.

"I got something for you," I said to Xia.

"You didn't have to bring me anything."

"I know I didn't. I wanted to."

I took the pills out of my pocket and gave them to her.

"It's ecstasy," I said.

She gave me an excited, surprised looked and threw her arms around my neck. She drew up to my face quickly kissing me softly with closed lips.

"Thank you," she said simply, putting the pills in her mouth.

We had a very flirtatious chat about nothing in particular and Xia seemed like she was well into me. Her body language said a lot. She was attentive and touched my arm gently several times. After a half and hour or so Xia went to socialize with the rest of her guests and told me that she would find me later to dance.

I went over to Kal and Miguel. They were talking to a short, fat guy wearing a three piece suit. He had his hair parted down the middle and plastered down the sides. The suit was an older one and I figured he was probably going for some vintage look that he wasn't quite able to pull off. He looked like a charlatan or a used car salesman from one of the prairie states, wearing that suit. He was holding a little vile in his hand. It was the kind with an eye dropper on top.

Snake oil?

"You want some?" Miguel asked, gesturing toward the bottle.

"What is it?" I enquired, directing my question to the car salesman, "Acid?"

"Not exactly," he replied casually, ambiguously.

I addressed Kal and Miguel.

"Did you guys take some?"

They replied that they had.

"Annnd…you're not, dead…Right?"

They indicated they were not.

"Alright. I'll try it," I said, having thoroughly considered the whole thing.

In retrospect, that might not have been the best idea. But the temptation was too much.

It didn't take long for things to start getting out of control. The whole apartment was consumed by a perpetual wave, which was both callus and familiar, Madness and Insanity.

Kal, Miguel, Jai, the girls and I were dancing when I notice the room and everything in it becoming a pinkish hue. It seemed very odd to me at the time that everything would be changing colors like that. I stopped dancing to figure out why such a thing might be happening. Kal probably noticed it too because he turned and said something to me I wasn't able to get. I just stood there looking at him completely bewildered. He repeated himself; but, still I couldn't understand a word he was saying. Then, it dawn on me.

He's speaking Punjabi.

"Speak English!" I shouted at him.

45

"I am!" he responded peevishly.

I think I understood that…Is he speaking English now…or…am I understanding Punjabi?

Kal continued to talk and I kept smiling and nodding as if I was listening; but, I had to tune him out. Whatever was in that charlatan's bottle was taking me over. I just stared as Kal and everything else turned pinker and pinker in color. Then, Miguel grabbed my arm from behind me. His grip was tight and rigid.

"You need ta stop it…ya need ta dis-intoxicate me!" he pleaded.

His eyes were wide and his voice told me he was on the verge of panic.

"You're fine!" I shouted to demonstrate that I had control of the situation even though I didn't. "It's just the drugs. It's supposed to be like this!"

That seemed to ease his mind. He lost his panicked look and starting dancing again. I danced for awhile longer too but the car salesman's drugs had an enervating affect on me. They were making me indolent and confused. I felt my energy flow from me in a stream taking my cognitive faculties along with it. Not that I minded it at all. In fact, I quite liked it. But, I could no longer dance. My body felt like a foreign weight I was burdened with.

I dragged myself to the edge of the room and leaned against the wall to rest. There were two guys standing to my right and as my head fell back against the wall one of them approached me and said with a thick German accent, "You must be the American!"

He's pretty convincing. It must be true.

I nodded my heavy head in agreement.

"Xia said she met you on the beach. We're her flat mates," he continued motioning to the guy next to him.

"It's nice to meet you," I said politely.

"Where are you from? New York?"

"No, no, no…I'm from Michigan–"

"Ahhh a real American!" The German exclaimed with exuberance.

He put his arm around my shoulder and rocked me from side to side in a gesture of friendship and well-meaning. I didn't have the power to resist so I went back and forth with him as he kept saying, "A reaaaal Ameeeericaaan…"

He paused the rocking and guzzled some wine from a bottle. Copious beads of the red liquid rolled down his chin, onto his shirt.

"So what are you doing–" He began before being interrupted by another German.

"LISTEN TO ME! LISTEN TO ME!" repeated a voice that reminded me of the Emcee in Cabaret.

We both turned our heads to see the other guy he identified as his flat mate storming off in the other direction. The guy I was talking to followed him and I was left alone against the wall. Strangely relieved he was gone, I allowed my body to slide down the wall until I was sitting on the floor with my knees against my chest. I gaped out at the pink chaos in front of me and waited for shadows and multitudes and languages to engulf me.

Time passed.

"What are you doing over here all by yourself?"

I looked up slowly and saw Xia standing next to me.

"I'm not entirely sure."

"Come on, get up let's dance."

"I can't. I'm too tired."

"Come on then. I want to show you something."

I got up slowly and she took my hand to lead me through the apartment.

"Where are we going?" I asked.

She turned her head around and said, "My bedroom," in a way that sounded like I should have already known that.

We entered her room and she shut and locked the door behind me. It was completely dark except for the light that intruded from under the door. It was surprisingly quiet in there. The party became nothing more than a low hum, like an auditory memory. I, at once, felt a thousand miles from it.

Xia went casually to her vanity and lit a group of candles that were on it. Their dull light reflected off the vanity's mirror barely casting enough light to see. The room was all shadows and I could only see what was near me. I looked at Xia and she had a long, thin, copper pipe in her hand. It was an ancient, oriental type, the kind glassy-eyed Chinese men used in the middle part of the nineteenth-century to smoke opium with.

"Wow," I said dreamily, "Where did you get that?"

"It belonged to my grandfather's grandfather."

She handed it to me to examine. The metal of the pipe felt cold and weighty.

"Would you like to smoke from it?"

"Sure."

She went back to the vanity and took out a small baggy from a porcelain box. I caught a glimpse, from the candle light of an opaque substance in the baggy.

"Have you ever smoked opium before?" she said as she prepared the pipe.

"No."

When she was done, she sat on the edge of the bed and lit the pipe. I sat down close to her as the smoke began wafting in the air. It had a peculiar, non-descript odor. She took a few small, gentle drags and passed it to me.

I felt the weight of the pipe again and took a powerful toke allowing my lungs to fill completely. The smoke was harsh and had a slightly bitter taste.

"Take another," she urged gently.

I did and relaxed back on the bed. I felt like I was falling weightlessly down into the depths an ocean.

I sat on the bed for a moment then I got up, thanked her and left. I left her room, and went out the front door of her apartment. A misty fog floated just inches above my head and I could feel the moisture of the sea deep in my lungs. I made my way leisurely back to my motel, taking time to appreciate the sound of the waves on the beach, nearby. My room was dark when I opened the door. I reached for the switch, flipped it upwards and then...POP!...an explosion of noise...shadows...dull light...candle light...I was still in Xia's room. I hadn't moved at all. She had turned on her CD player. The Velvet Underground streamed from it. I sat up lazily.

"You like the Velvet Underground too?" I said languidly.

"I love Nico," she whispered.

"Me too–"

Xia put her fingers over my mouth to stop my words. She was standing in front of me, arms hanging loosely to her sides, rocking seductively back and forth to the slow beat of the music. She raised her hand up slowly and rested it on her shoulder, never taking her eyes off me. She slid the strap of her dress off. It still clung to her body by the other strap. Her hand gradually drifted toward the other shoulder and pushed it off. The dress glided down to the floor revealing her small perfect breasts. She straddled my legs and sat on them, pinning me where I sat.

She kissed me slowly at first. She kissed my lips and neck caressing the side of my head with her petite hands. I smelled her

48

fragrance. It was an enticing, exotic scent. I put my hands on her hips which were still rocking to the beat of the music. She kissed me harder and began nibbling my neck. I kissed her dark breasts, surrounding her hard nipples with my mouth. I fondled them with my tongue, working her into a frenzy. She pulled my t-shirt over my head leaving my arms caught in it, above my head. I couldn't move them because I was so weak from the drugs. Powerless, she pushed me flat on the bed. She ran her hands over my bare chest allowing her nails to dig in lightly as she continued to rock gently to the music.

Again her lips kissed mine, very hard now, pressing them into my teeth. Then she bit my lips and my neck, harder than before. I could feel the sharp erotic pressure of her teeth on my skin. I felt her hands undoing my belt buckle. I looked at her face. Sweat glistened on her forehead. She looked devilish and angelic at the same time. She was beautiful. She brought her face toward mine and I kissed her mouth. Our tongues crashed into each other like waves, and then pulled gently back like the tide. Her mouth moved down my body to my lower neck. She bit me again, harder than before. My body tightened up for a second as the pain surged through me. The pain was followed by a rush of sexual excitement. She sensed this and moved her lips down and across my chest, biting me. I expected to feel my blood trickle from the wounds. I watched as she took off my clothes and then her underwear.

She straddled me again and began speaking to me tenderly in Chinese as I slid inside her. I closed my eyes and listened to her mysterious, alluring words. I felt her tight slender body on mine and concentrated on the pleasure of being with her. She rocked, still to the slow tempo of the music until we climaxed and collapsed into the foreignness of each other.

Helli

The first time I saw Helli, was some weeks after I got back to Manchester from Greece. In fact, it was just after the second semester started. The six or eight weeks between my return and the time Helli entered my life flew by so fast, remembering them is like trying to capture images from a speeding train. General impressions tend to be persevered while details blur into the landscape and are lost. I do know that I spent quite a bit of time hanging out with Solis, Miguel and Mikko during that period. I would sip coffee or ale in Krö Bar or smoke pot with them in Solis's room while he danced like a freak to the music he always played loudly. We would waste away entire afternoons that way. We also went to parties or hit the clubs three or four times a week, quite often coming home in the early morning hours with strange girls. I was meeting interesting and exciting people all the time, people like Helli. Indeed, I was on a speeding train then and my general impressions are of being happy and uninhibited. My memories are of being in the right place at the right time and knowing it. It was a time in my life when the city I lived in, the friends I had, the places I went and the things I did all formed a specific synergy that I had never felt before and hasn't been replicated since.

Of course, this is only selective memory. There were mundane chores which needed to be done. I cleaned my room and watered my plant. I had to take out the trash and check emails. My strained relationship with my father had a way of creeping up from time to time. I also had to attend lectures and seminars during that period. I had books and articles to read and papers to write. That's why I was in the library that day. I was doing research for a paper on distributive justice. I was walking around with a stack of books tucked under my arm like a nerd when I noticed her. She was working at a computer, in one of the various clusters spread throughout the library. Her eyes were intently focused on the monitor and her fingers were pounding the keys furiously. She had an intense look in her eyes that contrasted with the soft, yet impish beauty of her face. I noticed her hair first. It was light blond, hanging straight down to the small of her back. She was tall and gorgeous, baring a resemblance to the singer Nico.

Ohhh Fuck! Who's that?

I rarely had this kind of impression when I saw a girl but she wasn't just a girl, she was amazing. There was something about her.

Maybe it was the confidence of her movements or the audacity of her beauty. I'm not sure what made her amazing but it was something intangible, a uniqueness about her that appealed to me much more than any girl ever before. I thought about going up and talking to her. I really wanted to, in fact, but I couldn't. I had nothing to say. It would have been too awkward approaching her like that, so I just continued to walk by.

That was on a Friday. I remember that, because the next day, Saturday, Mikko's girlfriend Darcy had a party. The party was pretty unexciting and I don't really recall much about it except that's where I saw Helli for the second time. She came late in the evening with a couple of other people. She just stood by the door with her coat on, waiting for her friends as they went in. It appeared like she wasn't planning on staying long so I quickly went over to her and stuck up a conversation. I knew I had a small window of opportunity and didn't want to waste it.

Now, I would like to tell you that everything went really well; but, that would be a goddamn lie. It was probably the worst pick up attempt I ever made. She was aloof and seemed bored like she was only talking to me because she had nothing better to do. I tried several of the usual conversation starters but she was unresponsive to all of them. The only time I got her engaged was when I asked her if she wanted a drink. It was a simple enough question but a very long and intimate answer followed. To be honest, I was a little shocked by the candidness of her response.

"Well," she said, "I'm not drinking tonight which is quite shit because I usually do. I quite like to drink. Mostly, I drink vodka, but sometimes I prefer a lager. Wine is also nice. But, my doctor told me not to drink alcohol until the results of my test are available."

"Test?" I questioned.

"You see there is this problem with my liver…"

Did she just say there was a problem with her liver?

She then went into graphic detail (which I will spare you) about the problems she was experiencing with her liver. She described invasive photos that were taken of it, how it was discolored and rife with decay. The image it conjured was vivid and grotesque, a stark contrast to her outward beauty. At some point, I wished she would just stop talking; but, she just banged on about it—how it felt, what it might be, etc.

We talked for maybe a half an hour. Or more to the point, the conversation lasted about half an hour. Out of that, I spoke for maybe three minutes. She talked about herself and her liver all the rest of the time. When she finally left, I wondered how a girl could be so smoking

51

hot and at the same time so crass. I wasn't surprised so much about the self-centeredness, how she dominated the conversation speaking about herself. Quite honestly, I expected it even before we started talking. I figured that anyone of her caliber probably would be, at least to some degree. No, it was her lack of character that I was surprised by. It was especially unexpected because I was so physically attracted to her. It seemed like it would have been easy to find something about her personality that I liked, or could at least tolerate.

Only one thing about her, except her looks, interested me. She told me she was Finnish. I don't know what it was about those people that fascinated me so much then but they did. At that time, I hadn't been there and only knew about it from the stories Mikko told me. I guess that I sort of saw Finland, tucked away up there in the far reaches of Northern Europe as maybe The Emerald City or something like that. Except, instead of being inhabited by a bunch of singing midgets, it was full of beautiful, sophisticated, intelligent women that I wanted to shag. To be fair, Helli's just being hot was enough for me to go after her but hot and Finnish…I was hooked.

I was going to try and get her phone number before she left, but when her friends came back she was out the door, just like that. She only said a quick "bye" as the door was closing behind her. I thought it was pretty rude of her to leave like that. I felt like she could have at least given me a proper goodbye.

Oh well fuck it I said to myself after she was gone, *she's got Jaundice or some shit anyway. Baggage…Issues.*

I went back to the party and forgot about her. But, obviously that wasn't the last time I saw her or else I wouldn't have named the whole goddamn chapter after her. I ran into her again, weeks later at a bar called Big Hands. Mikko and I had stopped in for a night cap. The place was packed but I noticed her right away through the crowd. I really didn't want to talk to her though. I felt slighted by her hasty departure at Darcy's party. However, when I walked by her, I noticed her, noticing me. She was bobbing her head around tying to get a look at me through all the people that were between us. When a clearing broke, she was there in front of me.

"I know this sounds weird," she began, "but, don't I know you?"

Know me? Fuck! Better play this cool. She might want sex!

"Yeah, I think that we meet at a party a few weeks ago." I said.

I tried to down play the impression that she had made on me. So, I went through the whole "Oh, what was your name again, etc, etc."

technicalities. But, I remembered her name. I remembered the first time I saw her at the library pounding the computer keys, and how I was besotted by her slender curves and shiny, golden hair. I knew exactly that I meet her at Darcy's and that she stood in the doorway the whole time, never bothering to take off the puffy, white down coat she had on. I recollected what we talked about and could have probably recited the conversation verbatim. I had wanted to play it cool though. I didn't want to fuel her ego.

I stood there maybe fifteen minutes and conversed with her for the second time. Actually, I mostly listened to her talk about herself again. She told me about some drinking exploit she had recently had and of course she brought up her ailing liver. Apparently, she had gotten her test results back and things didn't look so good. She didn't go into details and it looked like she was either hiding something or somehow in denial. She had a beer in her hand and I could tell that it wasn't her first.

"What the fuck is this chick's deal?" I said to myself over and over as I watched her beautiful lips, glistening slightly move enticingly with each word. It pained me to hear her talk about her grotesque medical condition like that. She was so attractive but the image of her liver was horrifying. Finally, I couldn't take it any longer. She was so boring and had this awful condition. She also seemed self-centered and attention hungry. Logically, she was not a girl I should have been interested in at all; and yet I found myself standing there listening to the drone of her words and nodding my head up and down like an idiot. She was reeling me in like the song of a Siren. And it was all because she looked really good and I wanted to shag her. I imagined having sex with her in explicit detail as she talked, the feel of her skin, the noises she would make, the positions we would do. It was solely a base and animalistic attraction and I was intellectually repulsed by this realization. Yet, I indulged it, encouraged it in a depraved and wanton manner.

It was all wrong and I knew it, so I made a very bold decision, right then and there. A decision, I wasn't sure I could really follow through on because it would mean a major lifestyle adjustment. I decided not let my depravity get the better of me. I would not try to shag her or any girl for that matter solely because I found them attractive. I would no longer lower myself to it regardless of how hot they were.

I told her that I had to go talk to my friend and that I'd chat with her again later. However, I had no intention of that. My intention was to begin living out my decision, to begin my new life. I left her and went to find Mikko. He was having a drink with some people he knew from his course. I had a drink with them and left by myself without talking to Helli again.

***

I woke up the next day, as I did most days, in the early afternoon. I got out of bed, stretched a little, flipped on the radio to listen to the news and turned my phone on. I was accustomed to having phone messages when I woke up. Most of my friends, classmates, associates, and the rest of society for that matter, would have had hours of productivity before I arose from my slumber. But, I liked to follow the wise words of Ben Franklin, "Later to bed, later to rise, means no more hangover or red eyes."

On this particular morning I had only one message, a text message that said something to the effect that I was an inconsiderate jerk for not saying goodbye before I left the night before, but if I wanted to, we could go out sometime. It was signed, Helli.

Helli? Couldn't be.

"Fucking Mikko, I gotta wake up to his games..." I said quietly to myself. I thought that Mikko was playing a joke on me because we had talked a couple times about Helli. He knew how hot I thought she was. He knew her a little bit as well. They had met a few times through mutual friends.

I called Mikko and asked him what was up with the message. But, it turned out to be authentic. According to Mikko, after I left, Helli went up to him and asked a few casual questions about me. Were Mikko and I friends etc. etc? Then she asked him if he thought that I would like to go out with her. He gave her my number and that was that. She sent me a message.

At first, I wasn't going to reply. I had made a major life decision the night before. I was going to change my ways. I wasn't an animal and I didn't have to act on all my libidinous urges. I was, in fact, a human being and should look for more in a companion than physical beauty. But then, I reconsidered. Fair enough, I was a human; but, I was also an animal. And besides, if I kept running into her in random places and if she went through all that trouble to get my phone number, something larger than animal attraction was at work. Indeed, it seemed to be Karma and I didn't want to fuck with that.

54

I called Helli and we set a time to have drinks a few nights later. Drinks were her idea. This didn't really surprise me though. I was beginning to suspect she may have had a modest drinking problem. She was only twenty-eight years old and had already developed some type of hideous liver disorder and yet, she chose to go out for drinks. It was a little sad but at the same time I sort of admired her bravado.

We decided to go to Krö Bar, which was my idea. Ever since the day I went there with Akal, I had been almost daily. It had both a convenient location and a good atmosphere. It was close to the Library and the building where my seminars were. I would pop in after class quite often. It had a nice, comfortable, relaxing ambiance that was hard for me to resist. It was chic but not presumptuous. It was, to me, the best place to have a drink in all of greater Manchester.

I also chose Krö Bar because I thought that it would be good to have the date on my turf, so to speak. I had been a little apprehensive about the date ever since I made it. It wasn't so much the fact that we were going on a date. That much I actually liked. It was more the fact that we were going to have drinks together, which I think is particularly tricky for a first date. Going out for drinks on a first date is a double edged sword. On one side you are entering into a situation where drinking is involved. This automatically increases the likelihood of sexual intercourse and is clearly a positive. However, on the other side, you are forced to sustain a conversation the whole time. This is not always an easy thing to do, or endure. Sustaining a conversation with Helli might have meant sitting there, bored out of my skull and acting like I was interested, while she rambled endlessly about all the times she got wasted or about her Cirrhosis or whatever it was she had. Nevertheless, having drinks was the date and I wasn't going to back out.

I got there first and waited outside her. I didn't have to wait long and we went in. We picked out a table near the front window and I got a couple of drinks for us. Then, we started in on the small talk. She told me that she was studying film, a topic that I had more than just a passing interest in. We discussed the nuances of Stanley Kubric's work and some of our other favorite directors and movies. She told me that one of her favorite movies was *I Am Curious, Yellow*. Although she was Scandinavian, I would have never guessed she would appreciate such a movie. We discussed other things as well, like the places we had traveled and the literature we liked. She was impressed by my knowledge of *The Kalevala* and I was impressed by her appreciation of Philip Roth's work.

55

The two of us sat there drinking and talking quite comfortably. After two or three drinks, I began to realize that she was actually a little bit interesting. I was having a good time. She had barely mentioned her liver and the conversation was lively and unforced.

We were already five drinks into the night and far from ready to end it when Krö Bar closed. We continued our date at Big Hands where we had a few more drinks and really started to loosen up. We got on the subject of movies again, by that time we were both pretty drunk and speaking openly. I told her that when I was in high school I tried to write a movie script, but it turned out to be horrible, even to my untrained eye and I gave up on it. Then she told me that she had actually just finished a script of her own.

"Oh yeah? What's it about?" I asked curiously.

"It's a porno," she replied without a change in her expression.

"What?" I asked, unsure if she was kidding, "A porno...really?"

"Yes, really," she responded defensively, "I wrote a porno script."

"Well, what's it about?"

"It's a porno script! It's about sex and fornication, what else?"

"Yeah, I know what pornos are about. I mean what's the plot?"

"It doesn't have a plot. It's not that kind of movie."

There was a pause.

*A porno...sex and fornication...It doesn't have a plot...*Her words swam around my head, arousing my mind, arousing my body.

"Where did you get the idea to write a porn movie?"

"I like sex and I like watching sex movies. I want to direct one sometime."

She went on to talk about some of her sexual fantasies. She didn't go into much detail but the intimacy was certainly there. I found this and the rest of the conversation exceptionally interesting. Until that point, I had only seen her as sexually attractive, not as sexually proactive. That is, it never occurred to me to think that she had wants, desires and urges of her own. And she didn't seem to have any qualms talking about these desires and urges. She was the embodiment of sexual liberation. She was *Curious* and I was enamored. I don't know why I didn't think about it before. Of course she had desires, everyone does. I was just too absorbed in my own sexual fantasies. But, once she told me hers, I couldn't stop thinking about them.

When Big Hands closed, we stumbled, drunkenly, onto a bus and went to her house. We staggered into her bedroom and plopped down

56

on the bed like sacks of wheat. Even though we had all the talk about sex and there was certainly an energy there, we were too drunk to try. Before I passed out though, I slid my body next to hers. I pressed my chest against her back and moved my legs behind hers. I felt the contours of her body and smelled her hair. Each time she took a breath I could feel her perfect figure. It was a precise mixture, a perfect combination of muscle and bone and skin and hair. I wanted her badly and not just in a physical way. I wanted to consume her. I wanted to ingest her whole being. At that moment, I knew I could endure her idiosyncrasies, for a little while anyway. She wasn't someone, I saw myself being with forever, but after all she certainly did have qualities.

***

I had to cut out early the next morning because I had to attend a seminar on human rights. I invited her to come with me but she wanted to keep sleeping. She kissed me on the forehead and, before rolling over and falling back asleep, said that she would call me later.

All in all things went well for a first date. She seemed to be into me and I was unexpectedly into her, although to be fair, it was still more of a physically attraction on my part.

A few nights after our first date, we decide to go out again. I suggested that we go out to dinner and then for a couple cocktails afterwards. I knew a quaint Spanish restaurant on Deansgate.

At the restaurant, we ate tapas and washed it down with several pitchers of sangria. I paid particular attention to the way she drank. She seemed to almost relish each taste as if it might have been her last. I thought about the possibility of her having a drinking problem again. I really didn't care if she did. She never got too sloppy drunk and she could function just fine in her daily life. She went to school and paid her bills. She even managed to do quite well in her coursework. I liked her the way she was. She was sort of a party girl. She was also a sexually free, slightly debauched woman. I couldn't argue with that. Anyway, what did I care if she had a drinking problem? What did I care if she was destroying her liver? It was her liver, not mine. Besides, it was fun to associate with a girl who could consume alcohol at the same pace as me. It kept the nights long and allowed for all types of Madness and Insanity.

After dinner we decided to go to a place, near Canal Street called Tri Beca. The place was a pseudo-trendy watering hole that catered to a mostly gay and yuppie crowd. I really liked this place, although I didn't fit the scene exactly and neither did she. But that didn't really matter to us or anyone there. Since it was in the gay district people didn't really mind if you fit the scene or not. The Canal Street district was pretty much tolerant of anybody who was tolerant of it.

At Tri Beca, Helli and I got into another long discussion about sex. She was so open, such a libertine. That really turned me on. I stared at her well defined, high cheek bones and long blond hair. She had a traditional Finnish look, with the poise of a model. She did speak with a monotonous, flat voice but for some reason I found it irresistible. I liked it because she spoke about sex the way a scientist talks about their research, dispassionately but clearly moved by the subject.

Late in the evening, we were sitting next to each other on one of the couches that were scattered around the bar. She was talking and I let her droning, soothing voice put me in a trance. I looked intently at the way her flaxen hair brushed against her cheek.

"David...David!"

She put her hand on my leg. It seemed to move, from her body to mine, the way it would through water.

"Are you listening to me?" she asked.

"No."

"Why not?"

"I'm admiring you."

She gave me a flattered smile and said, "Let's get out of here."

She said it flatly but it had tremendous sexual overtones. Her voice and her words were almost paradoxical. It was so to the point. I kissed her and ran my hand the length of her thigh.

"Not here," she said.

We went back to my room and smoked a joint. I sat on the chair and she was on the bed. When she was done smoking, she passed the spliff to me and without a word, without provocation, she took off her shirt and bra. She sat only feet away from me but seemed oblivious to my presence. She stared out into space and started touching her breasts. She stroked them roughly and pinched her nipples.

"I love my tits," she said in a matter of fact way. "I think that they are my best part."

They were small but well formed with tiny erect nipples. Her stomach was flat but with little definition. I could tell that her figure came naturally because of the lack of muscle tone that comes from exercise. Still, her body was faultless and I watched as she groped it. She touched herself, it seemed, almost to mock me. I wanted to touch her;

58

but, she was getting so much enjoyment from touching herself. I just watched for the moment. She closed her eyes and let her hands caress her breasts and her shoulders and abdomen.

I went to shut the lights off and she heard me getting up.

"What are you doing?" she asked.

"I was going to turn off the lights."

"No. Keep them on…I want to see you…I want you to see me."

That aroused me mentally even more than I had become physically. I wanted to see her and I liked that she wanted to see me.

She undressed herself unceremoniously and then ordered me to do the same. I did as she said and stood there naked, surveying Helli's nude body, the whole time remembering our conversations about sex, recalling her fantasies and thinking of my own. I felt an urgency, internally, mentally, physically while I anticipated the sensation of her slender, warm body touching mine.

***

What the fuck?! I asked myself as I rolled off her sweaty, rigid, inanimate body.

As you might imagine from my initial reaction, the sex didn't live up to my expectations, at all. To be fair, it was by far the worst shag that I had ever been a party to. I was astonished. I didn't know how it could have happened. I replayed everything in my head. She was a chic beauty and a self-professed sexual dynamo. She should have been great. She should have been more than great. But she wasn't. She just laid there on the bed, motionless with her eyes closed, making squirrel noises and flaring her nostrils like a charging bull. She was a sexy woman but for Christ's sakes this was not a sexy sight, by any stretch of the imagination. Afterwards, she kept talking about how much she enjoyed it which I don't doubt because I had tried so hard. But to me, it didn't seem like she enjoyed it; it looked like something was wrong. At one of the more nasty points, I considered stopping and making sure everything was all right. I was a little concerned that she may have been experiencing liver failure or something to that effect. It was a complete disaster. I wasn't even able to climax. I felt the same way that I did the first time I saw the movie *Who Framed Roger Rabbit*. I didn't get to see the movie for a few weeks after it was released and everyone kept telling me, "You got to see that movie, it's the best." and so on and so forth. After three or four weeks of hearing about how great the movie was, I finally got to see it. When I did,

59

I was extremely disappointed. In later years, after watching it again, I actually took the time to analyze why I felt that way about the movie. I concluded that it wasn't the movie itself, but rather that I had subconsciously put too high of an expectation on it. I don't think that any movie could have lived up to those expectations. I learned a valuable lesson from Roger Rabbit and thought that perhaps my experience with Helli was the same kind of situation. That is to say, I considered the possibility that the sex really wasn't as bad as I thought and that I had just put unreasonable expectations on it. This seemed entirely plausible, so I decided to give it another go. Only this time I attempted to be completely objective. Unfortunately, the second time was miserable as well.

I felt cheated, like she had somehow swindled me. I felt like she had misrepresented herself or lied to me. She didn't seem at all the sexual creature she led me to believe she was. I didn't even feel like talking to her afterwards. I felt like making her leave and letting that be that. I didn't, of course, because that would have been rude and inhumane. Also, an obscure, yet somehow influential voice in my head convinced me that a monumental sexual event would eventually happen with this woman. All the signs were there. She was beautiful and sexy. She was fond of pornography. She appeared to be well into me. On paper, it seemed like a sure bet so I acted like nothing was wrong and fell asleep with her.

In the morning, I skipped class with Helli and we smoked weed together all day. We got out of bed early, around eleven and she was hungry. I went to the kitchen and got the only food that I had, half a baguette and a bottle of Merlot. It wasn't exactly the breakfast of champions but it had to do.

When I got back to my room Helli was going through some of my pictures that had been sitting out on my desk. One was of the horizon of Lake Michigan.

"Do you know what is aava?" she asked me.

"No, what is it?"

She replied in a way that seemed both poignant and enlightened, "It's a Finnish word, aava...It's the most important thing in my life."

"Well, what's it mean?" I asked with genuine interest.

"If you look it up in a Finnish to English dictionary, it will tell you that it means openness. But, that's not right."

"You explain it then."

"It has to do with the sea. When looking out over the sea, aava is half what you see and half what you feel. It is an openness of your self-being and your practical viewing."

"I'm not sure I understand."

"Have you ever been out to open sea?"

"Yeah...of course."

"And looked out over the water?"

"Yeah."

"What did you see?"

"Nothing. Just water."

"You didn't see the sky?"

"Yeah, and the sky too."

"And how did you feel?"

"I guess, I felt—"

"No. Don't tell me. But, that feeling you get when you look out over the water and all you can see, all around you, is where the sky meets the sea. That's aava. Not so much what you see, but how you feel. That feeling, aava...is the most important thing in my life. It is the only thing in my life, really."

"Why is it the most important thing for you?"

"I love to sail. I love to be out on the water, experiencing aava. It is complete liberation. It is a deliverance you can only find when you are at sea."

"A deliverance from what?"

"Everything you can't see."

***

Things never really went anywhere with Helli. We went out and shagged a few more times; but, at some point I decided the sex wasn't going to get any better and it certainly wasn't worth the bother of having to listen to her talk about her liver and all the goddamn time. It didn't take long for me to lose track of her and I was glad for that. I knew she would fade and she soon did. Well, mostly she faded...

61

Head above Water

I experienced a sense of relief when I broke it off with Helli. It was just one less hassle I had to deal with. In retrospect, though she wasn't completely awful. There were a few times I felt like we made a connection. I really liked it when she opened up to me and told me about aava and all that. It made her seem somehow more dynamic. But, it could have never worked and I knew it and so for a good couple weeks afterward I was comfortable and content with my life. However, as the weeks wore on, I slowly started to get preoccupied with a harsh, inevitable reality. The end of the semester was drawing near and like a balloon being inflated, Manchester was slowly swelling because of it. A blend of anxiety, stress, and sobriety was saturating the environment. This horrible mixture stayed trapped in the little student section of the city, trapped in the small circles of student accommodations and night clubs and student unions. You could feel it in the library, the halls of residence, the academic buildings and everywhere else in the university and the other universities in town as well. Everyday the pressure grew as the weather got warmer and people started 'buckling down' as my father, the cliché asshole would say.

I knew it would continue that way until the end of classes. There was no way around it. The city would continue to inflate until it would finally explode. We would need that explosion, to allow ourselves, to vent the stress and anxiety. The only problem was that the explosion was going to send my environment, my life sailing through the air in any direction. I wasn't concerned about where I was going to land because inevitably I would find solid ground. I was just concerned about the trip I would take before I landed. Because, I knew very well what force propelled such things through the air. It was Madness and Insanity and I could feel it near. But, this wasn't my own personal Madness and Insanity. It was the whole city's. I knew things were about to get out of hand and there wasn't anything I could do about it.

Now, no drug subjects a person more to the whims of Madness and Insanity than Cocaine. However, it is also the drug that Madness and Insanity is most forgiving of. Since I had been living in Manchester, I had learned quite a bit about it, ever since Rhodes. Madness and Insanity, you see, is a river. Alcohol, Marijuana, LSD, Ecstasy, Mushrooms, Benzedrine, Codeine, Demerol, glue, or whatever one takes, will cause you to float and drift upon this river differently. If you are lucky you bob in the water completely subjected to it until you are washed safely onto its banks. If you are, however, unlucky you sink to the bottom and drown. But, cocaine is somehow different. With cocaine, you don't just float. You swim with the current. This has both advantages and disadvantages. Since you are swimming you are able to keep your head above water. However, you are also quickly paddling yourself headlong into unknown waters, waters that transverse and flow over dangerous, unseen hazards. Cocaine will keep your head from going under, but it may very well take you over a waterfall, so to speak.

I knew that the end of the semester was going to be a furious river. I could feel it and to be honest I was a little nervous about the whole thing. In Manchester, and even in Greece, I had experienced crazy, wild times, but I had always fallen into it. This was the first time I could see it from a distance, like it was a big tsunami tidal wave rolling in. It was going to be massive. It was going to be dangerous. And, I knew that my friends and I were situated too close not to be pulled into it when the waters came. We did have a choice, though. We could drift or we could swim.

Two and a half days later, I pulled myself onto the bank of the river. I was weary. But I was alive.

***

I discussed the impending deluge with Solis, Miguel, and Mikko. I shared with them my theory of Madness and Insanity being a river about to wash us all into a treacherous course. Although, they had no idea what I was on about, they were keen to the idea of scoring some blow for the last day of classes.

We just had two problems: locating the cocaine and paying for it. Coke, unlike marijuana and ecstasy was relatively hard to get a hold of especially at short notice. Trust is vital. Before anyone will sell it to you they must trust you first and of course you have to pay up front. After we pooled our money together it quickly became evident that establishing trust was going to be a lot easier than paying up front.

We needed a plan to make sure this thing happened and a division of labor was rapidly set up. Solis and I had to obtain the money and Miguel set off to line up a dealer.

It didn't take Miguel long to find someone. He had a knack for these things. Even though he had only been in the city for as long as I had, he had tons of connections for nearly everything. If you wanted some blow or tickets to a Manchester United match or even an out of print book, he was the one who could get it. Not that he always utilized all his connections; but, he kept them just in case. The coke connection was the typical friend of a friend scenario that makes everyone uneasy, but we were in a pinch and didn't have much of an option. Already, I could feel the cold waters rising to my toes.

The guy who said he could get the cocaine for Miguel told him that the deal needed to go down quickly or his stash would be gone. We knew that it was true. Dealers, especially low level ones never have a lot and never want to hold much because it's too risky. My friends and I were under a time restriction. Solis and I had to get the money. I asked Solis if he had any ideas.

He responded with wide eyes, "Mate, en fac I do hafe an idea. We can wait by da cash machine an rob some motherfuckas!"

"Solis, mate, that's a poor idea," I said.

"No, mate, hear me out. You jus go up ta some ri-tch look'en motherfucka right after he get some monies and ya ask him what is da time or how ta get som place or any shit and den, I come and hit him en da fuck'en head wit a stick or a bat or my shoe or some shite like dat."

"We're not going to fucking rob anyone, jackass."

"Okay den! You have any ideas?"

"Maybe we can act like we're working for a church and ask people to donate money for some cause like feeding homeless people."

"Mate, look at you. No motherfucka will believe dat you are getting monies for to feed the homeless. You look like the type dat da church give the soup to! Hehehehe…"

"Yeah that's cute…Alright maybe it's not the best fucking idea, but it's a lot better than your idea."

"I have an idea," interjected Mikko who had been quietly watching on, "why don't you just ask your parents for the money."

"Is good, mate! Is good idea!" exclaimed Solis.

I wasn't so sure that it was a good idea. Of course it was the first thing that I thought of, but I didn't know how difficult it would be getting money out of my father. Normally, it wouldn't be extremely difficult. But, at that time I had to be tactful because I knew my father hadn't forgotten about the whole drunk driving fiasco. However, he was my only real chance at getting the money. I wasn't going to rob or steal or even con anybody for it and there wasn't enough time to become gainfully employed. Not that getting a job was a realistic option for me anyway. I mean, I really did want the money but not enough to work for it. My father was the only way. I knew what I had to do.

***

On my way home, I stopped into to a pay phone and called my dad.

"Hello."

"Hey! Dad! How's it going?"

"What is it, Dave?"

"You see dad it's like this. I need two hundred dollars—"

"What for?" he interrupted curtly.

"Well, dad, ah..." I suddenly realized that I should have thought up an excuse beforehand.

Think damn it. Think...

"Ahhh...I need the money for books."

"For books?" he replied suspiciously. "What happened to all that money I gave you at the beginning of the semester to buy books?"

What did happen to all that money?

"I already spent that on books a long time ago," I lied.

In actuality, all the books I needed for the semester where available in the library, so I didn't purchase any of them. Instead, I spent the money on marijuana and alcohol. But the part about it being spent a long time ago was the truth. I blew the whole wad the weekend I got it.

"Your mother told me that you've been working hard. It's good to see you finally getting serious about life. I'll send you the money this week sometime."

"That's fantastic!...Only one more thing. I need the money in two days."

"What do you think I am, a goddamn ATM? You'll get the money when you get it."

"Ah...well you see, the books I need...um...I already ordered them from the bookstore and they'll only hold on to them for two days."

"And that's my problem?"

You know, he really was a fuck. He always said shit like that, like everything I did was somehow a hassle for him.

"No it's not your problem. It's my problem; but, I need those books for a project. Look, you're the one who says I need to work hard, well I can't work without those books so can I have the money or not?"

65

"Fine," he said stubbornly, "I'll give you the money; but, you need to be more responsible…"

My father, like always found a way to turn the conversation into a responsibility lecture; but, I really didn't mind all that much this time. I was getting the money for the cocaine and one hell of a party was going to happen. There were only three days left of classes and the river had suddenly swollen to my knees. My friends and I were getting prepared for the ultimate bursting of the levy, when the wild surge would take us downstream.

***

The money from my father came two days later. Three minutes after I got it in my hand, it was in Miguel's along with the money Solis got from his mom. In total, we had enough for four grams plus a little left over for wine and grass. The score turned out to be no problem. Miguel got the product the day before classes ended. Solis got us some grass from his guy and Mikko and I went to the store and bought a couple bottles of wine and a bunch of beers. It was difficult not to sample the stuff; but, I knew that if we did it would quickly get out of hand. We sat on our stash and waited. There was no point getting into it then. We knew we where going to need it later.

My last class was actually a few days before most of the other students as was Mikko's. Therefore, we spent the last official day of classes drinking at Krö Bar. We sat outside in the front having Bloody Maries and carefully observing the events of the day. I could tell that it wasn't like any other day. There was a general excitement in the air, a buoyancy that was ubiquitous. Mikko and I felt that way too.

For two weeks I had been dreading this day and fearing what horrors awaited me. But then, sitting at Krö Bar having drinks with Mikko and watching my fellow students, I no longer felt apprehensive. Madness and Insanity was coming, that was for sure; but, I realized that she had always spared me in the past. I had no reason to think that that night would be different. I was actually a little anxious. I was ready to get all fucked up, to just dive in and see what would happen. After all, all I had to do was keep my head above water.

In the late afternoon, Mikko and I went to his flat, made some dinner and then sat around watching the television and drinking some of the wine we bought. We thought that it would be good to get some rest before the night really started. We were in the middle of a Knight Rider re-run when Miguel and Solis showed up with the powder.

"You got it I asked," trying to be composed.

Miguel smiled and pulled a bag out of a pocket in his denim jacket. He dropped it on the coffee table and I picked it up. I held it in the light and bounced it in my palm gauging the weight. Satisfied, I opened the bag, poured some on the table and cut four fat rails, one for each of us. When I looked up my friends had the look of hungry wolves.

"Same time?" I asked.

"Same time." They all agreed.

The four of us lowered our heads to the table and snorted our lines simultaneously.

***

The stuff got to Solis the quickest. In less than a minute he was already unruly. He had just sat next to me on the couch when he suddenly jumped to his feet.

"Ah papa, is good mate, is good mate!!!" He shouted with feral emotion. "Let's git some bitches tonight...I wan ta shag like fuck!"

"Yeah man, let's go to Prague V," I suggested. I was feeling a little feral myself.

Mikko and Miguel also liked the idea and we went down to Oxford Road to catch a number 32 Magic Bus toward the city centre. By the time we got to the bus stop, we probably didn't even need to take the bus; we were so high we could have flown.

A blue bus came sliding to a stop in front of us and the four of us got on. There were two sets of seats opened in the middle rows, across the aisle from each other. Solis and I took one set and Miguel and Mikko shared the other. After the bus rambled down a few blocks Miguel kicked my shoe to get my attention. He had taken out the small baggy with the cocaine. This was a very audacious thing to do. In my time in Manchester, I had seen people smoking dope in public at least once a day. But, I had never really even heard people talking about cocaine in public. Heavy narcotics where frowned upon. Mancunians like their drink, they like their cannabis and they even like kicking the shit out of each other. But, they had to draw the line somewhere. Honestly, I don't know exactly where that line lays; but, I did know snorting coke on a public bus was crossing it. There was a good possibility that someone would inform the police or even that some civic minded individual with a hero complex would make a scene.

I wasn't the only one aware of this. Mikko also sensed trouble and quickly intervened.

"Hey, put it away." He said, covering the bag with his hand. "There's a lot of people watching."

Miguel looked around the bus and responded in a determined but non-confrontational voice. "No, is okay. Solis, verdad?"

Solis looked over at Miguel, not having been paying attention, "Que?"

"Is alright ta do some more now?"

"Yesss…Ah papa, la cocaína papa. Dame la cocaína. Give me dat shite. I don give a fuck about any of dese mother fuckas." He looked around the bus and then continued, "Es'cept for dose bitches up dere. I know dose bitches, an dey need DICK! And I would like to give it ta dem…."

He turned to the front of the bus where a couple of good looking women sat.

"DICK! They need DICK! QUIERAN BECHA, PUTAS? HEEHEEHEE….AHHHHH PAPA, LOOK AT DA BITCHES. LA COCAÍNA PAPA, WHERE IN THE FUCK IS LA COCAÍNA???"

He turned to Miguel, "Where is da cocaine by da way?"

"Yeah man, fuck it. Who cares if we're on the fucking bus? What the fuck is anybody going to do?" I said.

I figured that if no one would do anything when a bushy-headed, shifty-eyed freak like Solis started screaming obscenities and sexual harassments at innocent women, they surely wouldn't intervene if they saw him start using cocaine.

"See." Miguel said, directing this comment to Mikko.

"Alright man, you convinced me. Give it here." He replied with a cheeky smile.

***

We got off the bus near the Palace Theater and walked the short distance to Canal Street. I remember walking fast, with my arms swinging quickly beside me; but, I don't recall my feet ever touching the ground. I was energetic and excited. Solis was too, only he had sort of lost control. The whole walk to Prague V he was raving like he did on the bus only it got worse. He kept shouting crudely at random women. His eyes bulged. Spit flew from his mouth.

"QUIERA BECHA...DICK!...YOU WANT DICK!!!AHHHHHHH!"

Outside of Prague V, we had to wait in line before we could enter and Solis became inpatient.

"AHHH...BECHA, THEY WANT DICK, AHHH," he screamed insanely in my direction.

The cocaine has finally done Solis in. He's fucking lost it.

"AHHH...HEEE...HEEE...BECHA? AHHH...AHHH...PAPA...LA COCAÍNA ...BASUCO WE NEED BASUCO!!!" he continued, becoming more dramatic. His lips glistened from the spittle that accumulated there and he made wild, pornographic gestures with his hands and groin. People started to stare uneasily at him. He was acting like a schizophrenic or something.

"Hey, calm the fuck down or they won't let us in!" I pleaded.

He managed to calm himself down and a few minutes later the bouncer opened the door for us revealing a dark, smoky club filled with people. Prague V had two stories, the upper level where we had entered from which had a bar and tables for sitting and conversing and a lower level with another bar and a dance floor. The four of us headed down a wide, set of contemporary, wooden steps to the basement level.

There were some patrons on the dance floor but not as many as I imagined it would have. Still, I noticed some good looking women out there. Mikko, Miguel and I gauged the female prospects for a minute or two before we started off for the bar to get a drink. Solis, wasting no time, went to the dance floor directly. His libido was in overdrive and it was evident he was on the prowl for some girl to shag.

I found him a short time later dancing in his usually bizarre way near the back of the dance floor. I came up next to him and started dancing too. There were two girls dancing by themselves on the opposite side of the floor. I nudged Solis and brought them to his attention. Although, it was dark I could see them quite well because of the strobe lights. Both were attractive. One was a petite blond who wore a see-through black mesh shirt. The other, who I preferred, was taller and had shoulder length black hair. She wore a tight-fitting, blue tank top which was cut low on the top revealing an enticing bit of cleavage made by her abundant breasts. The shirt came down about two inches above her waist. The gap between her shirt and pants exposed a section of smooth, white skin in a wholly seductive and sexual way. However, although her shirt was revealing she did not seem to be particularly slutty. She had a gracefulness about her. I was instantly intrigued and titillated watching her body move as she danced.

I was trying to make eye contact with her. Her face was soft, with round cheeks, beautiful, full lips and intense, yet aloof eyes. I was just about to catch her eye when Miguel came up to me.

"Are you ready for some more?"

I nodded my head yes and said, "Let's go into the bathroom."

Prague V was actually a nice club but you would never guess that by looking at the bathroom. It was filthy and unkempt. A toilet had overflowed and spread urine and shit all over the floor. The smell was so foul and overpowering it made it hard to breath. On the wall a mirror was shattered and drops of dark, red blood dripped from it covering the grimy, mildew stained sink below. I treaded through the inch deep toilet water toward the toilet stalls. In one of the stalls I could hear two men engaged in some type of sexual act. I went into the stall next to them and shut the door. I looked at the toilet and it didn't appear to be terribly infectious so I shut the lid and sat on top of it. The stall was covered in all sorts of profane and explicit graffiti. There were names and telephone numbers, crudely draw pictures of penises and animals all over the place. Directly in front of me, on the door was a large picture drawn in black marker of a penis spraying semen on the word 'cunt.' Although I usually enjoy public works of art, I found the technique of this particular piece to be rudimentary and the subject matter trite. I couldn't help feeling that maybe they could have done a better job.

Miguel went into the stall next to mine and I heard a faint sniff…sniff coming from him. Then he whispered, "Here."

I looked down and saw Miguel's hand poking through to my side of the divider. He was holding a portion of a drinking straw with the blow all set for me. I took the straw and snorted the cocaine in one powerful inhalation.

SNIFFFFF…*FUCK! ROCK AND ROLL!*

I rubbed my nose, tried to clear my throat from the gritty sensation in the back of it and we went back into the club.

When, Miguel and I got out of the toilets, we found Mikko and Solis upstairs sitting down, talking to some strange girls. We went over and heard them talking about a party they were going to later on. After flirting with them for a while, we went back downstairs to hit the dance floor again.

70

Just before Prague V closed, it was decided to go to the party the girls had talked about earlier. At two, the music stopped and Solis and I headed for the exit while Miguel and Mikko went to the bathroom. We stood near the exit to wait for them. As we were waiting the two girls we had been watching on the dance floor, earlier, walked by.

Solis, still in shagging mode, stopped them and asked where they were going. The tall one, the one I liked, replied something drunkenly that I wasn't able to pick up.

"We are go'en ta a party. Do you wan ta come?" Solis offered. Then, out of nowhere, without any sort of indication or provocation, the taller girl stepped up to Solis and started kissing him.

Lucky bastard.

She was really hot and drunk and she appeared really up for it. The shorter girl grabbed her by the arm and pulled her a few feet away so they could converse. They looked over at us a few times while they talked and Solis and I stood up straighter and smoothed out or shirts to appear more presentable. The shorter one came over and asked me where the party was. I was just about to give her directions when I heard something to the effect of, "Jeg er kvalm!" It was the taller girl. She had her hands cupped over her mouth and her face lost all its color. The two girls rushed toward the bathrooms.

"What an unfortunate turn of events," I said to Solis after the girls were gone.

"Aye." He replied, disappointedly. "An she wan DICK, like FUCK, too!"

***

We took a cab to the party. Or, I guess more accurately, we had it drop us off six blocks away from the party. This was an exercise in what my friends who studied finance called, 'fiscal conservatism.' The idea was to have the driver drop us off a short distance from our destination. Since your trip is shorter, you avoid paying the entire fare. After a period of time you can actually save quite a bit simply by walking a portion of the trip. It was a very good way to save money. There are also variations of this system. The first is to walk the initial portion of the trip and then take a cab when you get tired. The second is to take a bus for as much of the trip as possible then get a taxi. The third system, which I developed, was the one we employed this particular night. We told the driver to drop us off somewhere near our destination and then split without paying him.

This was by far the most 'fiscally conservative' approach. Plus with a head full of snow there was no way any cabbie could have caught us. We'd just book it like mad, all coked up. Besides, no driver in Manchester would be stupid enough to leave his car to chase somebody for not paying a fare. If he was lucky enough not to be clobbered and robbed, chances are his car wouldn't be there waiting for him when he got back to it.

We were out of breath from running away from the cab fare when we arrived at the party. We stopped and stood on the sidewalk for a moment to catch our breath.

The house was a hive of activity. It was bursting with party goers. There were so many that they had overflowed to the outside. There were people in the front yard, in the driveway, on the sidewalk, in the street, on the balcony, in the neighbor's yards and up an ornamental tree. People were hanging out of the windows. There was also debris: beer cans, wine bottles, cigarette butts, condom packaging, takeout food wrappers and the occasional article of clothing littering a three house radius of the party. The noise was extraordinary as well. It was a dissonance of voices and music which together formed a long unwavering clamor that sounded like a train in the distance. Every time somebody opened the door the noise poured out like a rush of water and filled the entire neighborhood. The whole scene looked like something out of *Animal House*.

Solis had been relatively calm since leaving Prague V; but, the sight of the party got him excited again.

"AHHHHHH PAPA! IS GOOD MATE, IS GOOOOD! LES GO IN! MATE…DER ARE BITCHES EN TH'AIR. DEY WANT DICK!!! AHHHHHH BECHA…."

"Fuck, yeah man." I responded, heading for the door. "Let's go in!"

The inside was as crammed as it appeared from outside. There were people packed in every room of the house especially the living room and an upstairs bedroom. They were set up in proper rave fashion with flashing, colored lights, smoke machines and DJs playing really good drum and bass music for the mass of pill freaks that had jammed themselves in and were dancing like lunatics.

The four of us went into the living room and wasted no time in starting to dance. I was having a great time and must have danced non-stop for at least two hours before I had to pull myself away to go to the bathroom. I fought the crowds through several rooms until I found it.

72

Much to my surprise, it was unoccupied. I went in and shut the door, locking it behind me. After I went, I washed my hands and splashed some cold water on my face. It was almost shocking to feel the cool water against my hot, flushing face. I dried my face off with a hand towel and caught a quick glimpse of myself in the mirror. Suddenly, I was struck by a sudden impulse of genius.

Why not take a peek in the medicine cabinet? I asked myself. *See what you find.*

At first I tried to reject this urge because, well let's face it, it's tacky. But, then again, I was alone in there and I was the only one who would know and basically I didn't give a fuck. So, I opened the cabinet door and rummaged through it. There was some cough medicine, a couple toothbrushes, toothpaste, a razor, a bottle of perfume and a stick of deodorant.

"Rip off!" I said to myself and started to shut the door. Before I did however, I decided for some reason to take a whiff of the perfume. I picked up the bottle and smelled it. It was a very nice, soft, feminine fragrance. I was about to put it back on the shelf when I noticed something I hadn't before. There was a prescription bottle sitting behind where the perfume had been. I didn't bother to look at the label; I just stuffed it in my pocket and closed the door. Just before I walked out, though, I reconsidered what I was about do. Something didn't feel right about it. I turned around and went back to the medicine cabinet. I opened the door again and swiped the cough medicine, too, for good measure.

That's better.

I blazed a path back to the living room to dance some more. My friends were still there dancing like freaks. They hadn't slowed down a bit. They had huge, drug-induced smiles on their faces and that was a magnificent sight. I went over to Solis. He looked like he was having the most fun. He was dancing in his erratic, crazed way like he was having a seizure standing up. I loved the way he danced. He looked ridiculous doing it but he didn't give a fuck. He did it because he had fun doing it.

I started to imitate his dance techniques and he threw his arm around the back of my neck bringing my head against his, holding it there as we jumped up and down.

The night continued in a cloud of Madness and Insanity. We danced. We drank. We smoked pot and we did coke. I don't know how much or for how long; I'm not sure. All quantities, especially time, had become meaningless to me by then. Seconds, minutes, hours passed like waves crashing on an empty beach, perpetual yet unnoticed.

Sometime after sun up, we decided to make a move. As we were leaving the party I noticed a cordless phone sitting on a table next to the door. No one was looking so I boosted it. To be honest, I'm not really sure why I did it. I just felt sort of malicious.

When I got out the door and walked down the sidewalk some, I showed Solis, Miguel and Mikko the phone.

"What the fuck are you going ta do wit dat?" questioned Miguel.

I shrugged my shoulder because I hadn't had an intention for it.

"AHHHHH MOTHERFUCKA!!!!!!I HAVE AN IDEA!" Screamed Solis. "Wait here!"

We watched as he jogged across the street to a news agent's that was just opening up for the day. He came back a few minutes later with a cheap porn magazine.

"What are you gunna do, wank on it or something?" I asked.

"No mate letmme see dat shite," he said indicating the phone.

I handed it to him and he flipped to the back of the magazine. He found a number to a sex line that was advertised for and started dialing.

"HEHEHEHEHEH!" He laughed as he punched in the numbers.

"Lis'en to dis Motherfucka!" He said.

We passed the phone around for a few minutes to hear the sex recording and then Solis hid it under a bush next to a fence without hanging up.

"HEHEHEHEHEH Dose motherfuckas will say, you call dat fuck'en number and den da other will say no motherfucka, it was you!!! And dey will blame each other, but dey're fucked. Hehehehe…" Solis said.

Mikko, Miguel and I looked at him, then each other and broke into a fit of laughter. It was a really immature prank but that was the beauty of it. That was the beauty of Solis. Although, he was a very complex person, he was also very simple in a sense, like that prank. He found simple pleasures and was never afraid or embarrassed to admit or embrace them. That's one of the reasons, I think, his sex drive was so high or why he liked pot so much. They're simple pleasures and he saw no reason not to enjoy them. There's a genius in that thinking as well. He realized that most of life is a bunch of bullshit. People have to worry about grade point averages, electric bills, mortgages, student loans, promotions, raises, leaking faucets, buying snow tires, mowing the grass,

CFCs, greenhouse gas emissions, global warming, polar cap melting, overbearing fathers, asteroids, hemorrhoids, cheating spouses, gun violence, bombs, war, terrorism, the list goes on. The whole fucking adult world is a mess. So why not do drugs and fuck like a rabbit in heat? At least you can forget about all the other shit for a little while. It lets you forget about your own fucking misery long enough not to kill yourself. It makes you feel good for Christ's sake and Solis understood that.

***

Mikko received a phone call on the way home from a friend of his telling him about another party. I looked at my watch. It was half past six but I wasn't tired in the least. No one was. There was no decision to be made. We headed for the party Mikko's friend told him about. On our way to it, we saw two girls walking by. They were wearing skimpy party clothes and appeared like they had been out all night. Solis stopped them.

"Hello," he said in a soft, innocent tone.

"Hello," they replied in stereo.

"We are going ta a par-dy, why don you come wit us?"

"Sorry we're going to bed," one replied.

"Dat's okay ya can come ta bed wit me," Solis quipped suggestively.

"Why don't you fuck yourself?" exclaimed the girl.

Although the comment was probably warranted, it managed to set Solis off again like he had done on the bus and waiting to get into Prague V.

"HEHEHEHEHE...BITCH SUCIA...SHE WANT DICK...AHAHAHHHAHAH...BETCHA, QUIERA LA BECHA, I KNOW DISSSS...AH PAPA...AHHHHHAHAHAHHHAAAAA!!!"

He was out of his fucking mind.

It took us ages to walk to where the other party was supposed to be and when we got there the place was empty. Luckily, it was only a few blocks from Mikko's flat so we decided to go there instead.

When we got inside I showed Solis what I had stolen from the bathroom. He snatched the bottle of pills out of my hand, opened it and swallowed three like they were candy. It didn't even occur to him to read the label or ask what it was.

"Motherfucker!" I exclaimed. "Do you even know what you're taking?"

"No! Hehehehee..." He responded. "Do you?"

75

"Give me that fucking bottle," I commanded.

I snatched the container back and looked at the label. It was OxyContin .

"They're birth control pills, man!" I exclaimed, maintaining a straight face.

"WHAT? Lemme see dat shite!" He exclaimed with an excited, worried look in his eyes, like a wild animal sensing danger.

"Just fucking with you man. They're pain killers."

I took four out of the bottle. I popped one and crushed the other three into a fine powder with my lighter. I made two lines with the powder on the table and snorted them with a rolled up five pound bill. After that Mikko and Miguel followed suit and snorted some too. However, from that point on, my recollection of the night becomes somewhat opaque. I remember doing the last of the blow, drinking wine from the bottle, finding a bottle of rum and drinking it with warm Diet Coke. I also remember smoking spliffs until the pot ran out as well.

Between doing the drugs, or maybe after they were all gone, I slipped in and out of consciousness. I saw light and then it was dark and then it was light again. I laid down on the floor at some point and let my eyes fall shut. I felt like I was falling or actually drifting into a bottomless pit. When I opened my eyes again, I looked around for my friends. Mikko was on the couch. Miguel was on a chair and Solis was lying next to me. They were motionless and their limbs dangled lifelessly at odd angles to their bodies. Their hands and faces where horribly distorted as well. They looked bloated and chalky.

Maybe they're dead? I thought with eerie calmness. *Maybe we've gone too far.*

Then there was blackness again and the drifting sensation. In the dark, I heard voices whispering above my head, "...the river's not going to stop...It's too late... your friends are dead....you're going to die..." The voices were that of children's and had a playful, mischievous tone. They sounded like the voices of ghosts and made me excited and frightened. I began perspiring and my heart thundered.

Ah fuck! Ah fuck! Are they dead? Am I next?

Shut up. Shut the fuck up. I tried to shout at the voices but the words refused to leave my mouth. I felt helpless and weak. My heart pounded faster, my clothes were soaked with sweat. My mouth was dry and the back of my throat burned. I continued to slip in and out of sleep, completely unaware of how much time was passing.

76

Then, I heard music, "*Stood by the gate at the foot of the garden…*" I opened my eyes and the music stopped. I saw my friends lying around the room exactly where they had been the last time I saw them. *How long ago was that?* I pulled myself up onto a chair and sat for a moment. The room was becoming illuminated by the first light of the morning easing its way in. It was revealing a huge mess around the whole room. There was half-eaten food: kebabs and yogurt festering on the table and empty Diet Coke cans on the floor. A wooden chair lay in pieces, scattered across the room. The rum bottle was broken and the couch cushions were inexplicably stuffed into the fireplace. There was also a weird, foul odor permeating from some unknown part or parts of the flat.

I was confused. I knew where I was but not how I had gotten there or what had happened. I got up slowly and walked into the bathroom. My entire body was sore and stiff.

I flipped on the bathroom light. The intensity of it burned my eyes. I looked in the mirror. My whole face and shirt were cover in dried, crusted blood. I knew, from the pattern it had come from a nose bleed. I felt nauseous and ached.

I started to remember the things that had happened Prague V, the party, the pills…

What time is it?

I looked at my watch. I couldn't believe it.

Could it be?

Not only hours had passed, days had as well. It had been nearly sixty hours since the whole thing began, since Miguel brought the cocaine over and I had cut the four lines. It had been over two days since I jumped into the river.

How long was I passed out? Twenty hours? More? There was no way to tell.

I had never been swept away for so long, nor had such a rough ride, but there I was, tired, thirsty, a little bloody but for fuck's sake I was alive! At least I thought so. I examined myself more closely in the mirror to make sure. I could barely recognize my own face. I turned on the water and washed the blood off from it, letting the warm soapy water run down my neck and chest. I patted my face dry with a towel and looked in the mirror again. That time I saw myself. I looked horribly disheveled but I was, in fact, alive. It had been a frenzied couple of days and a good little run. But, in the end, everything went according to plan. I managed to keep my head above water.

I shuffled past the sleeping bodies of my friends, into the kitchen and put on coffee.

St. Sunniva

Things slowed down in Manchester after the second semester ended. There wasn't much going on anywhere. Most students had moved back home. So when I saw a flyer posted on the exterior door to my flat that read, "Acomb House Party" I was a little interested, although, normally I wouldn't have been. I didn't know many people who lived in Acomb House and there was a reason for this. It was designated for graduate students and for whatever reasons most other graduate students lacked my vivacity. Indeed, they spent so much time with their course work and research that they ignored the simple pleasures of life like booze and drugs and copulating with the opposite sex whilst drinking booze and taking drugs. Of course, I spent time on my course work as well; but, there were limits.

One time, I had the misfortune of going to another party in Acomb House. It turned out to be a big fiasco for no reason at all really. I ended up getting kicked out because I got really drunk and spilled some wine all over a couch. Being kicked out, I felt was completely ridiculous and unwarranted. For the life of me, I couldn't understand how someone could get so upset about a stained couch that wasn't even that nice to begin with. Moreover, how could someone expect to have a party without anything being spilled? The fact that I spilled the wine on purpose is inconsequential. These people were squares.

That's why it was reluctantly that I decided to go to the party. But, I didn't have anything better to do and besides, I reasoned, even if the party was really lame I could just go and cause trouble. The city may have slowed down but I wasn't about to.

I spent the whole afternoon before the party smoking pot and drinking beer at a barbeque in the park with Solis, Haruki and some Spanish guys that Solis knew. It was a pretty good time. The rain held off, I cooked some cheeseburgers on the grill and we threw around a Frisbee. When it started to get dark the barbeque died down and I tried to talk Solis and Haruki into going with me to the Acomb House party but they declined. I left for home by myself to change clothes and get ready for the night.

I had just gone through the black, iron gate to Witworth Park and was ambling down the path home when I ran into Dang, my flat mate. It looked like he had just come back from exercising. He was carrying a squash racket in his hand and had on a pair of hot pink gym shorts that were scarcely coming down past his ass cheeks, way to short for his skinny little legs. On his feet were white tennis shoes and black, knee high athletic socks that were pulled up all the way. This, I must admit was quite the ensemble but the *pièce de résistance* was his orange and black Garth Brooks tee-shirt. I have no idea where he got a hold of an item like that but for fuck's sake he wasn't shy about sporting it. He was on the path ahead of me and I got it into my head to invite him to come to the party with me. Although he was my flat mate, we never hung out. The party was a good opportunity to change that. He rarely went out and I didn't have anyone to go with me. I snuck up behind him.

"Good game!" I said, smacking him on his petite, womanly ass.

"Oh!" he exclaimed with surprise and confusion.

"Hey! Dang! What's happening?"

"Herro, Kerra."

"Dang, I'm going to go to a party tonight. It's upstairs in Acomb House. You want to go with me?"

"Oh! Yes." He answered, delighted.

"Good, alright man, so be ready in twenty minutes and we'll go up there."

We went into our flat and parted ways to get ready. I took a shower, shaved, put on some clean clothes and in twenty minutes was standing in front of Dang's door. I gave it a light rap and Dang answered, still in his squash clothes.

"What the fuck man! I thought you were getting ready," I said to him, dismayed.

"Oh, ah I am," he replied.

"You're going to go like that?" I asked, not sure if he had understood what I said about being ready in twenty minutes.

"Rike what?"

Fucking great!

I thought about explaining to him the errors of his wardrobe and the pain it was causing me but decided not to. For all I knew he might have been dressed in the height of Chinese leisure wear and anyway his other clothes might not have been much better.

"Never mind. Let's just go."

I was confident that going into the party with a guy dressed like that was a definite liability in the economics of casual sex; but, I couldn't do much about it, really. I would just have to go with him as is. It was still better than going alone.

We left our flat together and went around the building to the stairs leading to the upper flats. As we ascended, I started to hear music playing. I couldn't make it out initially, but as I got higher I could hear better. Halfway to the top, I could tell it was techno. I almost turned around when I realized this. Not that I had anything against techno especially, it was just that I was in no mood for it. All the drinking and smoking had made me tired and I was hoping to meet a girl. This environment was probably the worst type for that. I didn't have the energy to dance and it was most likely going to be too loud to talk. The later point was extremely important because I wouldn't be able to explain to any girl that I happened to meet why I was with a guy who looked like he just came from the beach. Not that I had much of an explanation anyway.

As we approached the top step, I gave Dang's clothes a final *coup d'oeil* and was overcome with an impending sense of doom. I realized right then that the night was going to be a wash. There was no way I was going to get laid and I would almost certainly be embarrassed at some point. But, being the stoic that I am, I continued determined to make the best of the situation.

"We'd be better off just going home and whacking off, don't you think?" I asked Dang as an aside.

He gave me a confused look.

"Never mind," I said and continued up the stairs.

I stopped on the landing that looked much like my own and paused briefly to catch my breath before I opened the door. It entered straight into the fairly dark lounge that was lit only by a couple of black light lamps. Through the black light, I could see that the place was actually full of people. The lounge was mostly empty of furniture but there were lots of partiers standing on the periphery of the large room drinking and talking and several more dancing in the middle of it. Dang and I walked in and were immediately greeted by a short, muscular, black guy with a Caribbean accent.

"Welcome," he said with a big smile revealing "help yourself ta som drinks."

He pointed to a card table that was set up in the corner of the room. "They're over there."

On the table was a big punch bowl, eight or ten bottles of wine and an assortment of snacks.

"That's quite the spread, man. What's in the bowl, punch?" I asked.

81

"Das right, mon. But titis a special punch, like un de eylands, mon!"

"Oh Yeah? What's in it?"

"Oh somma dis, somma dat. Who knows…Rum, fruit juice, Vodka, Kerosene… maybe?"

"Fuck yeah man! I'm gunna get some of that!" I said and nudged Dang to come with me.

I poured Dang and myself a couple of cups of Caribbean punch then stood back near the wall to scan the room and take in the whole scene. I must admit it was better than I expected. The punch was potent, there were a few good looking women scattered around and some people were passing around a joint over by the window. I was just about to ask Dang if we should fire one up ourselves when my attention was caught by a light coming in from the outside door. A small group of people were entering. My interest was drawn to the front of the group, to a big breasted, dark haired girl. Her eyes were incredible, so fragile looking it was almost as if she could break down and cry at any moment. Not that she looked sad. She didn't. It was more that her eyes were delicate and cordial and I could tell that about them even at a distance and in poor lighting. I could tell because I already knew them. So too, did I, the beautiful sheen of her hair and the fullness of her lips. It was the girl who kissed Solis at Prague V and then puked.

***

I was standing across the room from where she entered. As she walked in, I watched her closely, taking in every movement. To my surprise, I caught her looking back at me. Our eyes locked briefly before she shyly turned away. I suddenly became very nervous for no particular reason. My heartbeat quickened, my arms became weak and although I wasn't able to see myself, I think that I blushed like a school girl. This, of course, was not my usual reaction to making eye contact with a girl. I felt very strange.

It had been a few weeks since I had seen this girl in Prague V. And that was the first and only time I had ever seen her. But, from the beginning, I felt that there might be an attraction. Since that night, I had thought about her several times. Not that she became an obsession or anything, but I would, however, keep an extra keen eye out for her whenever I went some place. There was a certain aura of mystery about her, too, which intrigued me. I had been in Manchester for nine months

82

and had only seen her one time. I would see familiar faces everywhere I went. Whether it was walking down Oxford Road, in the library or at a club, faces tended to reappear. Except, hers never did. Why hadn't I seen her before? What was her story? Who was she?

These were all questions that needed to be answered; but, first I had to pull myself back together. Once, several years ago, I attempted to talk to a girl whilst in a similar condition. That time, foolishly, I didn't settle down before I went over to her. My performance, as you might imagine was less than par. After complementing her on her socks and playfully punching her in the arm a couple times, I realized I was making a huge jackass of myself and slinked away in embarrassment. I couldn't let that happen again.

I downed my drink and went for another to calm my nerves. Seeing her again anywhere would have been good; but seeing her in a confined place of social interaction, like a party, constituted a genuine opportunity. It was good Karma and chances were that I would never see her again. I had to act then. I just needed to wait until the right moment. I didn't want to just walk up and start talking to her. That was too aggressive, too transparent. I needed an opening.

My opening came about an hour later when I saw an acquaintance of mine talking to her. He was a compatriot from somewhere out East named Pete, but you would never guess that he was American by the way he talked. It was sort of a mix between Eastern socialite and British gentry. It was bizarre that he spoke this way, but I never questioned it. He was studying literature at the University. He was also an inspiring novelist and a mad chain smoker. He smoked mentholated cigarettes and would easily finish a pack off before most people smoked three. I had enjoyed his company quite a few times at Krö Bar over pints of Boddingtons. Although he was an aloof, sort of melancholy guy, I felt really comfortable talking to him. I couldn't have asked for a better opportunity.

He only spoke with the girl for a few minutes and then walked to the refreshment table. I followed him there.

"Pete! How ya do'en?"

"Ah David, nice to see you?" Smiling at our chance encounter, "What do you think about those Red Sox? They should be pretty good. Huh?"

"Yeah, Yeah, they look good," I answered distractedly.

"What's wrong David? You don't seem your usual self?"

"Nah, it's just ah…Hey, who was that chick you were just talking to?"

"Which one?"

"Over there, the dark haired one."

"Oh that, that is the fair and lovely St. Sunniva of Norway."

"Norway?" I questioned, titillated by the very word. Norwegians fascinated me like the Finns.

"Yes. That fair creature haft voyaged her way here, to this island, to rape and plunder just like her Nordic ancestors. Only she seeks not the spoils of war but the pillage of my heart."

"What? What the fuck does that mean? You got a thing for her."

"How could I not? Just rest you eyes upon her and you shall be hard pressed to turn away."

"Yeah. I know what you mean," I said a bit dejectedly.

"Why David, has this Siren caught your ear?"

"Yeah man, she's a fox."

"Then I must introduce you at once!"

"But, I thought that you liked her."

"Ah, yes, but you see I have drank two bottles of Shiraz and have got a good start on my third. St. Sunniva is lovely indeed, but there are other lovely women here as well. And to be quite candid in my state they don't really have to be lovely at all!" He said with a devilish grin. "Come, behold the beauty and magic which is Norway."

**

Pete and I waited a few minutes until Sunniva was alone and walked over to her. Pete made a hasty introduction of the two of us and then left. And just like that, I was alone with her. This, of course, was very fortunate, and what I had wanted; but, I needed something cleaver to say to get the ball rolling.

"So ah…you having fun?" I asked.

Immediately after those idiotic words flew from my mouth, *I thought Ah fuck! I can't believe I just said that. She's going to think I'm some kind of an idiot.* I felt like I could have done better.

"Yeah, the party is quite nice." She replied in a sing-song Norwegian accent. "There are quite a lot of interesting people here. Did you see the one who was wearing pink shorts?"

Pink shorts!

"No. I didn't see anybody like that," I lied.

84

"Yeah, he's just over there," she replied, pointing behind me.

I turned around and there was Dang standing by the refreshment table. His head was bent down and he was shoveling cake off a paper plate, into his mouth. He must have sensed somehow that we were watching him because he looked up in our direction and smiled at me, inadvertently allowing gobs of cake to fall from his gapping mouth. Sunniva chuckled. I turned around and quickly tried to change the subject.

"So, are you studying here?"

"Look that guy is waving to us," she said.

"Nah, nah, he must be waving to somebody else," I said sensing my chances with her were about to be ruined.

"No, look he is waving to us."

I was forced to turn around again. When I did, I saw Dang smiling from ear to ear and waving his arm from the elbow in an over-exaggerated motion that covered far more range than would be expected of the average human. I smiled and waved back.

"He's a friendly sort isn't he?" I said turning around again.

"Yes, he seems to be. Look, I think that he's coming over here."

I turned around and saw Dang looking for a place to throw his plate away.

Ah great, he's going to come over here and fuck everything up. I need to do something fast.

"Hey, Sunniva would you like to go into the kitchen for a few minutes. It might not be so crowded in there?" I said almost pleadingly.

"Sure," she replied quizzically and off we went to the kitchen to hide from Dang.

The kitchen adjoined the lounge so we didn't have to go far. But in that few steps, I noticed something about Sunniva that I hadn't while talking to her. She was really bombed. It was very strange. She didn't slur her speech at all, but when she walked she looked like Otis the drunk from *The Andy Griffin Show*. What was even stranger was that she still managed to maintain a level of gracefulness and sex appeal, well quite a bit more than Otis anyway.

The kitchen was dark except for the black light that crept in from the lounge. The purple light reflected eerily off the white appliances. Other than the occasional person opening the refrigerator, the kitchen was nearly empty. I leaned up against the counter and Sunniva stood right next to me. The near blackness and isolation created a brief moment of awkward silence, but I was able to break it without too much effort.

"So, are you studying here in Manchester?"

"No, I have a job," Her voice seemed to have an even more sexual quality about it in the dark.

I probed further, "Oh really, what do you do?"

"Nothing, actually."

"You don't do anything?"

"I got sacked."

"For what?"

"Because, my boss is an angry bitch who hates my whole department," she responded with frustration in her voice.

"Well, what were you doing before you got fired?"

She then proceeded to tell me a bunch of complicated things about molecular biology and cells. Actually, that's just speculation. I don't know if it was really complicated or even about molecular biology for that matter. After about six seconds, I stopped paying attention. However, it really wasn't my fault. I tried to pay attention but I kept getting distracted by the silhouette of her breasts bouncing ever so slightly as she talked. This of course led to envisioning a barrage of explicit things I would like to do to those breasts and the rest of her. The more she talked, the more I fantasized. Eventually, she stopped talking and looked at me waiting for a reply. Only I didn't have anything to say because I hadn't paid attention. With every second that passed and I remained silent the pressure mounted. I needed to say something but I had no idea what. If I had listened to her then I would probably have had some type of comment or follow up question or something. But I had none. I just stood there like a mute trying to come up with something to say. Finally, after what seemed like a half hour, I just blurted out the first words that came to mind.

"You wanna make out?" I said moronically.

She looked at me and before I even had a chance to cringe at my crassness and indiscretion, she threw her arms around my neck and started kissing me. She kissed me gently; but, moved her hands across my body aggressively, digging her nails into my back and chest. I became aroused. I grabbed her thigh and ran my hand up and down her leg. I pressed my chest against hers to feel her ample Nordic breasts. She responded by digging her nails into me deeper. We became frantic, rapturously discovering each other's bodies.

I could taste the familiar flavor of vodka in her kisses. I felt the sweat from her cheeks and brow. I smelled the sent of smoke in her hair and on her skin and I absorbed it all with sordid pleasure. I knew that taste, the faint yet distinct essence of booze and cigarettes from a strange girl's mouth. It is the flavor of Madness and Insanity. It was the taste of random sex, a rare and oft sought variety. It is especially rare when a girl of this caliber is involved, regardless of her level of inebriation. Things looked quite a bit better than they did when I was walking to the party with Dang.

After about ten minutes of going at it, I moved my mouth away from hers and whispered in her ear, "You wanna get out of here?"

I felt her hand squeeze my chest tight, then calmly release and slide down my torso, stopping midway on my stomach before reaching for my hand. Without saying a word she gently locked her fingers with mine and led me out the back door of the flat.

***

Sunniva continued to lead me by the hand all the way down the stairs and didn't let go until we where outside. The drone of the city night was considerable quieter than the party we just vacated. Sunniva dropped my hand playfully and spun around with her arms fully extended outward, like a child at play. She stopped spinning right in front of me. There was a seductive but innocent smile on her face.

"So David, where is it that you want to go?" she asked coquettishly.

I felt a boyish excitement rush over me. I looked at her and smiled the most genuine smile I have ever given. She seemed so lively and uninhibited. I grabbed her and kissed her passionately.

I needed to decide where to go with her next. The obvious thing was to bring her to my flat. But it wasn't that clear cut. It was actually a hard decision to make. On the one hand my room was really close and very convenient. On the other hand, it was a piece of shit and I was embarrassed to bring her there. In the end, I decided it would have to do. Proximity was the key factor.

"I just live on the other side of the building. You want to come to my place for a drink or something?" I asked.

"Sure," she said simply and we walked together, holding hands, around Acomb House, to my flat.

87

I opened the door to my room. I had left the light on which instantly revealed a huge mess of drug paraphernalia, empty beer cans and the copious notes I had compiled for my thesis, scattered on my desk. I went over and half-heartedly tried to straighten up a little; but, she stopped me with a soft giggle after I knocked over a half-full can of stale Boddingtons on my desk.

I invited her to sit down and play some music if she wanted to. Sunniva sat down at the desk and started thumbing through my album of CDs.

"Hey, do you want a drink? I have some wine or possibly some beer," I asked while she was picking the music.

"Beer sounds good," she replied not bothering to look up.

I left the room and went to the kitchen to get us some beer. When I got a few steps down the hall I could hear her playing Lou Reed with the stereo going full blast. I could feel it echoing through the hallway and noticed it shaking the doors to my flat mates' rooms. I figured they would find this noise to be a nuisance but did nothing about it. I really didn't give a fuck. I wasn't going to have her turn it down. I wanted to shag her. I just continued into the kitchen in search of beer.

I opened the refrigerator and to my chagrin noticed that I not only didn't have any beer, I didn't have any wine either.

Fuck man!

I looked in the freezer on the off chance I had some booze in there keeping cold but there wasn't any. I found myself in a pinch, with limited options, so I did the only thing I could. I swiped a couple cans from Dang and went back into my room.

When I opened the door, Sunniva had her back to me and was dancing like a Druid to the music. She had her hands above her head and was spinning around in circles. The door shut behind me and apparently startled her. She stopped dancing and spun around suddenly. There was a confused and panicked look on her face.

Up until that point things were going well and pretty much as one would expect them to. However, for whatever reason, when she heard the sound of that door closing her behavior became erratic. I extended my arm and offered her a beer, but she just looked at me like a deer stuck in headlights then babbled some nonsense under her breath.

"What?" I said.

"I gotta go, I gotta go!"

She pushed past me in a flurry and flew out the door. I was stunned. She just left. There was no goodbye or anything, let alone an explanation. I stood there, like an ass hole, trying to decide what to do. At first, I thought, *Fuck her!* But then, for some reason that I am not entirely able to understand myself I gave chase. It might have been that I still wanted to shag her or it may have had something to do with the feeling I got when she walked into that party. It may have even had something to do with Karma. I don't know why I did it. I didn't think about it; I just ran out the door after her. When I caught up she was halfway to the gate.

"Hey, wait a minute," I shouted to her as she just kept walking away, "Can I get you a cab or walk you home?"

She stopped, her back still turned toward me, and said in an accusatory tone, "You just want to shag me!"

She's fucking psychic!

"I don't," I replied taken off guard by her abruptness.

She turned around and looked at me. There was a hurt look in her eyes and it was hard to tell if she was about to cry or if the light mist of the Manchester night made it look that way.

"You don't want to shag me?"

"Well...I guess I do."

"See...you see...you FUCKING BASTARD, you just want to shag me!"

I had absolutely no idea what had just happened. I had no clue what caused the storming out, all the business about shagging her or anything. I was becoming irritated though. The whole thing was bizarre and I didn't feel like being bothered by it anymore. She was hot; but, I wasn't going to put up with all that for a shag.

"Fuck you!" I said.

She didn't respond.

"Forget it!" I continued, "I don't want to shag you anymore!"

It wasn't that I was angry. I was just fed up. I turned away from her and started walking back to my room. I was content to just jerk off and get some sleep.

"Wait!" She called to me with sudden composure.

I stopped and turned around slowly to see her coming back to me. She took my hand again almost apologetically.

"Come on; let's sit on the grass and talk," she said softly.

Reluctantly, I sat with her on the damp grass. We sat for a moment without saying anything as the mist began to build on the tops of our heads. Then, she laid down and started rambling on about tennis shoes. The topic was completely random, truly pointless and I have no idea why she brought it up but it was entertaining nonetheless. She was funny and had several insightful comments about shoelaces of all things. When she was done saying her piece about shoes, there was another brief silence between us that was filled with the clamor of a fleet of emergency vehicles passing by on Oxford Road. I was about to comment on the fire trucks and ambulances when I saw her give a shiver from the damp night air. It wasn't a helpless shiver like the kind some homeless kid in a Dickens novel would give. It was more of a controlled shiver, a quick shifting of her shoulders. I saw in that shiver a self-possession that I admired, something quite different from the unpredictable behavior I just witnessed.

"It's getting late. You should go in...You want to stay at my place?" I asked cautiously not wanting to provoke a repeat of the earlier episode.

"I'll sleep on the floor and you can have the bed if you want." I added not that I really intended on sleeping on the floor.

"Okay," she said a bit reluctantly.

I helped her up and held her hand back to my room. The music was still blaring when we entered and I shut it off.

"You know, you don't have to sleep on the floor," she said plainly.

Of course, I immediately assumed that I was going to have sex with her; but, she must have sensed what I was thinking because she followed it up with a direct, "What you think is going to happen tonight isn't going to happen." She seemed serious about that point so I decided not try anything major with her. I didn't want her to go schizo and storm out again. So, we just fooled around for awhile and then went to sleep.

In the morning, as soon as it was light, I felt her get out of bed. I opened my eyes and watched as she hastily threw on the clothes which I had managed to work off her the night before.

"Are you leaving?" I asked as she was tying her shoes.

"Yes," she replied indifferently with her eyes still on her laces.

"You wanna get some breakfast?"

"No."

What goes on in your heart? What goes on in your mind...

I probably should have been annoyed by this; but, I actually found it intriguing and sexy in a remotely masochistic way. I really wanted to see her again. Her strange behavior coupled with her physical appearance appealed to me.

"I want to see you again," I said sincerely.

"Okay, give me your number," she replied with apparent indifference.

And that was that, I wrote my number down on a piece of paper, she took it from me without saying a word and left with only a quick "bye" and a cheeky smile.

***

After Sunniva left, I tried to go back to sleep but couldn't. My mind kept running through the events of the previous night. It had all been so strange: making out with her in the kitchen, her running away and then coming back, and especially her quick exit in the morning. I had no idea what to make of the whole situation. One thing was for sure, though, she really looked good. However, I had no real sense of her personality. It was just a hunch; but, I didn't think that she behaved like that all the time. I thought that I probably caught her in rare form. But maybe not; who knew? The only thing I knew was that I would never find out unless she called me and judging by the way she split that probably wasn't going to happen.

Since I couldn't go back to sleep, I decided to get up, shower and go work on my thesis. I went to the library and worked for a few hours but I got tired and went home for an afternoon nap. When I woke up it was nearly eight. I decided to give Solis a call and see if he wanted to score a bag and get high. Not surprisingly, he did.

I went to his flat and rang the bell. Jill, Solis's flat mate opened the door. I really didn't like that girl and neither did Solis. I didn't like her because she was always complaining about things every time I was over there. Solis didn't like her because she wouldn't shag him that time he ended up whacking off all night and because she looked like a horse.

"Where's Solis?" I inquired not trying very hard to be polite.

"I think he's in the shower," she answered curtly.

She escorted me down the hallway to the bathroom. I had been there a thousand times and didn't need to be shown where it was; but, she walked with me regardless. This made me feel very uncomfortable. She probably thought that I would steal something if I was left alone. She was a bitch.

When we got to the bathroom, the door was wide open. Steam poured out into the hallway like fog. I could also detect the unmistakable smell of marijuana. There was a radio sitting on the toilet blasting out

Fleetwood Mac. Solis was in the shower singing loudly along with the music.

"Solis?" I called out.

He flung open the shower curtain to see who was calling. He was standing near the back of the shower, fully aroused. There was a lighter and a pipe in his hand. Jill let out a shriek and quickly turned her head. Solis made no effort to cover himself up. He just started laughing.

Jill turned back to Solis. She held her hand up to her eyes like she was shielding them from the glare of Solis's penis and testicles.

"Damn it! Solis you need to be respectful!" She shouted.

I could tell she was really pissed; but, I thought it was funny. I stated laughing which made her even madder.

Solis didn't reply he just laughed with me, all the while standing there with a hard on and a dope pipe in his hand. Jill turned away in a huff, stormed into her room, slamming and locking the door behind her.

"DAT'S RIGHT! GO TA YOUR STABLE, YOU HORSE LOOK'EN BEA'CH!" He yelled when she was out of sight.

"Hurry up, man," I said, getting down to business. "Let's go smoke some weed!"

"Alright mate," Solis replied calmly having already forgotten about Jill.

He got out of the shower and started drying off.

"I dan know why dat beatch is always complaining, mate...She need dick! I know dis!"

"Yeah, man, that's probably it; I'm sure that that's all it is," I said sarcastically. "Hey, did you call your guy yet?" I continued.

"Ah yes he say to meet him outside da Hog Head. We shad go, right now."

Solis threw on some clothes and we went across Oxford Road to wait outside of the Hog's Head. A few minutes later, a small, unassuming car pulled up to us. In the driver seat sat a sharply dressed Pakistani man with a button down shirt and a gold bracelet.

"Dat's him," said Solis.

We got into the back seat and Solis's connection drove away. Solis introduced me to the dealer.

"Sal, mate, dis es my mate, David."

"Alright then, niceta meet ya." He said and glanced around to acknowledge me. When he did I was bowled over by a cheep looking prosthetic eye lazily floating around in his left eye socket.

"Alright ,Solis, what will it be den?" Asked Sal, getting down to business.

"Mate, giv me fiddy worth."

Sal reached over to a duffle bag sitting on the passenger seat and pulled a bag of grass out. He discreetly passed it back to Solis. He held it lightly in his hands bouncing it up and down to gauge the weight and then lifted it up in the light to assay the quality. This wasn't a particularly clever thing to do while we were in traffic. Sal didn't think so as well.

"Jesus Christ, Solis, put that shite down!" he exclaimed obviously upset at Solis's indiscretion.

Solis put the bag down on his lap and handed Sal the money. Sal drove around the block and dropped us off in front of Witworth Park. I could tell that he was still mad about Solis flashing the dope around in the car.

"What was that all about?" I asked after we got out of the car. "I thought you bought from this guy all the time."

"I do."

"Then what was that about? Why did you check out the bag so much? You know that he has good stuff."

"Is jus dat… you ken never tell with des motherfuckas!"

"What?"

"You saw da motherfucka's eye, verdad?"

"Yeah, man, I saw it."

"You know dat, my uncle said to me, when I was liddle. He say never to trus a motherfucka who has a fake arm or a leg, or enny shite mate!"

"Why?"

"'cus ya never know how dat motherfucka got da shite, mate!"

I looked at him to see if he was serious. He was. I was about to argue with him; but, I decided that it would have been futile to debate this topic. Besides, somehow it seemed like there was some logic to what he said.

We went back to his place to have a smoke. Solis put in some music and we just spaced out a bit in silence while we toked away. I thought about St. Sunniva and re-ran the events of the previous night in my head. Eventually, unable to come to any conclusions, I sought Solis's advice.

"Hey man. Listen to this shit," I said and then proceeding to recap the whole ordeal.

When I was finished he looked at me as if he was in deep thought, trying to absorb it all.

"What?" He finally shouted, "You did not shag her?"

"I told you she didn't want to."

"Wha da ya mean she did not wan dat shite mate, of course she ded. Dey all wan dick!"

"Not this one."

"Of course mate…she ded."

"Alright whatever…But, you know who it was, this girl?"

"Who?"

"That chick that kissed you that night a Prague V."

"Which one?" He asked curiously.

"The one who threw up afterward, remember?"

"Ah!" he exclaimed as if he were in the midst of an epiphany but stopped.

"Which one?"

"Remember that fucking time, you and me and Mikko and Miguel did all that blow for like two straight days?"

"Ah dat night…" He stared up at the ceiling trying hard to remember, "Ah I remember dat beatch. Why didn't ya shag her, mate?"

"I told you I tried; she didn't want to."

"Wha do ya mean she didn't want dat shite?"

"It was complicated—"

I was interrupted by my phone ringing. I took it out of my pocket and looked at it. I was receiving a text message. It said, simply "Good Nite" I looked at the number it was sent from. I didn't recognize it; but, I knew it had to be from Sunniva. My heart quickened somewhat with excitement. I thought for a moment about how to respond and decided to play it cool.

"Good nite Sunniva," I wrote.

"That was her. That was the girl I was telling you about," I told Solis excitedly.

"Which one?"

"The one from last night."

"AHHHH…Ya know wha dat mean mate?"

"What?" I asked, eager for some insight.

"Dick! She want dick!" He replied and then broke into a fit of laughter.

This was the man I consult regarding matters of the heart.

I looked at him and couldn't help but to smile. I loved this man unequivocally. He was, despite all his vices and faults, a true friend. I also smiled because I thought he might be right about Sunniva.

***

Sunniva called me a couple of days later. She wanted to know if I was interested in going out "drinking" with her. I remember quite specifically that she used the word drinking and did not say something like go out for a drink or get some drinks. No, she said, "Do you want to go drinking with me tonight?"

Now, I had gone out drinking many times and I had gone out for drinks many times; but, the two are not the same. Drinking, and having drinks, although not diametrically opposed are very different. You see, when one goes out for drinks there is a highly social element to it. The focus is not on the alcohol per se, but on personal, human interaction. When having drinks, the conversation or entertainment is likely the key to the evening. In contrast, however, when one goes out drinking the focus is set more upon the medicinal qualities of intoxicating liquors. It is the act of consuming alcohol that is important. One does not go out drinking simply to have fun. One goes out drinking to get drunk.

Thus, it seemed a bit odd that she would ask me to go out drinking with her for what would be our first actual date. Maybe she just didn't understand the subtle difference between the two the way I did. This was quite possible seeing as how English was not her mother tongue.

She told me to meet her outside the front entrance to the Central Library in St. Peter's Square. It was pouring down rain when I got there so I waited for her under the portico. The Central Library was a beautiful building designed no doubt to inspire. It was made of white Portland stone and laid out in a perfect circle. In the front, leading to the main entrance, where I stood, was a giant Corinthian portico. Above, circling the second and third floors was a Tuscan colonnade. The fourth floor was topped with a leaded roof that, during the odd time when the sun would shine, glimmered like white gold. The building was constructed in the early nineteen thirties, which of course, was a period of great economic hardship the world over. Manchester was not immune to this; but, they built the library at that time regardless. This to me stands as a testament to the commitment the city has for scholarly and literary endeavors. After all, Manchester was home to many great authors, scientists, and philosophers, including Anthony Burgess, James Joule and Fredrick Engels. In fact, Burgess used this very library, no doubt molding his then young mind toward literary greatness. I was using it for what one might consider far less lofty motivations. It was keeping me dry and I was using it as a place to meet a girl and possibly get laid.

Sunniva showed up right on time. She was wearing a pair of tight blue jeans that accentuated her voluptuous proportions. As she moved toward me, she walked with a confident but modest swagger that I found most alluring. We met each other with a friendly kiss and despite the steady rain, walked down Peter's Street to a place called Jar Bar. It was only a short distance from the library to Jar Bar so we filled the time with mindless chit-chat about umbrellas.

"You don't have an umbrella either?" I asked.

"No, I don't like them," she replied.

"Really, why not?"

"I just can't be bothered with them."

"Yeah, me either," I said, "I don't like carrying them around once I'm inside. I never carry one. People think that I'm stupid because I live in Manchester and I don't even own an umbrella. But it's not stupidity, it more like—"

"Laziness?" She interrupted and flashed a mischievous smirk.

"Yeah, laziness," I said smiling.

When we reached Jar Bar, we were both drenched and the rain had caused Sunniva's mascara to run. Her eyes were surrounded by the black makeup and it was starting to streak down her face. We stood outside under the awning so she could fix it before we went in.

Jokingly she asked, "How do I look?"

"Very lovely," I replied.

"No I don't. I look like Alice Cooper."

We both laughed. It was a good sign, I thought, that she didn't take herself too seriously.

Jar Bar was a slightly upscale spot with a dance floor and a modern motif. It was a little ostentatious for me, but I was content being there as long as I was with Sunniva. As soon as we entered we moved directly to the bar. She ordered us both double shots of vodka. I supposed then that she did understand the subtle difference between drinking and having drinks.

We took the double shots down, one right after the other, and I ordered us a couple of beers.

96

We stood near the bar sipping our ale for a moment or two in silence. I scanned the club for a place to sit. It was probably only at half capacity and I noticed a few empty tables in the back. I asked Sunniva if we should take one.

"No," she said decisively, "I don't feel much like sitting and talking if you don't mind."

"Okay?" I said, "What do you want to do then?"

"Let's dance!"

"You want to dance right now? There's no one on the dance floor."

"So, we'll be the first…trendsetters," she said nudging me with her elbow.

"I don't know…"

"Ohhh, wasss a maaater? Youuu don't daaaance?" She said in a playfully teasing way.

"No, I dance."

"Well then, let's dance."

She took the beer from my hand and set it on the bar next to hers. Then she led me by the hand out to the dance floor and we started dancing. From that moment on, until the place closed at two, we were dancing practically the whole time.

We danced close to each other from the start. I placed my hand lightly on her hip and let my body glide with hers as we moved rhythmically to the music and each other. Our motions were smooth and ingenuous. We looked each other in the eyes. Oddly, we didn't talk to each other more than a few words. But, although we didn't use words in a strange and wholly nonverbal way, we were communicating.

As the night wore on and the songs became slower, she pressed her body closer to mine. This made my heart race, just as it had done the other time that I was close to her. I pulled her tighter and brushed her glossy, dark hair back behind her ear revealing her neck. It was smooth and firm and beautiful and glistened slightly, from perspiration. The sight of it made me want to just loose control, to devour her neckline in a sexual frenzy. But, I composed myself and took a more measured approach. I pressed my cheek against her cheekbone and held my lips there slightly parted against her soft, moist skin. I was cautious, not knowing exactly how she would react. I moved my lower lip softly, just enough to be detected. When I did, I felt her take a little inward gasp of excitement. I proceeded unhurriedly with my lips down her cheek to the top of her neck. I kissed her gently on the side of her neck and behind

97

the ear. I tasted the salt from her sweat and smelled the mixture of alcohol and perfume that was wafting from her. I wanted that taste of salt and her scent and the feel of her skin. I wanted her with all my senses.

I felt her head start to pull away a little and I stopped kissing her neck. I drew my head back too until I was looking in her sapphire eyes. I was frozen there captivated by her taste and fragrance and the blue of her eyes until she leaned in and kissed me, pressing her lower lip to my upper while she moved her hands up to my shoulders resting them there. It was a soft, but extremely erotic kiss that made my body almost weak. Things were getting good. Unfortunately, just then the music ended and all the overhead lights came on. The sudden brightness hurt my eyes and seemed a physical manifestation of my disappointment. Jar Bar was closing. It was already two. I could hardly believe it. I hadn't even noticed the time going by let alone cared that it was getting so late.

As the club got brighter, people piled out of it but Sunniva and I stood transfixed on the dance floor looking at each other intently for the moment. It could have been one of the most sexually charged moments I had ever experienced.

I'm getting laid!

"What do you want to do now?" I asked finally.

"I have to go home and pack," she said a bit dolefully.

"Pack?" I asked showing my surprise and reevaluating my assumption.

"Yes, I'm going on a holiday back to Norway for a week."

"Well, when are you leaving?"

"My plane leaves at six-thirty."

"Tomorrow evening?"

"No."

"Six-thirty, in the morning?"

"Yes."

"And you went out tonight, even though you have an early flight?"

"Yes"

"Why?"

She looked at me with a slight wonderment and lightly bit her lip, just enough to expose the bottom of her top front teeth.

"I wanted to," she answered candidly. A rush of emotion flooded my body and made me blush heavily on my arms and chest.

Because, she wanted to.

I looked at her and could only smile.

"Maybe you can help me pack," she said after a short silence.

"Yeah, that sounds good," I replied not trying to sound over eager.

I am going to get laid!

Outside the rain had slowed to a sprinkle and the streets were busy with the remains of the night clubbers and the homeless people who relied on the charity of the intoxicated. Sunniva put her arm through mine and we strolled to the edge of the sidewalk to hail a taxi. Before long one pulled up and she opened the door. Just before she stepped in, she turned back toward me exposing her fragile, honest eyes.

"What you think is going to happen tonight," she said "isn't going to happen."

"I wasn't thinking anything," I lied, trying to hide my disappointment.

She smiled a girlish grin and took my hand to gently pull me into the cab with her. She gave the driver her address and off we went.

***

We drove down to Oxford road, toward a section of Manchester called Withington. Ten minutes later, the taxi turned down a narrow road lined with identical dull, red brick townhouses on both sides and we stopped in front of a townhouse with a gate in front of it. Sunniva paid the driver and we walked up to the door. I could hear her fumbling around for her keys in the quiet of the night for a moment before unlocking the door.

"You have to be quiet." She whispered, pressing her index finger to her lips. "I have flat mates."

It seemed like a very provocative gesture, although I knew it wasn't designed to be. Sunniva took my hand to lead me through the dark house. We passed the vestibule, went down a hall and up a flight of stairs, ending up in her bedroom.

She flipped on the lights revealing the room to me. I was slightly overcome with an excited feeling, not sexual, but voyeuristic in a way. I was seeing her personal space for the first time. I had never even tried to image this before. When I had thought about her previously it was in the abstract. Seeing her bedroom then she became somehow more real. She became more dimensional. I was seeing her for the first time and more importantly, although she may not have consciously thought of it in this way, she was opening herself up to me.

The room was a little messy and I could tell that she hadn't planned on company. There were pictures of her friends and family, framed and sitting on the dresser. There was a Björk poster and a concert ticket stub hanging on the wall above her bed. There were bottles of lotion and perfume on a dressing table and a bathrobe hanging from the opened door of her armoire. On the night stand was an ashtray, a dirty wine glass and an empty bottle of wine.

"Nice place," I said.

"Thank you, but it's a bit messy right now. I haven't tidied up in ages."

"No, its fine."

"Do you want some wine?" she asked.

"Yeah, I'll take some...red, if you have it."

"Okay, I'll get some."

She left and I sat on the bed waiting for her. It took quite a bit longer than I expected for the wine and I started to feel a bit awkward sitting there in her room by myself. I looked around trying to find something to occupy me. I spied some papers lying on her desk and was tempted to look at them but decided against it. I just sat there on the bed looking at a print that was hanging on the wall in front of me.

Sunniva returned a few minutes later with the wine and some cheese and crackers as well. She set the food down and poured the wine.

"Do you like it?" She asked, indicating the print.

"Yeah, I was just looking at it. It's Munch right?"

"Yeah, it's his Madonna. So, you know Munch?"

"Of course."

"You know he's from Norway."

"Is that right? I didn't know that."

"Yeah, it's true."

"How about that? Edvard Munch is Norwegian...So is that eighties pop-rock band, Ah Ha right?"

"Yeah they're Norwegian too," she answered as she sat on the bed next to me.

"Well, that's quite the contribution to Western Culture," I said jokingly.

She picked up a pillow and hit me with it playfully. Then she grabbed the wine glasses and handed me one.

"Skol!" She exclaimed then took a big drink, which emptied half the glass.

"Skol!" I repeated and did likewise.

"You like to drink?" I quipped.

"Sometimes, but it's mostly that I had a bad week."

"Oh Yeah, why so bad?" I asked interestedly.

"I'll tell you all about it," she began, "if you reach into the dresser drawer next to you and roll us a spliff."

I got out the stuff and started to roll the spliff.

"Did I tell you I got sacked from my job?" She began.

"Yeah, you mentioned something about it, the other night at that party."

"Well my termination is under review and my union representatives told me that they don't think they can get my job back, which really pisses me off. They're having a meeting with the management the week after next and I'll find out then. That's why I'm going on holiday, because I don't have fuck-all to do."

"If you don't mind me asking," I ventured "why did you get fired?"

"They accused me of ruining half a milliliter of primary antibodies, by leaving them out of the freezer."

"What's that," I asked, completely ignorant.

"Antibodies are the things that fight viruses and things like that."

"Oh I see. So they got all bent out of shape over half a milliliter? What's the big deal?"

"It's like two thousand American dollars worth of antibodies."

"What, two grand, you got to be kidding me!"

"No it's true. Things in labs are really expensive. You should see how much the equipment costs."

"Like what?"

"You know what a centrifuge is?"

"No."

"It looks sort of like a machine that makes bread, only it spins things really fast."

"Yeah."

"They cost like ten thousand dollars, American."

"Fuck!"

"Yeah, so that's why they're all pissed off."

"I see."

There was a silent pause.

101

"So, ah…" I began cautiously, "did you…ahhh…did you do it?"

"Do what?"

"Did you accidentally ruin those antibodies?"

"No."

"Really? That sucks that you're getting fired for it then."

"Well, it wasn't an accident I did it on purpose!" She said, with a heavy, sardonic laugh. "But they have fuck-all for proof that I did."

"What?"

"Yeah, I did it on purpose, but they don't know it was me. My boss just put the blame on me because she's a bitch and hates me."

"You're kidding…right?"

"No, it's true."

"Why did you do it? I mean you just felt like vandalizing something or what?"

"No, that's not it at all. It wasn't vandalism. It was a kind of a protest," she explained. "It was micro-terrorism."

"What?"

"Never mind, let's smoke that spliff and start packing."

I dropped the subject and lit the joint. I took a few relaxing drags and passed it to her. After she took a few hits, she pulled a duffle bag out from under her bed and started packing her clothes in it. Her packing was neither neat nor methodical. Pants, shirts, socks were all shoved in the bag in a disorderly way. When she was packing her underwear, I took a particular interest, which of course I did my best to conceal. When she finished packing them she looked at me sternly, like a mother would look at a child she was about to discipline and said jokingly, "I know you want to touch them you sex pervert!" She took a pair of red lace panties out of the bag and threw them at me. They hit me in the chest and fell unto my lap. She giggled and I laughed also. After packing some toiletries in the bag, she zipped it up and proclaimed, "That's it!"

She looked over at her alarm clock. "Good, I still have almost two hours before my cab arrives."

We spent the next two hours sitting in her room talking. We talked about quite a few things in that time. Mostly the traditional, get-to-know-you topics like what our hometowns are like, our families, music likes and dislike and so forth. It was actually a very good conversation and I felt like we were starting to connect. We both had an affinity for classic jazz and we had the same tastes in movies, drugs, books, and art. I was feeling really good about her.

When it got closer to the time her cab was supposed to arrive, we went downstairs and waited for it. It showed up right on time and she offered me a ride home before going to the airport.

I got in with her. The taxi drove us to my flat and pulled to the side of Oxford Road, across from Witworth Park.

"So when are you going to get back to Manchester?" I asked.

"Sometime next week," she answered with a flirtatious vagueness.

"I see," I said pretending to be uninterested, keeping the coquetry alive.

"How about, I'll call you," she said softly with genuineness in her voice.

"I'd like that," I replied with equal genuineness.

She leaned over to me gently and kissed me goodbye with a long, slow, delicate kiss, which was very different from the passionate, alcohol fueled kisses at Jar Bar.

I said goodbye and got out of the car. I shut the door and stood on the curb. The taxi pulled away making a u-turn in the middle of the street. Sunniva waved as she rode past. She looked buoyant and vernal. I felt buoyant and vernal. It was strange that she could make me feel that way. Helli never did. I didn't even know Sunniva that well, but I knew that I was going to see her when she came back from Norway and I felt the initial stages of something burgeoning between us. After Helli, I pretty much decided that I wasn't going to bother with any kind of a relationship; but, with Sunniva I didn't really care how disruptive it might become to my life. She made me feel good and after all wasn't that all I ever wanted anyway? Why not let my life get complicated? Simplicity is for amebas.

When Sunniva's cab drove out of sight, I crossed the road and walked back to my flat. As I opened the door, I noticed the sun starting to come up. It was beginning to illuminate the overcast sky that hovered above the wonderful city.

***

The next night Solis, Miguel, Mikko and I were relaxing on the lanai of Krö Bar. We were just shooting the shit and otherwise having a good time like we always did. After a few drinks the conversation came to Sunniva.

"What da fuck do you mean, micro-terrorism?" asked Miguel.

"I don't know that's what she said."

"Are you sure that she did it on purpose?" questioned Mikko.

"Yeah, she said she did it on purpose."

"How much does something like that cost?"

"The antibodies?"

"Yeah."

"She said like, fifteen-hundred quid or something like that."

"FUCK!" exclaimed Miguel and Mikko, in stereo.

Then Mikko asked me, "Why did she do it, really?"

"I don't know, she didn't say."

"Maybe she's unstable," he replied half-jokingly.

"Maybe…Fuck I don't know. She seems alright though. I kind of like her."

"You wan ta know, what I tink?" asked Solis. "Dat's da kin of bea'ch dat will cut your throat, in the med-dle of da night, mate!"

"What the fuck are you talking about?" I replied.

"Is true mate! In Costa Rica we have des womans like dat too. You never know how dey will behave. One minute dey ruin'en anti-bodies, in a lab…an da nex dey are cutting you fuck'en throat, when ya are a-sleeping!"

"Shut up, Solis. You don know what you are say'en," protested Miguel.

"No! Is true…Is a fact! Is 'cause of deir hormones an da menstruations!"

"Shut up," I responded shaking my head.

"Das fine, mate. You tell me, 'shut up,' but wen you are dead by dat bea'ch, I will say ta you, MOTHERFUCKA! I tol you a-bout dat shite!"

"Lot of good that will do me, if I'm dead."

"Den, I will kill dat bea'ch, jus for you mate."

"Thanks Solis. You're a true mate."

Rare is the Occasion

I talked to Sunniva a couple of times the week she was in Norway. They weren't long conversations, no more than ten minutes each; but, they were good nonetheless. There was no getting around it. I was starting to like her. I found myself doing things that I normally wouldn't have. For example, I developed a keen interest in things like Norwegian history and Norse mythology, for no other reason than to impress her with my knowledge of her country. I even found out a little information on the real St. Sunniva.

Sunniva got back to Manchester on Saturday afternoon. I had plans to go out with Solis, Mikko and Miguel that night, so I asked her if she wanted to go out, just the two of us, early in the evening and then we all could go out later. She said that was a good idea.

She suggested that we see a movie playing at the Corner House that she had wanted to see. It was a Spanish film called *Lucia y el Sexo*. I had actually just seen it three days earlier but I told her that I hadn't. Now, this may seem like a very romantic and giving thing to do and it was to a certain degree. She really seemed like she wanted to see it and I didn't want to rain on her parade. Although I must admit there were some selfish motives behind my actions as well. The movie is filled with tons of romance and sexuality. I figured that if she saw the movie with me the romance and sexuality would, through osmosis or whatever, seep into her subconscious. There, like a seed it would grow slowly throughout the night eventually blossoming into the flower of uncontrollable sexual desire. The movie in itself would be a powerful aphrodisiac and afterwards we would consume large quantities of alcohol, which would help in the cultivation of this sex flower I envisioned.

The Corner House is a small theater and art gallery that specializes in foreign and avante garde films. I would drop in there from time to time with Matti or Miguel to catch a movie or art exhibit. It occupies the street level of a triangular building in the city centre nearly to the northern end of Oxford road, across from the Palace Theatre. I got there twenty minutes early and decided to get a drink in the café as I waited for Sunniva. I ordered a beer and sat down at a long thin counter that ran the length of a window overlooking Oxford Road. This was a nice place to sit by myself and watch the bustle of the street. The congested traffic filled the street like two rows of worker ants. On the sidewalk random people of every description trekked to unknown

105

destinations. I peered out the window watching all of it voyeuristically. It wasn't raining at the time; but, it had rained earlier. The road and sidewalks were wet and shallow puddles of water had formed in places. The damp pavement reminded me of something I had just read a week or so earlier.

In 1835, the French philosopher, Alexis de Tocqueville visited Manchester and remarked that "On this watery land, which nature and art have contributed to keep damp…humanity attains its most complete development and its most brutish; here civilization makes its miracles, and civilized man is turned back almost into a savage." That was, like I said, in 1835 but his words could have been written the day I stared out the Corner House Café window watching the traffic pass by.

Manchester is Dickens'. Or at least it could have been created in some Dickens novel. During that coarse epoch in history called the industrial revolution, cotton mills and factories covered the city. They dotted the landscape like flaming, smoking arms reaching for the promises of heaven. They filled the city with riches, indeed it was the richest place on earth at the time; but, they also filled the city with pollution as ubiquitous as the bourgeois wealth. Thick black smoke lofted from factory chimneys high into the air only to fall again to the earth as soot and choke any life form that had the audacity to attempt to live. It certainly wasn't a nice place to exist at the time but all that was in the past. The Manchester I knew had no industry to speak of. Manchester's industrial grandeur has faded and become just a collective memory that was bottled up and placed upon a shelf or in a display case in a museum.

During the industrial revolution, the people of Manchester shuffled from place to place in misery, plagued by their place in life and an environment which caused irritated red eyes and chronic sore throats. Present day Manchester doesn't have the pollution problems it used to have however, sitting there at the Corner House observing the main thoroughfare of the city, I realized that the people still shuffle from place to place in misery just like they did in de Tocqueville's time. I looked hard at the people in the cars and walking past and saw economic hardship, alcoholism and violence in the exhausted, hardened faces of the Mancunians. Their eyes trapped the dimness and clouds and rain that filled the sky. Their faces were fixed with a rugged stiffness. But in every one of the faces there was something more. I noticed individuals that refused to break just as the red brick buildings that decay and crumble at their feet refused to fall. The people I saw stood in defiance of the rain and poverty that pounded down on them like physical sadness. That's their most complete development, a sort of emotional Darwinism. They find ways to adapt and live despite their troubles. That's why I think that the nightlife is so popular in Manchester. The people of the city adapt through music and drugs and alcohol and dancing and copulation and violence or anything else that enables them to forget about the social stratification and inequality that imprisons them. However, this adaptation is sort of a regression to the brutishness de Tocqueville talked about. It relies on the ability to embrace primitive pleasures. The more animalistic you allow yourself to become, the less human suffering you have to endure. In that statement, underneath the violence and poverty and deterioration of the buildings and souls of the people, lies the real Manchester.

There are really two Manchesters and I know them both because the longer I thought about it the more I could identify myself with the Mancunians. It wasn't so much how long I had been there. It was more how I felt. I know the Manchester where humanity reaches its highest level of development; and I also know the Manchester where humanity becomes its most brutish. I know them because in Manchester I was becoming both my most developed and most brutish all at the same time.

I spotted Sunniva coming down Oxford Road shortly after I finished my drink. She was wearing a light-blue rain slicker and blue jeans. She looked good to me even though she wasn't really dressed up. I liked that she dressed so casual. It spoke volumes about how comfortable she felt with me. I rapped on the window as she passed by. She looked through the glass and noticed it was me. She gave a quick, excited wave and smiled. I left my seat and met her at the door.

"Hi," I said greeting her with a kiss. "How was your trip?"

She told me about her flights and some of the things she did while back in Norway. The sing-song quality of her voice seemed more vivid in person than it did on the phone when she was gone. I listened intently to what she was saying. We chatted for a minute or two then decided to go purchase our tickets. I went up to the ticket counter and bought two. We went into a small theater with terrace seating and sat in the center of the very back row. We made small talk for a few minutes, while we waited for the film to start. The lights dimmed and the theatre got quiet. Sunniva reached over and held my hand.

***

After the movie, we decided to have a drink before we met up with my friends. We went back into the café and sat down at the window where I had been earlier. It was night by then and Manchester looked different. Once the sun went down it took a more sinister form. Nothing changed with the landscape, of course. The change was in the people. After dark, was the time of day the brutishness and savagery began.

We sipped our gin and tonics slowly while we discussed the film and enjoyed each others company. I was having such a good time I considered making a change of plans and just hanging out with Sunniva the whole night; but, then I thought better of it. I was getting to like her, fair enough; but, Mikko, Solis and Miguel were my mates. I wasn't about to stand-up my mates. Just before we finished our drinks, I received a text from Miguel that said to meet them at a place called Po Na Na, which happened to only be a block or so from where we were.

I was happy with the choice of venue. Po Na Na had a nice speed for the night. It always had good music to dance to and was really dark. Most of it was subterranean and if the upper portion had windows I never noticed them. The place was really cozy as well. It resembled a Central Asian opium den with loads of private enclaves situated throughout it. You could draw a curtain across the entrance and sit on the pillows and cushions that were spread across the floor from wall to wall. It was nice to get really high and lounge around in those enclaves with a drink.

I wanted to walk quickly once we left the Corner House café. I was anxious to get there. I wanted to hang out and I was also interested in seeing the dates Mikko and Miguel said they were going to bring. Apparently, they met a couple girls on the bus a few days earlier and asked them out. It was going to be sort of a date night for all of us, except that is for Solis. He didn't want any part in bringing a date because as he put it, "Ya dona brin milk ta da cow!"

Sunniva and I found Mikko and Miguel laying down in one of the private enclaves with their arms around their dates. Their dates looked similar to each other as if they were sisters. It was hard to tell; but, they both had auburn hair and big tits which they were not shy about either. They were wearing low cut tank tops that exposed a good deal of cleavage. I could tell they were Mancunians before they said a word by the gaudy, gold jewelry they wore. Miguel introduced his date as Nicole and Mikko introduced his as Samantha which I thought was odd because she was wearing a necklace with gold letters that said, "Chloe."

Solis wasn't in the grotto and I enquired about him.

108

"Where's Solis?" I asked as Sunniva and I laid down on the pillows.

"He's left," replied Mikko with a cheeky smile.

"Already?" I queried knowing by the look on Mikko's face there was more to the story.

"He was talking to some bird and the next thing I knew he's left."

This of course meant he was shagging the girl.

"Did you know who she was?" I asked, fighting back a chuckle.

"I've never seen her before."

"He knew her?" I continued, fairly certain he hadn't.

"It didn't appear that way."

Mikko and I flashed each other a smile of approval. We made them very discreet however, because we didn't want our dates to think that we encouraged such behavior. I thought about changing the subject but my curiosity wouldn't let it drop.

"So, was she hot?" I blurted out.

Mikko and Miguel burst into laughter.

"What?" I asked.

Finally, Miguel managed to get himself together enough to say, "Nooo. She was a fuck'en wildebeest!!!"

Everyone laughed at the unabashed candor of Miguel's observation.

"Not really picky that guy. Is he?" I said shaking my head.

This caused Mikko and Miguel to laugh even harder. The fact was he wasn't really picky. As long as she was female that was good enough.

After a good laugh, I went up to the bar with Sunniva to get drinks for us. We each ordered a shot of Finlandia and a beer. We took the shots at the bar and went back to our cushions with the beer. When we got back though, the rest of our party wanted to go out on the dance floor. We set our drinks down and joined them.

There was Indie dance music playing and the DJ had the crowd really going. Sunniva and I got into it as well. We each had one hand on the other's hip and danced just close enough for our bodies to touch but not press against each other. I could feel the heat from her body radiating and soaking into me. I put my head next to hers so that I could smell her hair and brush my cheek against hers. She breathed deliberately slow, hot breaths on my neck. It was very sexy in a subtle, teasing way. I remember thinking that the night was going really well. The movie had worked out and so had Po Na Na.

109

After a few songs we all went back and lazed on the pillows. That's pretty much how we stayed for the rest of the night except for the occasional run up to the bar for more drinks. Mikko and Miguel ended up making quite a few trips to the bar actually and I could tell it was putting off their dates, however Mikko and Miguel didn't seem to care in the least. In fact, I think they may have been regretting asking those girls out. Nicole and Samantha or Chloe or whatever her name was turned out to be poor conversationalists. They didn't join in any of the discussions and Mikko and Miguel spent more time talking to Sunniva than they did their own dates. My friends seemed to like Sunniva which made me feel good. Not many people's approval was important to me. For example, I could give two shits what my father thought; but, I did care what Mikko, Miguel and Solis thought.

Toward the end of the night just before the club closed Miguel and Mikko's companions left together without them. Mikko and Miguel left together shortly afterward. By that time they were barely able to walk and certainly too drunk to care that they got ditched.

That left just Sunniva and me.

"So you ah …you want to ah, do something now or something?" I asked.

I was tying to be cautious but admittedly ended up sounding like a fucking idiot.

"We could get a take out and go back to my flat if you want," she replied.

"Sure," I said warily optimistic that something good might happen at her place, warily optimistic that sex might actually happen.

We left Po Na Na and stood on the sidewalk outside the club. There was a soft, cool mist in the air. Above us, the lights from the Palace Theatre's tower lit the street with a hazy red glow. It reminded me of the lighthouses in Michigan, and then made me realize how far away from there I really was. Michigan seemed almost like a foreign place to me then. Sometime, I'm not sure when, Manchester became my home. Things there became my life and things from Michigan became apparitions, shadowy images of a former life. Michigan was intangible. It wasn't real anymore. Manchester had become my life. Manchester had become my reality. Solis, Miguel, Mikko, they were part of that reality. Sunniva too, I realized, was becoming part of that reality.

There was a mob of people outside Po Na Na. Everyone was leaving all the clubs around there in the city centre and walking toward

Oxford road in the hopes of getting a taxi. Somehow Sunniva managed to flag one down almost right away.

It slid to a stop next to the curb, Sunniva opened the door and started to get in. She had one foot in the door then stopped to turn around and face me.

"You know," she said in a familiar tone.

I know where this is going?

She continued, "We don't have to get a take out if you don't want to."

"Let's just go back to your place," I said.

She started to get in the cab again grabbing my hand to pull me in with her. I shut the door and the car started moving.

***

We got back to her flat and the place was empty. She took me into the living room and turned on the lights. There was an entertainment center with a big screen TV and stereo against the wall, opposite a couch. Standing next to the entertainment center were two giant speakers on either side. The walls were decorated with framed prints. There was a Van Gogh, a Duchamp and some others. The furniture all matched but it wasn't very expensive. The room had the aura of shabby sophistication that is indicative of young professionals.

Sunniva sat down in the middle of the couch and I sat next to her, just close enough that the sides of our legs and arms touched.

"Where are your roommates?" I asked.

"They've gone away for the weekend."

"So we don't have to be quiet?"

"No, why?"

"Let's listen to some music. You want to?"

"Sure."

"What do you want to listen to?"

"I don't care; you pick something."

I walked over to a rack of CDs near the entertainment center and looked over the titles. There was a bunch of Sugar Cubes and Björk disks as well as a lot of ones I'd never heard of.

I wanted something that would set a nice mood. She had some Marvin Gaye and Barry White but that was too obvious, too crude. I needed something better. I wanted it to be mellow, but also upbeat.

111

I thumbed through them until I came across four or five different Charlie Parker disks.

This'll be good.

I read the backs to see which songs were on them. I picked one out that had mostly slower songs.

"How 'bout this one?" I asked, turning around to show her the disk.

She was leaning down, over the coffee table rolling a joint and looked up.

"Yeah, that's a nice choice," she said with an approving smile.

I put it in and sat back down next to her. She finished rolling the spliff and sparked it up. She took a couple of puffs and handed it to me. I took a nice long drag and let it out slowly through my nose. I leaned back all the way and put my feet up on the table. She did likewise and we smoked the entire joint that way, just listening to the music, relaxing and not saying much.

I felt really comfortable sitting there with her, even though we weren't talking which is, admittedly, a bit odd when you don't really know a person all that well. But, it didn't seem to bother her either. We just reclined on the couch next to each other and spaced out.

I stared at a fish tank that was sitting on a side table in the other room. The lights were off in that room but I would see the fish clearly by the tank light. I watched the fish dart through the water from here to there with seemingly no direction or purpose in mind. They would swim maybe an inch or two and then *boom*, change direction as fast as they could, only to do it all over again three seconds later. A couple of times two fish changed directions toward each other and ended up colliding. Then, they would get themselves in a panic and dart in five or six directions in about two seconds. It was chaotic. I loved it.

"I'd like to be a fish," I said out of nowhere, still staring at the tank.

Sunniva laughed.

"What?" She asked after she stopped laughing.

"I was just looking at the fish in the other room and I was saying that it'd be cool to be a fish."

"Why's that?"

"Ah, it's just like all they do is swim around and they don't really do anything. They just like go one direction and then dart off in another," I said turning around to face her.

112

We both cracked up laughing. When we stopped we were looking at each other and there was an awkward bit of silence. She broke the discomfort by leaning in quickly, playfully and giving me a peck. Then she jumped up from the couch and headed for the stairs, without saying anything.

"Where are you going?" I asked, a little afraid that I might be experiencing a replay of the night she stayed over in my room.

"I'm going up to my room; I'll be right back down," she answered with mysterious brevity.

I heard her run up the stairs, knock around up there for a minute and then run back down the steps. She came back with a little porcelain jewelry box.

"What's in the box?" I asked.

"Wouldn't you want to know?" She said in a teasing voice, hiding it behind her back, like a child playing a keep-away game.

I made a few playful, flirtatious grabs at the box, not really trying to get it.

"You want to see what's in this box?" She asked in the same teasing voice.

"Yeah," I said, making it a game.

"Well first, you have to tell me how great I am."

"You're great," I said flatly.

"No! Say it like this: Sunniva you are the best. There is no other one that compares to you in the whole world. You are a queen."

I looked at her suspiciously.

"Say it!" she demanded in jest.

I obliged, "Sunniva you are the best! Every other woman in the whole world fails to achieve your beauty and grace! You are a true queen and I am honored to even be in the same room as you!"

"That's better. Now give me a kiss."

I stood up and gave her a peck on the cheek.

"That's it? That's all I get for what's in this box?" She questioned.

"I don't even know what's in the box," I replied.

"And you won't unless you give me a real kiss."

I put my hand on her cheek and caressed her face delicately with my thumb. I moved my mouth slowly to hers and then kissed her aggressively, dominantly. She shut her eyes and I could feel her body relaxing.

"How's that?" I asked after stopping.

"Well....I suppose that will do," she said teasingly.

113

We sat back down on the couch. She put the box on the table and opened it. I could feel my eyes getting bigger as I viewed its contents. There was about a quarter of a gram of cocaine in it.

"Fucking nice one!" I exclaimed.

"I thought you might like that. I've been saving it for a special occasion."

She poured the powder out onto a coffee table book on European migratory birds and started cutting some lines. I got up and changed the CD to another of Charlie Parker's, one with faster songs. When I sat back down, Sunniva had four lines set up. She hit two using a little straw then passed it to me. I followed suit. The powder exploded up my nose and into my blood stream.

A rush of euphoria, power and energy hit me almost immediately, electrified me, animated me.

"That's fucking nice!" I said rubbing my nose.

"Yeah," she said simply nodding her head.

"Hey, you said it was a special occasion? So what's the occasion?" I asked.

Without answering, she smiled at me and picked up the remote control. She pointed it at the stereo and turned the music up louder, as loud as it could get. The whole house shook from the noise. The flat was filled with the hysterical, whimsical sounds of Charlie Parker's saxophone. The music echoed and reverberated off the walls until it eventually slammed into my inner ear making an impression on my brain. The prints on the walls rattled from the vibrations and threatened to fall.

"You know they call him The Bird," Sunniva said indicating her pleasure with the music.

"Yeah, I knew that," I said giving her a shared look appreciation.

I could feel The Bird's tempo race even faster than my cocaine filled blood rushed through my veins. The drums thundered all around me. My body ached for action and motion. I felt great, lively, alive.

"Salt peanuts! Salt peanuts!" echoed throughout my head, and the room, probably the whole house, maybe even the neighborhood or the world for all I knew. There was no way to tell, nor did I give a fuck. The music could have been waking people up in Australia but I was having a blast. My heart hammered against the inside of my chest. My thoughts raced. And I listened intently to every note of music pounding my head.

This was the sound of Madness and Insanity. It was quick, fierce, and capricious but always somewhere deep in the back-beat, often hidden

114

or too complicated to understand there is an order, a harmonious force, a coercion of some sort, that keeps the river flowing.

Sunniva gently nudged me back, with the palms of her hands, so that I reclined on the couch, sinking into it. She sat on my lap facing me with an unruly look in her eyes. I was overwhelmed. I felt myself getting hard and the muscles in my chest and arms tightened.

She pulled her shirt up over her head trapping her long black hair in it as it went up. When her shirt crested the top of her head, she let it drop, releasing her hair back down on her shoulders like a waterfall.

I felt my heart beat still faster; it felt like it was lodged in my throat. I took my hands and put them on the sides of her torso, just under her ribs. Her skin was filled with goose bumps from the chill of the damp Manchester air. I rubbed my hands firmly and slowly against the sides of her body warming them until the goose bumps disappeared.

The Bird went into a frantic improvisation and Dizzy Gillespie blew his trumpet at him. They went note for note, in double time, then triple. Sunniva and I unconsciously quickened our tempo as Parker did his.

She reached behind her back and unfastened her bra. She grabbed each strap with the opposite hand and pulled it away from her body to slowly reveal her breasts to me. They were large but her nipples were small and erect. She leaned forward to me, pressing the middle of her chest against my face. It was almost completely encompassed by her breasts. I kissed her chest and her neck then she pulled back and grabbed my shirt. She clenched it at the bottom and tugged at it forcefully. She couldn't get it off so I lifted my arms and she was able to pull it over my head. She tossed the shirt across the room too impatient, too wrapped up in the moment to do anything else with it.

I ran my hands across her firm breasts, grabbing them, feeling her nipples with the tips of my fingers. She touched my bare stomach and chest. Parker thundered strange, abstract sounds and we sat there feeling each other, exploring each other as Columbus must have the shores of a new land, thoroughly, lustfully and ecstatically but cautiously, nervously.

This was a special kind of Madness and Insanity. It was especially intense and especially dangerous. It was shared and reciprocal. It had consequences of an unknown nature. It was new and exciting and different, but like all Madness and Insanity once it starts, you are captive to it.

Sunniva stood up deliberately slow and went to turn off the lights. It was completely dark, except for the small light coming from the fish tank in the next room.

I could make out the silhouette of Sunniva's face and body as she walked back toward me. Her hips swayed slightly from side to side and her hair bounced against her shoulders. She was mysterious to me, still, but compelled me with a beauty and longing that I never felt before. She sat down again on my lap and leaned close putting her mouth next to my ear. She exhaled hot, wordless breaths on my ear and the side of my neck.

She put her mouth even closer to my ear, so that her lips almost touched it. Charlie thundered. Fish darted. Cocaine flooded my body. My heart raced. She whispered into my ear deeply, sexually, as if the words themselves were tangible. "Do you know why it's a special occasion yet?"

***

Sunniva and I had breakfast on Sunday, although we didn't wake up until two in the afternoon. We made some eggs and toast and drank coffee. The food was pretty good; but, the best part was that we were able to talk without any of the awkwardness generally associated with seeing the person you just had sex with for the first time, the morning after. I was in an exceedingly good mood because the sex somehow had made us closer. It was a nice feeling, a little strange but nice nonetheless. I really did feel better when I was with her. And it was like the sex was a physical manifestation of the inner feeling she gave me. Although, I couldn't read her mind, it seemed like she felt pretty much the same way I did. That's probably why there wasn't any awkwardness between us. There was no reason for it. We were on the same emotional page.

After breakfast, I went back to my place to wash clothes and work on my thesis. She and I made plans to go and have a proper date at a place called Solomon Grundy for the following night. That day, she was expecting the results of the appeal her union filed at work. She seemed nervous about losing her job and felt like going out would at least be something to look forward to if things didn't go her way.

Solomon Grundy was a quaint little bistro in Withington that combined, quite nicely, a traditional old world feel with an atmosphere of urban savoir-faire. It was a good place to go, in and of itself, but it was especially good since Mikko got a part-time job there. On the front door, there were two stickers showing that they accepted both Visa and

116

MasterCard, but that didn't matter much to me. In the two weeks that Mikko was gainfully employed there, he had managed to, as my Marxist friends would say, "redistribute" hundreds of dollars of alcohol. This, not coincidently corresponded with an increase in my, Miguel and Solis's patronage to the establishment.

I was supposed to meet Sunniva there at ten for a few drinks. I put on a sport coat and tie for the occasion, to class it up a little. I got there about a half an hour early to talk a little with Mikko.

When I got there the place was crowded for a Monday. It was the usual mix of students and young professionals. Mikko was behind the shiny wood and brass bar pouring a beer. When he saw me, he stopped working and said, "Hey man, how ya doing!"

"Good, man, good. I'm supposed to meet that chick, Sunniva here, in awhile."

"Nice one, man. So how did it go the other night?" He asked raising his eyebrows.

"Things went well," I replied vaguely.

"Well?"

"Yeah, they went fairly well, I'd say."

"You shagged her right?"

"Who?" I said pretending to be innocent.

"You know who."

"A true gentleman doesn't talk about such things!"

"Kal already told me—"

"I don't know where Kal is getting his information…" I interrupted.

"He said you told him."

"He said that? Well you know how Kal is…"

"Solis and Miguel said the same thing."

"What did they say?"

"That you shagged her."

"Who?"

"Fuck off."

There was a brief pause.

"Mikko, guess who I shagged the other night?" I continued.

"Yourself?" He replied.

We both laughed.

Just then Sunniva came through the door and smiled when she saw us. She approached the bar and I was reminded of the way she seductively walked toward me the other night after she turned off the lights. She was wearing a tight, black dress that hugged firm against her curvy body. The three of us talked for a while then Mikko opened up a private banquet room so that Sunniva and I could have some privacy.

Sunniva and I sat making small talk for a few minutes; but, I could tell that something was wrong. She seemed distracted and aloof.

"So…ah did you get some bad news this afternoon?" I asked carefully.

"I lost my appeal," she said dejectedly.

"I'm sorry to hear that," I said commiserating.

"That fucking bitch lied through her fucking teeth."

"Who?"

"My old boss. She said that she saw me do it and warned me about it and all this; but, it wasn't true. She lied because she's a lying bitch who lies!"

I could tell that Sunniva was really upset so I declined to point out the redundancy in what she just said.

"So what are you going to do now?" I asked.

"I guess I'll have to find another job."

"Yeah, I suppose you will."

She paused as if she was in thought.

"But first…" she said crossly, "first I'm going to get even!"

There was a malevolent look in her eyes. It wasn't a malevolent look like someone who was planning a practical joke either. It was a menacing, vindictive look. I could tell right away she was serious. I had no idea whatsoever of her intentions; but, her eyes screamed mayhem; her words rang havoc. There was an unmistakable aura of Madness and Insanity hovering around her. I knew I wouldn't be able to resist this aura for long. But, it didn't really matter; I was overcome by something myself. I was, at that moment more attracted to her than I had ever been to anyone in my life. She was dangerous. I had never seen anyone's eyes reflect mischief so willingly and recklessly. It was thrilling and sexy and exciting and scary all at the same time; and I didn't even know how she intended to get even. All I knew was that she was serious and would invoke Madness and Insanity to help her.

"What do you mean get even?" I asked, partly intrigued, partly apprehensive.

"I'm going to break into the lab!" she answered as though she hadn't given it much thought.

"Yeah, and do what?"

118

She thought for a moment. "I'll sabotage it! I'll break and smash everything I can get my hands on! Some of that stuff is expensive."

I didn't say anything.

"What do you think?" she finally asked after my silence.

I gave it a thought. I looked at her anger. I considered her resolve. I weighed the situation objectively, scientifically and answered.

"Well, if you want my opinion, if you're going to break into the lab to vandalize it, you might as well steal some shit from it. After all, like you said, some of that stuff is really expensive."

"You're right! I met a guy, at a conference, who does research using the same anti-bodies that my lab uses. He works at the University in Tallinn and he complained to me how it's hard for him to afford the antibodies and that his work is in jeopardy because of it. I bet he'd pay for some. I know he would!" she said with wide-eyed optimism.

I had one hand laying flat on the table and she delicately put hers on top of it. Gently she started stroking the back of my hand with her index finger.

"But…" She continued slowly in an almost powerless voice. "I'd need help…"

Right away I knew it was a bad idea, the look in her eye, the breaking and entering, the shady Estonian biologist, all of it seemed problematic to me. But, at the same time I couldn't say no. I didn't want to. I was swept up by her voice and eyes, and breasts and recklessness. I was swept up by Madness and Insanity. And, let's be quite clear about something. There are things that a man will do for a woman and there are things a man will do for money and financial independence from prick fathers. Rare is the occasion when he can do it for both.

Besides, what's the worst that can happen?

>|()|()|<

After we left Solomon Grundy we went to Sunniva's house, drank six bottles of wine and made love until about five thirty in the morning. We had only been sleeping for about an hour when the alarm on my phone went off. I had forgotten that I set it and the noise startled me. I was disoriented and sat straight up in bed for a second trying to figure out what the fuck was going on. Then I remembered.

I jumped out of bed to shut off the alarm before it woke up Sunniva. I found my phone in my pants, under the bed and turned off the alarm. I looked over at Sunniva to see if it had bothered her. She was still sound asleep.

I needed to hurry. I hunted for my clothes as fast as I could, which was really difficult. The faster I looked, the faster the room spun as a result of the all wine. I was able to find all of my clothes except for my boxers and a sock.

Fuck! I thought franticly. *Ah fuck it; I guess these'll have to do.*

I threw on all the clothes that I had, managing to snag a couple pubic hairs in the process of zipping up my pants. After lamenting for several seconds over my missing short hairs, I decided that I couldn't be bothered to tie my tie or tuck in my shirt.

I clocked myself in the mirror and accessed my appearance. I looked really bad in contrast to my normally presentable nature. My hair was sticking up and all over. My eyes looked sunken in and dark and my face was a chalky white. I tried to comb my hair down a little with my hand but that only seemed to make it worse.

While I was checking out my hideous appearance, I noticed a foul odor wafting from me. It was the smell of heavy body odor, stale wine and marijuana smoke. To be fair, I had become a little accustomed to this particular smell however, this morning it was especially potent.

I noticed a bottle of perfume sitting on Sunniva's dressing table. I gave myself a few squirts to mask my scent and then looked at my watch. It was time for me to go. I went over to the bed and kissed Sunniva on the forehead.

She stirred and asked, "Where are you going?" in a sleepy voice.

"I have to pick my friend up at the airport. Remember?"

"Okay," she said, then mumbled something unintelligible and rolled over.

I looked at my watch again.

Fuck! Better hurry!

I darted down the stairs and out the front door. Just as I got outside, I could see the bus pulling up to the stop at the end of the block. I needed to catch that bus because, the next one wouldn't come for at least a half an hour. I didn't want to be late so I decided sprint. I took off, in a mad dash, going as fast as I could, which was difficult wearing wing tips and missing a sock. I was surprisingly fleet of foot however, and managed to get to the bus just before it pulled away. It was a fine achievement in athleticism.

I boarded the bus which was empty except for the driver, paid and sat down in the first row. I was winded and sweating from my sprint.

I tried to sit quietly for a minute and recover from my exertion but things started to go horribly wrong. My chest began to ache painfully and my head started spinning even worse than it had earlier. The spinning caused an uneasiness in my stomach that kept intensifying until, my mouth began to water...

The next thing I knew, I was hunched over, puking watery, brown vomit all over the aisle. At first I tried to be silent, so I wouldn't make a scene; but, it hurt too much to be quiet. I had to give it my all. This apparently, was very loud because the driver heard me and pulled the bus over.

"YOU LIT'LE FUCK'EN CUNT!!!" The driver shouted at me. He got out of his seat and opened the door of his booth, to see the damage.

After staring, in dismay, at my pool of vomit and smelling the putrid odor that was filling the bus for several seconds he screamed "GET OUT!" and not in a nice way.

I tried to protest but when I started talking I got sicker and puked again, this time more fiercely. The vomit exploded out of my mouth and went all over the seat across the aisle. As I was bent over, vomiting for the second time, the bus driver grabbed me by the back of my jacket and started pulling me out of the bus. I thought about hitting him; but, all the vomiting had made me weak and vulnerable. I just let him pull me off the bus, like I was a trespassing wino. All I could do was watch as he climbed on the bus, got back into his cage and started to shut the door.

"FUCK YOU!" I shouted, but it was too late, the door was closed and the bus was leaving.

I got dropped off, or I guess more accurately thrown off, by a small shop and decided that I should get some gum and a Coca-Cola to help with the vomit taste in my mouth. Then, I walked a couple of blocks until I came across another bus stop. I sat there chewing gum and drinking my Coke while I waited for the next bus. After the soda I started to feel better.

Another bus came alone after awhile and I rode it all the way to the airport without any complications. When I got there, I looked at the monitor and saw that I had still made it in time. My friend's plane had landed and was just about to disembark. I walked to his gate and saw a slim, brown haired guy wearing blue jeans and a t-shirt coming through the door. His face was unshaven and stubbly. He walked quickly and kept looking around like he was trying to find somebody.

"Carl!" I shouted.

Carl was a friend of mine since our freshman year as undergraduates. He lived on the same floor as I did and he liked to drink. We hit it off instantly. He was an interesting sort and a little complex as well. For example, I hardly ever saw him talking to girls; but, he would always talk about them. Except, he never talked about his ex-girlfriends. I didn't know any of these women personally, but I imagine they were initially attracted to his quiet, socially aloof, straight forward demeanor, and were later tortured by it. Carl also like to complain about events that were out of his control, political events, social events, economic events, movie schedules, weather conditions, TV show plots, the price of eggs and then he would make outlandish statements like he was going to move to New Zealand or buy a commercial fishing boat. It was hard to follow his logic at times, but he was a good friend, nevertheless.

He noticed me and walked over. The only luggage he had was a hiker's backpack, which he wore swung over his slender shoulder. We hugged each other and talked for a few minutes.

I took him over to exchange some money then we went outside and caught a bus back to my place. We sat in the upper deck of the bus directly in the front to get a good look at the cityscape. We were the only ones up there, so I cracked a window and lit up a partial joint that I had left over from the pervious night. I took a couple of hits and then passed it to Carl. He took it from my hand and looked at it musingly for a moment. He blew the cherry to get a big ash off and took three or four powerful full-bodied hits that lasted several seconds each. There was a certain intensity about the way he smoked it. It seemed almost as if he was trying to catch up to something and in a way he probably was. We emailed each other at least twice a week and in my emails I would try to describe the level of Madness and Insanity which abound in Manchester. That's what he was after. That's why he came there. He wanted to experience this beast, Madness and Insanity, to explore it and be strong-armed into its devious whims.

I would make sure he got what he wanted. He was going to stay in Manchester for a few weeks and then we were going backpacking through Western Europe. His visit was going to be sixty-two days in all and it was going to be sixty-two days of Madness and Insanity. I didn't know what kind or how severe but I knew it. I knew Manchester. I knew Carl. And I knew myself.

A few weeks before the whole heist business came up with Sunniva there was a big thing on the news about a foiled robbery attempt. A group of thieves tried to steal over three hundred million dollars worth of diamonds that were being displayed in the Millennium Dome in London.

The gang plotted for four months. They cased the entire dome, including the room where the diamonds were kept. They acquired high tech communication equipment to coordinate their movements during the robbery. They even arranged for a speed boat to race them across the Thames, to freedom, after they lifted the diamonds. These were highly professional thieves with years of experience. They had financial backing from Russian gangsters, and their plan was intricate and well organized. Yet they were caught in the act by a Scotland Yard sting and eventually sentenced to fifteen years in prison.

After I told Sunniva that I would help her rob her laboratory, I started to do something that I should have done before I said yes. I started to think about it carefully. I thought about the Millennium Dome heist. I considered the possibility of spending fifteen years in prison and decided right away that I wasn't going to go the way of the Millennium Dome robbers. I wasn't going to spend the next four months planning some stupid robbery of a science lab only to end up in jail. No fucking way. If I was going to end up in jail, I sure as hell wouldn't waste four months planning for it.

The night Carl arrived, I had Mikko, Miguel, and Solis meet Sunniva, Carl and me at Krö Bar. I gathered them there under the auspices of meeting Carl. However, unbeknownst to everyone but Sunniva and me, my real intention was to solicit their help in the break in.

Sunniva, Carl and I got there first. We got drinks and found a secluded table in the back courtyard. It had been a nice spring day and some of the warmth of the afternoon was still lingering in the air. Miguel, Mikko, and Solis got there one at a time and I introduced them to Carl.

We all sat around drinking outside with the noise of the city in the background. Everyone was talking except for me. I sat quietly trying to figure out how to broach the subject. After a few minutes Solis provided me with the opportunity.

"Mate! Is som'tin on you mind, ya are'na say'n no'tin."

This detachment of mine was uncharacteristic so everyone was interested in my reply. They all stopped talking and turned to hear my response.

"Yeah, I ah, actually, I need you guys' help on something."

"Enytin, Mate, What tis it?" replied Solis with sincerity and concern.

I paused a moment, thinking about what to say.

"I'm ah...I'm going to ah, to break in to Sunniva's lab and loot it," I said calmly.

I could sense a feeling of confusion in my friends. They looked at each other and at me, uncertain if I was serious.

"You're joking right?" asked Miguel.

"No, I'm serious. I'm going to rob that fucking place!" I replied.

Everyone stared at me without speaking for a few seconds, still trying, no doubt, to determine if I was serious. The whole thing was a little extreme and somewhat hard to grasp.

Mikko broke the silence, "What, are you serious?"

Sunniva interjected before I had a chance to respond, "He's serious."

She spoke with a definitive tone in her voice that left everyone certain of my intention. There was another silence and a general uneasiness around the table. I took a drink of beer and then sat back in my chair looking around the table, eyeing each of my friends individually. Sunniva took a cigarette from a pack that was sitting on the table. She fingered it nervously for a few seconds in the silence before lighting it.

Then the silence was broken by Solis, "I'll fuck'en do it mate!" he exclaimed with the reckless exuberance of his that I had grown to know so well and admired and loved.

I looked at him and gave him a sincere smile of approval and adoration. There was never any doubt in my mind that he would be aboard.

"Have you loss your fuck'en mind?" Miguel asked Solis.

"I DON'T GIVE A FUCK!!! I ROB DOSE MOTHERFUCKAS, MATE, HEHEHEHEHE!!!" he replied.

"Alright, alright...good...that's fuck'en good. So who else?" I asked looking around the table.

"You loss your fuck'en mind!" said Miguel, this time directed to me.

"Nah man, it's foolproof," I said. Then I turned and looked at Mikko who hadn't said a thing. "What about you? You in or you out?"

"It seems like a really bad idea," he answered.

"Yeah, of course it's a bad idea; but, it'll make us fuck'en rich—" I responded.

"What do you mean rich?" Miguel interrupted.

Solis interjected, "It mean rico motherfucka, no puedes hablar ingles motherfucka?"

"Fuck you Solis, don't fuck'en interrupt me, motherfucka. What do you mean rich motherfucka?"

"Listen," I said looking Miguel in the eyes, "Sunniva knows some scientist motherfucker in Estonia who'll pay us for these anti-bodies that they got in that place. I mean top fuck'en dollar. Big money! Maybe seven thousand quid. Maybe more. Plus, they got some equipment in that fuck'en lab that costs tens of thousands of pounds. And the best part, the best fuck'en part, is that there's no guards…There's no fucking guards or anything… All we have to do is get in the fuck'en building; and that's it…So, are you in or what?"

Miguel addressed Mikko. "What do you think?"

Mikko was leaning back in his chair smoking a cigarette. He took a long drag off of it and exhaled, blowing the smoke in front of his face. There was so much smoke that I could barely see his eyes. He took another quick drag and exhaled slowly while he watched his fingers knock the ash off the end of his cigarette. He put the cigarette down in the ash tray and a stream of smoke floated up toward his face. He looked at me through his thick tortoise shell frames, through the smoke.

"What would I have to do?" he asked me with reservation in his voice.

"Drive the get-away car. You're the only one who has a European driver's license and the only one who can rent a car. That's why we need you."

"Are you sure we need to get a car?"

"Well, it's not as if we can take the fuck'en bus, now is it Mikko?" I answered patiently.

He picked his cigarette back up and took a puff. Then he put it back in the ashtray and took a drink of his beer.

"Are you sure about this?" He asked looking me in the eyes.

I nodded my head slowly in the affirmative without saying a word.

"Okay, I'm in."

"Good man," I said and then turned my attention to Miguel. "Y tú, a-mi-go?" I said smiling.

125

Miguel looked around the table as if he was trying to make a decision, but I knew, everyone there knew he had already made it.

"Okay," he said simply.

***

The day of the robbery I was all over the place. I got up early and went to take a look at the laboratory. I cased the building a little and planned our get away route and some alternative routes just in case something went wrong, although I must admit I was pretty confident nothing would. After that, I went to Krö Bar for some coffee and to think about the plan. Obviously, I had never done anything like it before and I wanted to make sure everything would go perfectly. I didn't want to over look anything. To be honest, I really liked scheming like that. It made me feel a little like James Bond or someone like that. I felt like I was in movie. Picturing myself that way gave me chills of anticipation and a hard on. Not surprisingly, I rolled with the 007 feeling. I took it for all it was worth. It made me feel big. It made me feel like I had never felt before. Not that I wanted to be that forever, but for the moment I lived it. Hiding in that illusion, I was able to suppress my reservations and nervousness. Hiding in the illusion, that is, combined with the drugs and alcohol I was increasingly consuming at the time. In fact, with my confidence in the plan and the gin and marijuana I was pretty much numb.

The plan was simple. Or at least as simple as a heist plan can be. I knew that the more complicated the plan was the more foolproof it would probably be; but, then again I also knew that if it was too complicated one of my friends or even I would probably fuck it up somehow. So I choose simplicity.

Miguel, Solis and I were going to be the ones who actually entered the building. We were going to go through a lavatory window. Sunniva was in the lab the day before to pick up her last paycheck. While she was there she unlocked the window. So, our point of entry was already covered.

Once we were in the bathroom we planned to make our way to Sunniva's laboratory. Sunniva had explained to me, in detail, how to get there from the bathroom. I must confess to you however, that my short term memory is not the greatest. This is a phenomenon which I am unable to account for, but suffer from chronically nonetheless. In order

126

to help me remember the directions, I scripted a little rhyme. This was, mind you, crafted for functionality not poetic beauty.

Through the double doors,
And stay to the right.
Go to the third door,
Kick with all your might.

Once we got into the lab each of us was going to grab one thing. Solis was supposed to get something called a photo-spectrometer. Miguel was going to get something called an ultra-centrifuge and I was supposed to grab the anti-bodies. Sunniva explained to us what each of the items looked like and where to find them.

After we got the goods, we were going to run out of the building through a side door which led to a quiet residential street. Outside, Sunniva and Mikko would be waiting in the rental car with a cooler filled with ice to put the anti-bodies in.

Carl had probably the easiest job, but it was crucial nonetheless. He was going to keep a look out, in front of the building. There was a bus stop where he could wait at without seeming suspicious. He was on special orders to do two things if the cops should happen to arrive. The first was to warn me by telephone and the second was to create a diversion. I knew the first would be no problem for him; however, I felt that it would be easier for him to have someone help create the diversion. For this, I incorporated the help of my good friend Kal. If the police arrived I told them to say they just saw a group of kids running away. Carl would say they went one direction, while Kal would say they went the opposite way.

I imaged this scenario in my head and it seemed entirely possible and highly comical, all at the same time. Carl would claim they went one way and then Kal would say in affected Pidgin English they ran in the other. Then the pigs would be completely confused and run all around the neighborhood shaking their batons above their heads, tripping all over each other and falling down like a bunch of Keystone Cops. It was even possible that one would get his foot stuck in a bucket of some sort or slip on a banana peel, although admittedly this was probably just wishful thinking.

Once Solis, Miguel and I got into the car, I would put the anti-bodies in the cooler as Mikko drove us away on one of the predetermined routes, back to his house and into the life of luxury and riches. It was perfect, I was sure of it.

After my second cup of coffee, I looked at my watch. It was almost eleven. I decided to get on the phone and make some calls. First, I called Solis and asked him to pick up some gloves and a flashlight for the robbery. He said he would. Then I called Mikko to make sure he was getting the car. He informed me he had already gotten it. Things were going smoothly, so I decided to go home and rest up for the big night that lay ahead.

***

Everything started out good. At the predetermined time, Akal and Carl were in position and so were Sunniva and Mikko. Miguel, Solis and I got there on schedule too. No words were spoken between us; but, everyone knew what to do. We put on our gloves and slipped stealthily around to the back of the sprawling, single story building that Sunniva's lab was in. As we did, I felt my pulse quicken. With only the aid of the overcast moonlight we found the bathroom window. It was exactly like Sunniva said it would be. I slid the window up. Somehow though that James Bond feeling I had left me as soon as I opened the window. It was replaced with an 'oh my God, what the fuck am I getting myself into' feeling. It was sort of an inopportune moment to have such a harsh realization come crashing down. For the life of me, I don't know how I was able to indulge the fantasy for so long. I was a grad student in Political Science for fuck's sake; I wasn't a spy or cat-burglar. I had absolutely no idea what I was doing. My hands started trembling slightly from this reality. It probably would have been much worse if I hadn't been so stoned. I thought about calling the whole thing off but it was too late. Miguel was already going inside. I couldn't back down. Not then. Solis and I followed Miguel's lead. We climbed through one at a time. The three of us were inside just like that with no problems at all.

The bathroom was dark, cave-like. It was nearly silent as well. The only sounds were a slow drip coming from the sink faucet and the pounding of my heart. A trickle of sweat ran down my spine and caused me to shudder. I nudged Solis and he flipped on the flashlight. The bathroom became illuminated; but, I was too focused to notice any features. It all seemed a mass of shadows and grays. We took a moment to regroup.

"Everyone know what to do?" I whispered, although I wasn't sure they could hear me over the thumping of my heart.

"Okay, les go," said Solis.

He slowly opened the bathroom door and I could feel pains of nervousness as I listened to the mechanical creak of the door. Solis stuck his head out of the door before it was completely opened then whispered back to me, "Which way is da lab?"

Through the double doors,
And stay to the right.
Go to the third door,
Kick with all your might.

"It's through the double doors," I answered.

"Wha do ya mean, da double doors?"

"You know, when there's like two doors next to each other."

"Yeah mate, I know wha is double doors, but which ones?"

"What the fuck do you mean which ones?"

"Mate, look fir yourself."

I peeked out into the corridor. There were double doors to the left and to the right.

Through the double doors,
And stay to the right.
Go to the third door,
Kick with all your might.

Fuck! Does stay to the right mean to go through the right-hand double doors or does it mean the lab is the third door on the right...Fuck! Fuck! Okay, okay...don't panic...fuck...okay, just make a decision...

"It's to the right," I said, pretending to be confident.

We filed out of the bathroom into the hallway which was lit by the glow of red emergency lights. The reflection of the red against the white, unadorned walls had a ghostly appearance; but, it also had a calming effect on me somehow. The red glow made everything seem surreal like the rest of the world was far away and forgotten. We went through the double doors on the right and I counted the third door. I stood in front of it, pausing briefly.

"This is it," I said.

Solis and Miguel looked at me in silence. The whites of their corneas captured the red of the emergency lights. They looked almost demonic.

"Okay Solis," I said as I felt another bead of sweat run down my back, "kick that shit open and let's do this."

"Wha ya mean, Solis kick dat shit...You kick it motherfucka."

Oh for fuck sake!

"Just kick the fuck'en door!"

"Mate, dat shite will hurt! You do it."

"Solis, mate, that's your job. Kick the fuck'en door."

"Mate, you not say no'tin about kick da fuck'en door. You say ta pilfer dat shit, dat photo-spectrometer shite."

Pilfer?

"Just—"

Miguel interrupted us. "It's not locked."

Solis and I turned our attention to him. He was holding the door open. We scurried in and Miguel followed.

The lab was illuminated by dull orange light creeping in from the street lamps outside the windows. Although it was dark I could see that the laboratory was large and white. Everything appeared to have a specific place. It was clean and institutional looking. It seemed enormous like the size of a football field; but, in reality it was probably closer to twenty feet by thirty or something like that. It was hard to tell because it was all open with no sort of partitions. The openness and orderliness gave it the sterile feel of a hospital.

Miguel and Solis went to get their equipment and I marched to the far corner where the freezer was tucked away to get the primary anti-bodies I was after. I threw open the freezer door and saw several trays of small vials. *This is it!* I grabbed two trays, one in each hand and nudged the freezer shut with my elbow.

I turned around slowly, not wanting to upset the anti-bodies. Miguel was standing near the door with a machine the size of a toaster oven in his hands. Solis was across the lab struggling to get a grip on his.

"Mate, is too heavy," he said grappling with the larger instrument.

I told Miguel to put down the centrifuge and help Solis. The photo-spectrometer was worth more money. The two of them picked up the photo-spectrometer and carried it out into the hallway. I was right behind them with my trays of anti-bodies. We walked briskly through the red light of the corridor to the far end of the building where our pre-arranged exit point was. Solis and Miguel had a little trouble keeping up with me due to the size and weight of their instrument; but, they managed.

We got to the exit door and stopped. I looked at my friends and was overcome by a sudden sense of pride and euphoria. I may not have been James Bond, but everything went perfectly. My plan was, as I said, foolproof.

"They're just on the other side of the door," I whispered, "You guys go first. I'll hold the door."

They nodded their heads to show they understood. I pressed the crash bar to open the door. In my head, I was already spending my share of the spoils when the door opened.

Then, there was the most frightening, God awful sound I had ever heard in my life.

DINADINADINADINADINADINADINADINADI NADINADINA...

It was the piercing, evil shrill of a fire alarm.

"FUCK!!!" we shouted.

I busted through the door and broke toward the car at top speed, completely forgetting to hold the door like I said I would. There was a flash of light and an outburst of pain as the door swung violently behind me, slamming into Miguel's elbow.

I turned around just in time to see the photo-spectrometer hitting the pavement. There was a sharp bang and the sound of glass shattering. The three of us stood frozen, helplessly looking at the instrument lying on the ground.

There was a shout from somewhere in the night. "Just leave it!"

It was Sunniva yelling from the car. "GET IN!" she pleaded.

I sprinted toward the car but halfway there I felt my foot catch something. I was tripped up and went flying though the air. I shut my eyes as I sailed powerlessly toward the ground. My knee hit first and the rest of my body followed. I felt a sharp pain in my knee and then a burning sensation. I was laying spread out on the ground, but somehow, miraculously I was able to keep the anti-bodies from spilling. I got up and limped to the car. Solis and Miguel were right behind me. I passed the vials to Sunniva. She put them in the cooler and the three of us shoved ourselves into the back seat of a tiny Fiat.

I slammed the door shut and Mikko floored the gas pedal. The tires spun in place, squealing deafeningly for a second and then we started pealing away. The backend fish-tailed a little and Mikko clipped the side mirror off a parked car before he got it under control.

***

We got back to Mikko's and waited for Carl and Kal. They got there about an hour later. We mixed up a few cocktails, rolled a spliff and sat around talking about the excitement of the break in. Although we didn't get any of the equipment, we still had the anti-bodies. The heist was a success and everyone felt an odd sort of pride. It felt like we just one a championship game or something. There was a jovial, celebratory mood in the room. We had gotten away without even a hint of the police and the only casualties were Miguel's bruised elbow and my skinned knee.

I was in the middle of replaying the getaway for Kal and Carl, captivating them with a story of epic heroism when Sunniva interrupted me.

"Dave, come here."

She was looking in the cooler and I couldn't see her face.

"I'm telling a story," I said not understanding why she couldn't wait.

"I know. Just come here."

I looked at my friends and shrugged my shoulders. Reluctantly, I went over to the cooler.

"Where did you get these?" Sunniva whispered, indicating the vials.

"What do you mean, where did I get them?"

I kept my voice down too although I didn't know what the secrecy was about.

"Do you know what these are?"

"Anti-bodies…why?"

"No, not anti-bodies."

"Okay, primary anti-bodies."

"No!" she said becoming slightly louder.

"What do you mean no?"

"They're not anti-bodies."

"Come on. What do you mean they're not anti-bodies?"

"They're not."

132

"Okay, fine. What are they then?" I said, confused.

"They're semen specimens!"

"What?" I asked in complete shook and disbelief.

"It's semen!"

"What the fuck do you mean it's semen?"

"They're semen specimens. You must have gone into the wrong lab."

How the fuck? Oh fuck, the goddamn poem! Fuck! Fuck! Bad, awful Karma-

"What's going on over there?" Mikko asked.

"Tell them," Sunniva insisted.

I turned around and faced my friends. I didn't want to tell them. I didn't want to ruin the celebration. I didn't want to disappoint them. But, I knew I had to. They would have found out soon enough. It wasn't like the Estonian was going to pay us thousands of dollars for cum.

"They're not the right thing," I said, dolefully.

"What?" asked Miguel.

"They're not the anti-bodies."

"What are they?" inquired Carl.

I took a deep breath to compose myself. "They're semen specimens...It's jiz...They're little fucking vials of cum."

A silence fell over the room as everyone looked at each other to see what to say. They had worked hard and taken a big risk. Now, I was telling them it had all been for nothing. They were shocked.

Five seconds went by, silence. The only noise to be heard was the tick of the clock...Ten seconds passed, more silence...Twenty seconds...Forty.

Eventually, Solis stood up. He looked at everyone in the room, finally resting his eyes on me. I waited eagerly for his words, keen to be freed from the silence.

"I DON'T GIVE A FUCK!" he shouted wildly.

The room broke out in laughter.

"Neither do I."

"Me either."

"Me either."

Etc.

Looking for Madness and Insanity

Being involved in that robbery made me realize something. I was really fucked up. I had suspected it before, but that solidified it. Not that that bothered me; it was just an accepted fact of life. People always talk about lives spiraling out of control because of drugs and alcohol. If my parents could have seen my life in Manchester, they probably would have said the same thing about me. However, this wasn't the case. I wasn't spiraling anywhere. I was simply adapting to my environment, which was fucked up. Hence, I was fucked up. Strange things happened in Manchester. They happened to me all the time and I knew it wasn't the drugs and alcohol doing it to me. It had to be something else. I had done plenty of drugs and booze in Michigan, but had never gotten involved in any robberies or spent two and half days strung out on cocaine. No, there was something different about Manchester, some type of environmental anomaly or psycho-social variant. I don't know exactly. I'm not a geologist or sociologist. I couldn't account for its presence; but, I knew for sure what to call it. Solis termed it for me the day I met him. "…Madness and Insanity!" he had said. They were just words then, without any sort of inter-subjective meaning. But, slowly, after time, I began to comprehend exactly what he was talking about. It was a force, a magnetism toward the substance abuse and sex and carefree attitude that made people say 'I don't give a fuck!"

I understood what I was dealing with. But the how and why of it, I had no idea. Where did it come from? How does it happen? Why Manchester? Why me? Why now? These were questions I thought I should know the answers to because Madness and Insanity had such an impact on me, such an impact on my world. I was pondering these questions in the days before my backpacking trip with Carl and I came to a bold decision. I decided to confront them during the trip. It seemed like the perfect opportunity. Whether it was a vision quest or pilgrimage or visit to the Oracle at Delphi, people throughout history never waited for what knowledge they sought. They went in search of the answers to their questions. That's what I was going to do, roam the earth until I comprehended this force, this energy, Madness and Insanity.

"What do you mean; you're going to look for Madness and Insanity?" Sunniva said.

She was sitting on the edge of my bed in her underwear, smoking a cigarette. The smoke circled her head like a nimbus. She had recently taken up the habit, right before the heist as a matter of fact and I found it sexy. It has a roughness about it that fit her somehow.

I was standing at my desk, hunched over a map of Europe, circling cities and places of interest with a red felt-tipped pen. A joint burned next to me in the ashtray. It was late and Carl was already sleeping in the lounge. He had been staying in there for the duration of his visit.

"Just what I said. I'm going to look for Madness and Insanity. I'm going to confront it."

"You're going to confront Madness and Insanity? How?"

"I'm not sure."

"What do you mean, actually, by Madness and Insanity?"

"I don't know…I can't explain it. I just know it when I see it."

"So you are going on a quest for Madness and Insanity, but you're not exactly sure what it is."

"Yes."

"And where are you going to look for it?"

I paused to think about that. "I don't know exactly," I confessed after giving it some thought.

"So you don't know where it's at either?"

"Well, it's not like it's in one place. It's everywhere."

"So you're going to look everywhere for it?"

"Well, I might have to narrow my parameters a little. We're going to stay in Western Europe."

"Anywhere in particular?"

"Not really. Our flight is to Pamplona, but after that we don't have any plan."

"What about Norway?"

"Probably not."

"That's good because I shouldn't think I've ever seen it there."

"That's cute. Go head, mock me."

I could tell Sunniva was really enjoying this.

"And how do you plan to find it?" she continued.

"With drugs and alcohol. That always seems to do the trick."

"Well it sounds like a perfect plan to me," she said, jokingly, sarcastically "make sure you ring me as soon as you find it."

***

135

I woke up at five the next morning. Normally, I wouldn't have been able to get up that early, but that day I had no problem. I was too excited about starting the trip. I was up even before the alarm went off. I eased out of bed quietly, so I wouldn't wake Sunniva. Since, the ill-fated robbery attempt, we had been spending a lot of time together. It was funny, although the thing turned out to be a big debacle, it had somehow strengthened our relationship. I consulted Solis regarding this matter and he said that it was probably because the robbery demonstrated to what lengths we would go for each other. This was, I believe, a very astute observation especially from a man that had, in the past, been quite suspect in his analysis of love. Although, he did tack on that she needed "dick." Regardless, our relationship was very strong. It seemed that there was a lot of truth in the old adage, "Those who steal together, stay together," or whatever it is.

The first thing that I did when I got out of bed was roll a big joint. Then, I went into the lounge to wake up Carl. Earlier, I told him that this was going to be the kind of trip that changes a person's life. I realize that that is a very corny and cliché thing to say; but, regardless, I had every intention of making it happen. I was positive that I would make serious insights and observations of one kind or another. I was going to confront Madness and Insanity, just like I had said. I planned to just throw myself deep into its depths, deeper than I had ever gone before and see what would happen. I think Carl understood this too although, we never really discussed it. He must have sensed it in me the days after the heist. That's why we decided to start our trip off where we were going to. We felt that there couldn't possibly be a better place to plunge head first into the raging waters of Madness and Insanity than the festival of San Fermín, which is, of course, where they hold the running of the bulls. Nothing says Madness and Insanity quite like a confused and angry, two thousand pound bovine chasing down drunken festival goers. For fuck's sake, if that's not Madness and Insanity, what is?

Smoking the joint at quarter after five in the morning was all part of the plan. It was setting a tempo that would eventually lead to a full and unconditional surrender. This unconditional surrender was the key to the whole thing. For some reason, I felt that that was the only way to truly understand the force I sought. I had to get close to it. I had to get intimate with it.

I lit the joint and woke Carl up by blowing smoke in his face. He, as you might expect, didn't find it as amusing as I did. But, he slid his legs off the couch, rubbed the sleep from his eyes and sat up to smoke. We didn't say anything; we just smoked and passed the joint. Despite our tiredness, there was an obvious aura of excitement and nervousness, surrounding us.

Personally, I was nervous about the Madness and Insanity, but I was also nervous about my financial situation. I had already spent nearly every penny I had on plane tickets to the continent and my Eurorail pass. All I had was three hundred and fifty dollars in the bank and one hundred pounds in cash. This was a major problem. I knew it wouldn't be enough to see me through the duration of my trip. I knew it wasn't enough to sustain the Madness and Insanity. Despite this, I was going anyway. The way I had it figured, I could extort more money from my parents when the time came.

I had it all planned out. When I got low on money, I could call them and have them deposit some in my account. I would simply make up some story about why I needed the dough. Of course, this was a risky proposition and would no doubt have negative repercussions; but, I was sure that they wouldn't leave me broke and stranded in the middle of Europe. Well, I was fairly confidant anyway.

We finished half the joint and got dressed. We had already packed the night before, so by five thirty we were ready to go.

Before we left we went into my room and kissed Sunniva goodbye. She was still sleeping but the kiss woke her.

"Are you leaving?" she asked, sleepily.

"Yeah, we're ready to go," I whispered.

"I'll walk you to the gate."

"No, it's okay. You go back to sleep."

"But, I'll miss you."

"I'll miss you too…I'll tell you what. When I get back, we'll go away for a weekend, just you and me."

"That sounds nice."

I kissed her again, on the top of her head. She lied back down and shut her eyes. The sun was just coming through the window. A ray of light had invaded the room from under the shade and was shining on her face and hair. I ran the tips of my fingers over her hair, right above her ear. She had already fallen back asleep and stirred a little. I thought about giving her another kiss, but didn't want to wake her.

I turned to Carl, "You ready?"

"Yup," he responded simply.

"Let's make a move," I said as I heaved my backpack onto my shoulders.

I could already tell it was going to be a beautiful day. Although it was still brisk, the sun was shining and birds were filling the air with their flirtatious cacophony. We walked down the path, out the gate and over to the bus stop. I looked at my watch and noticed that the next bus wasn't scheduled to arrive for over a half an hour.

"Fuck it!" I said. "Let's walk."

The station was nearly two miles away; but, I really didn't give a fuck. It was such a nice morning, I was pleasantly stoned and we had lots of time. We headed up Oxford road toward the Oxford Road Rail Station. A little while later, we were there and hopped on the next train to Liverpool. We got off at the Hunt's Cross stop and took a bus to the John Lennon International Airport. I had brought the rest of the joint from earlier to smoke before we went in. So, we walked over to an ashtray outside an entrance and lit it up. It was the second smoke of the morning and it was good weed. By the time we finished smoking, we were really stoned, so much so that when we entered the airport, I became confused. Everything looked so big and complicated. It was almost too overwhelming.

We went up to the check-in counter and stood in line. There was only a middle-aged couple in front of us so it didn't take long at all. In a few minutes, we were standing in front of the customer service representative.

"May I see your passports please?" she asked.

We handed her our passports and she typed our names in the computer.

"Sir, did you have reservations?"

"Yes," I replied dreamily.

"When did you make them?"

"I made reservations a few weeks ago."

She looked at the passports again and retyped our names into the computer.

"That's odd," she said, "I can't seem to find your reservations. Were you issued tickets?"

"Yeah."

"Could I see them please?"

I procured the tickets from my backpack and handed them to her.

"Sir, are these tickets for EasyJet?"

"Yeah, they are. What's the problem, can't you find us in your computer?"

"I'm afraid I can't."

"Well, why not?"

"Because sir, this is the British Airways kiosk."

The British Airways lady pointed us to the right desk and we got in line. After we checked in, it was off to our gate and eventually to the plane. I eased my seat back and closed my eyes.

***

I woke up when we hit the runway in Pamplona. After we made our way through the airport, Carl and I stood outside trying to figure out where to go next. It was sunny and warm, exactly how I expected it to be. The weather energized us. We were ready to find the festival and get at it. There was a chart on the back of the bus stop but it was worthless. I could have gotten more utility from the fucking thing if I ate it. So, I gave up and asked some guy who was standing around smoking a cigarette which bus to take. Luckily, he spoke English and said that he thought we needed to take the number seven bus, but he wasn't sure.

Carl and I discussed the reliability of the information we had just received.

"What do you think?" I asked.

"Seven's lucky, right?" he answered.

"Yeah, lucky seven."

"I don't know, sounds alright to me. You want to take that one?"

"I don't know. That guy didn't seem like he knew what the hell was talking about."

"No. No, he didn't."

"But, on the other hand, Mickey Mantle wore number seven."

"Yeah, that's true."

"And that guy hit like over five hundred homeruns."

"That's a good point."

"Maybe we should take the number seven bus?"

"You want to take it?"

"Yeah, let's take it."

"Alright."

It was settled. We boarded the number seven bus in hopes of finding the festival. Carl and I sat across the aisle from each other because the bus had so many riders. Next to me was an old lady, who appeared to be at least eighty, maybe even ninety. She was clad entirely in black and looked like the quintessence of an old Spanish lady. She was short and frail looking and her head was covered by a babushka, or whatever they call them in Spain. She reminded me of every old world women I had ever seen in the movies or read about in books. She seemed like a walking stereotype of herself. She even had a small push cart filled with grocery bags and some rosary beads. After a half and hour on the bus and no sign of the festival, I began to think that Carl and I were on the wrong bus.

I knew from the movies that you can always count on a strange old woman like the one next to me for some sound advice. I leaned over and addressed her. "Pardon, Doña. Puedes Ayudarme?"

She replied to me, in weak but fluent English, "You're an American boy, no?"

"Yeah, that's right."

"Your Spanish is very bad, very bad," she said shaking her head, disapprovingly.

"I...ah...I know; I apologize."

"Is okay, you work on it," she chuckled, patting me on the knee. "How can I help you?"

"Can you tell me how to get to the festival?"

"Why doya wan ta go dhere?"

"Umm...it's just ah...my friend and I..." I gestured toward Carl who was resting his head on the window and starting out of it blankly. "we came here for the festival."

"Oh no, no, no, no. You don wan ta go dhere. Is no'tin but trouble for you dhere."

"Well, ah you know, it's just we heard a lot about it and it looks like it's a lot of fun..."

"You come to run with da bull?"

"Ahh...Yeah, I guess so, but that's not the only reason—"

She interrupted me. "Is'a no good. Is too dangerous. Much too dangerous. Dose bull are very big an dhey jus a like everybody else, dhey don like Americans."

"Is that right?"

"Is true, bu ya donna believe me and you are go'en ta go anyway. I know was in da mind of boys like you. You donna wan ta lis'en. So! I tell you, bu only if you promise ta be careful!"

She had a sincere, grandmotherly concern for me that I couldn't refuse.

140

"Of course, I'll be careful. I promise."

"Okay boy," she said, patting me on the leg again. "You on da wrong bus. Ya need ta take number forty-seven bus."

"That's it?"

"Dats it, it take you where you wan ta go."

"Alright. Thank you."

"Jussa remember ta be careful and keep an eye on dis one," she said pointing to Carl.

"I will."

When the bus got to the next stop, the old lady told me that we could catch the bus I wanted from there. I thanked her again and Carl and I alighted. A few minutes later, the forty-seven bus came by and we got on.

I could tell we were headed in the right direction when I started to see people walking around wearing white shirts, white pants and red scarves. This is, of course, the traditional garb during San Fermin. I think that it's supposed to resemble a bullfighter; but, I never actually bothered to find out.

We got off the number forty-seven when we started to see lots of people dressed in bullfighter costumes. We were in an old section of the city with narrow, winding avenues and brick buildings that had no space between them. Most of the buildings were three stories tall giving the street the feel of a tunnel.

As soon as I left the bus, I could hear music and the thunderous dissonance of a large crowd. There was a street vendor selling costumes across the way from us. Carl and I crossed over to buy some. The vendor wanted what worked out to be about forty-five dollars for the costumes. I felt they were a little expensive because they were, quite frankly pieces of shit. They were thin and hastily made. But, when in Rome...

I forked over the money and got my outfit. Carl did likewise. We went into an ally to put them on.

With our new costumes donned and our old clothes stuffed into our backpacks, we set off toward the music. We walked down a narrow street for a couple of blocks and as we turned the corner into a public square, I knew we had found what we were looking for. It was nothing less than absolute chaos, wanton and beautiful.

There was a stage set up on the steps of a building with a band playing traditional Spanish music on it. The band's rhythm section boomed and echoed, while the brass instruments cut the air like swords. They were playing an upbeat song that matched the expectations of the crowd and ambiance of the day. Thousands and thousands of happy, cheerful people filled the square. There were people in every direction and everyone was dressed the same, in the bullfighter costumes. It was a sea of white. I gazed into the square and was consumed by the giant ocean of people. It was impossible to take more than three steps in any direction because it was so crowded. There was a free-flowing disorder to the mob that was both hectic and charming. Some people sat, listening to the band. Even more were dancing to their music. Everyone was drinking wine and talking boisterously. There was singing and laughing and friendly shouts and jokes being made too. Kids were chasing each other around and twirling things in the air and making a racket. It was ubiquitous revelry. It was exactly how a festive should be. It was fun and exciting. I loved it instantly.

"Fuck'en, hell!" I exclaimed, not able to control my excitement. "Fuck man! Look at this! Look at this shit! This is great!"

"Yeah there're a lot of people here," Carl responded with a pretentious coolness.

"I think this'll be alright," I quipped with sarcastic indifference, mimicking Carl.

Carl nodded his head in agreement.

"Let's find a place to drop off our bags. Then, we'll get a fuck'en drink!" I said.

Carl nodded his head again and smiled. I was happy to be there with him. He was a good mate. He didn't even blink an eye when I asked for his help in the break in. He just did it. I admired that. I rubbed his hair with the palm of my hand, messing it up and we set off to find a place to put our bags.

***

We walked around the city centre to find a place to store our backpacks. It seemed the whole city centre was overflowing with festival goers. They were on the sidewalks, in the streets, and in the bars. Even the doorways and balconies were occupied.

We stopped in front of an old train station, where someone had told us we could keep our bags. Inside, there was a makeshift counter made from rectangular tables. Behind the counter were hundreds of numbered shelves crammed full of backpacks. It was three Euros to store a bag. Carl and I gladly paid the money to get rid of our cumbersome packs for awhile.

142

When I got outside, I stretched my back and shoulders. They were becoming stiff and tired from lugging my backpack around. As I was stretching, I caught the warm and familiar aroma of marijuana smoke. I looked around to see where it was coming from. Finding it wasn't hard for me because my nose is somewhere on the lines of a basset hound when it comes to detecting the sweet fruits of nature. It was coming from a couple of teenaged guys sitting on a nearby bench.

"Smell that?" Carl asked me.

"Yeah, of course…Wait here, I'm going to try and score some."

I walked over to the guys and two minutes later came back with a big lump of hash.

With the hash situation clearly in hand Carl and I found a convenience store to buy shag tobacco and papers to make spliffs. We also picked up some wine. It came in one liter paper cartons, which admittedly is not usually a sign of high quality. It did however, only cost a Euro per carton and since it was so cheap we bought four liters. The wine itself tasted horrible. It had a potent aftertaste that tasted like diesel fuel smells, but I was on a budget and we couldn't beat those prices.

When we left the store I noticed that the sun was beginning to go down. It was going to be dark soon and I knew what that would mean. Clearly, in a place like this Madness and Insanity would erupt. It had all the indications. Already, there were tens of thousands of people on the streets, most of who had been drinking furiously all day. Who knew how many more drunkards and lunatics would flock to the streets once it got dark? There certainly weren't any signs that things were going to slow down. In fact, I had already noticed a steady increase in people and they all carried a fresh excitement and attitude that was reenergizing the seriously drunk partiers who had been at it all day. Yes, it would certainly explode in grand proportions. I was sure of it. I wasn't scared though or even nervous. This is what I wanted. This was the perfect time for a stand off. I was going to meet Madness and Insanity head on. I was up for mayhem and trouble of almost any kind and I was taking Carl with me.

We found a spot at the public square, near the old train station, where we could sit down. I rolled a big spliff and Carl opened some wine. We sat back on a bench and listened to a three piece band play traditional Spanish music. The band grooved for a long time, cutting in and out of stylistic solos and complicated jams sessions. They had a great sound and I found them entertaining. By the time they stopped playing, Carl and I had smoked three spliffs and drank a liter of wine each. Needless to say,

143

we were smashed. We also had to go to the bathroom. We found a line of portable toilets to take a leak. There were several people in each line, so we decided to sneak behind them to relieve ourselves. Carl finished first and went out front to wait for me. I finished and came back around to find Carl. I didn't see him straight away and had to looked around for him, but everybody was dressed the same and it took ages for me to spot him. It was then that I realized there was a good possibility of becoming separated from Carl in that crowd. We decided to rendezvous on the steps of the old train station, if that were to happen. That way, we knew where to find each other.

A little while later, a couple of blond haired suffer type guys from California struck up a conversation with us as we were watching another band. I didn't catch their names; but, they seemed like they were pretty cool. I rolled another spliff and the four of us smoked. Afterwards, we toured around the city centre, to check out the different things that were happening like magic shows and juggling acts. We stopped periodically to drink and smoke and listen to music. Actually, we maintained a stiff regiment of marijuana and alcohol until the early morning hours. At around two a.m., the four of us went to get a sandwich, which is an ordinary and common thing to do. The events which transpired after we got our sandwiches, however, were not.

***

We bought them from a street vendor and sat in the doorway of a vacant building to eat. Before he started eating, Carl announced that he was going to go the bathroom again. He handed me his sandwich and walked away. As he did, I noticed him staggering pretty badly. He looked like a stiff wind could have blown him to the ground. This didn't surprise me. He had had quite a bit of wine and pot.

The two Californians and I started digging in as we waited for Carl to return. Five minutes went by and my sandwich was finished but Carl hadn't gotten back yet. I speculated that he was probably taking a shit and didn't worry. After ten minutes, I was positive he was taking a shit. After thirty minutes, I started to get nervous. But, I didn't panic. I ate his sandwich instead and wondered where he was at.

When forty-five minutes passed, I got worried. The Californians and I decided that we should probably go look for him. As you can no doubt imagine, this was an extremely difficult task. Not only were there a billion people in the streets, everyone was dressed exactly alike.

My first thought, which was rather cogent I felt given my own level of inebriation, was to look for a figure that was staggering around because I remembered how Carl had wobbled away. But, after about three seconds I gave up that idea. Carl wasn't the only asshole out there staggering around like a bum. As it turned out there were lots of people swaying back and forth, just like I had seen him do. Even the people who weren't swaying looked like they were because I was. I had to find him but I didn't know how. The task was Kafkaesque. It was a fucking nightmare. It was like trying to find a needle in a stack of needles.

We looked for over an hour but couldn't find Carl anywhere. Finally, the Californians convinced me the search was futile. They said that it would be better to look for him in the morning. I knew that they were right so, reluctantly, I gave up for the night, hoping I would find him in the morning at our rendezvous point.

Anyway, what's the worst that could happen to him?

The Californians offered that I could crash in their hotel room. I decided to take them up on the offer because I had nowhere else to stay. We started walking through the tunnel like avenues toward their hotel. When we came to a plaza the crowd got really thick. We had to walk in a single file line in order to snake our way through. Since, I was following them, I was the last one in the line. I was staring intently at the back of the guy in front of me so I wouldn't get lost. As we made our way into a particularly dense area of people some motherfucker crossed in front of me and stepped on my foot. It didn't hurt but I was momentarily distracted. It was probably for less than a second, but it made me loose track of the guy I was following. The Californians had vanished. Just like that they were gone, consumed by the crowd, consumed by the ocean of white and I was alone. I was alone and didn't know where I was. This realization was very disheartening and made me rather nervous.

They just fucking disappeared…Or no! Maybe they didn't disappear…Maybe, I did!

On a hunch, I looked around for Carl. I thought that when individuals disappear they might all end up in the same place. Unfortunately, I didn't see him anywhere.

Being alone in this type of environment was, as you can imagine, another self-actualizing moment for me. I was entirely by myself. I was intoxicated on red wine and marijuana. And I was in a foreign place that, not coincidently, was engulfed in Madness and Insanity. In short, I was fucked. And this conclusion was only based on a cursory examination of my situation. I tried to think what to do but I couldn't. I was too stoned and it was too depressing. I decided to get some sleep and think about it later. I trekked about three miles out of the city centre until I came to a residential area. I wanted to find a safe place to crash, where I wouldn't have to worry about getting robbed and beaten while I slept. I finally came across an area next to a highway that had tall grass and shrubbery for me to hide in. I laid down in the grass and went to sleep.

***

I woke up a few hours later. I was still fairly drunk and thought about sleeping some more but I couldn't fall asleep again. My back was sore and stiff from passing out on uneven ground and the sun had already risen. I got up and started walking back toward the city centre. I was very nervous about the whole Carl disappearance. I had no idea what had happened to him. He could have been dead for all I knew. I was just hoping that he would be waiting for me at the rendezvous point. I have no idea what I would have done if he wasn't. Miraculously, I wasn't confronted with this problem. A few minutes into my walk back, I noticed a peculiar little figure in the distance walking away from the city centre. He was disheveled, staggering and grasping his upper left arm. Although he was walking in the opposite direction of our rendezvous point, I could tell it was my estranged friend.

"CARL! CARL!" I shouted.

He didn't hear me so, I ran up to him.

"Carl!"

He turned around and stared blankly. I could tell that he recognized me, but I don't think he understood the significance of our chance encounter three miles out of town and several hours after last seeing each other.

"Fuck, man! Where the fuck did you go last night?"

He mumbled something unintelligible to me. I had seen Carl really fucked up before; but, I had never seen him like this. He had a spaced-out, absent look about him like he was a zombie or something.

What the fuck happened to him?

He was completely out of it. I grabbed him by the shoulders and forced him to look at me.

"What happened to you?" I asked slowly, like a parent asking a small child for important information.

"They beat me up," he responded vaguely and with little emotion.

146

"What? Who?"

He mumbled incoherently again like a drunken schizophrenic.

"You're speaking gibberish, man!"

He make another attempt to explain something, still incoherently and then began pushing his sweatshirt sleeve up. I watched with acute interest. He got the sleeve up to his elbow but couldn't get it further. With a huff of frustration he wrestled the sweatshirt off. He had a plain, white t-shirt on underneath. He pushed his t-shirt sleeve up and revealed the biggest bruise I had ever seen. It was the color of an eggplant and roughly the same size, covering his entire upper arm.

"Fuck!" I exclaimed, shocked by the brutality of the injury.

He mumbled about getting his ass kicked again; but, something just wasn't adding up for me. I pressed the issue a little further.

"They kicked your ass," I asked, "in the arm?"

This seemed very bazaar to me; but, I could tell by his condition it was going to be hard to get more information. It was obvious that he had had some kind of a traumatic experience so I figured that I should wait awhile before asking him a bunch of questions. I didn't want to fuck him up psychologically or whatever. It was probably best, I decided, to let it come out when he was ready. I just hoped he wouldn't start crying or shit his pants or anything like that.

We started for the city centre together in silence. On the way we stopped at a tiny café. I thought that it might be a good idea to get some coffee into Carl. The day was already warming up. The sun was shining down from a cloudless, blue sky. We took a table outside and sat in silence sipping ours coffees in the early morning Spanish sunlight. Soon, perhaps as a result of the caffeine, Carl started to come out of his daze a little. He was starting to show signs of cogency. He just seemed a little more alert.

"Where were you?" I probed again.

He answered quietly, like a shy child, "The hospital."

"The hospital? What the fuck?"

He shrugged his shoulders, uncertain of what to say.

I continued. "What happened at the hospital?"

"I dunno. They just looked at my arm."

"That's it?"

"And gave me some pills."

"Fuck man! They gave you pills?"

"Yeah."

"What did they give you?"

"I dunno."

"They didn't tell you?"

"I couldn't understand them. They were speaking Spanish."

"So you just took them?"

He nodded.

"Fuck man, I can't believe that they gave you pills being as drunk as you were…You got anymore?" I asked partially as a matter of scientific inquiry.

He shook his head no.

I reasoned that they probably gave him some type of pain killers although, there was no way to be sure. If they did, it could explain his strange behavior. It would also raise some intriguing questions regarding the national health system of Spain. But that was neither here nor there and I didn't have time to probe any deeper. Every morning of the festival, the running of the bulls was held at eight sharp and I didn't want to be late. I presumed Carl wouldn't have either, if he were lucid enough to make that determination.

Carl and I left the coffee shop and headed toward the city centre and the course the bulls ran. When we got there, I couldn't believe how many people were still out on the street partying. It looked just like it did when I left the night before. There were thousands and thousands of people drinking and carousing and they didn't show any signs of slowing down.

Carl and I stopped in the middle of a street that was on the course the bulls ran. I looked at my watch. It was seven thirty. I started to get a little nervous because it seemed that maybe what I was about to do was somewhat dangerous. But that nervousness quickly passed.

What's the worst that can happen?

Besides, I was in Pamplona and in Pamplona you run with the bulls. It wasn't like I had much of a choice.

We still had thirty minutes before they let the bulls out so I decided to engage Carl in a little conversation to pass the time. He looked really pale and weak and tired.

This will never do. I need to buck him up a little or he might be in some fucking trouble when the bulls start charging.

"You ready for this shit!" I shouted to him, tying to arouse some emotion.

He gingerly shook his head yes.

"Thata boy!" I said.

148

I admired his gusto although, I must admit, I wasn't completely convinced he knew what he was ready for. But, that was beside the point. The point was he was up for it, goddamn it!

"So, ah…you remember anything from last night?" I asked with care, trying to see if he would volunteer any more information.

He shrugged his shoulders.

"Well, where did you go off to?"

"I remember that I was going to cross a street…then the next thing I knew I was in an ambulance…I got my ass kicked."

"Fuck man! So what happened? Who kicked your ass?"

"I dunno, some guy."

"Who? What did he look like?"

"I dunno, I didn't see him…but his name was Otto."

Otto! Probably a fucking Nazi!

I investigated deeper, "Otto? You know his name?"

"The guy from the ambulance told me."

"What…What the fuck? How did he know the guy's name?"

"I dunno, but he kept saying it. He kept saying, 'Otto Booze kick yo ass, Otto Booze kick yo ass…'like he knew the guy or something."

"Otto Booze…Otto Booze" I repeated aloud.

Then it hit me. "Autobús! Motherfucker! Autobús! It means bus. You got hit by a fuck'en bus!"

This revelation seemed to hit Carl pretty hard and had an enervating effect on him. He gently grasped his injured arm and sat down in the street, trying to absorb this information.

"I just need to rest," he said weakly, staring up at me with pleading eyes.

I responded nonchalantly, so as not to concern him, about the danger of such an action given the looming bovine stampede. "Come on man. You can't sit there. There's gunna be bulls running here in a few minutes."

I took his good arm and helped him back to his feet.

"I can't do this," he said, still in a fragile voice.

He started to walk away. I grabbed his arm, pulling him to a stop. I knew that I needed to do something. If I let him walk away and miss the running of the bulls he would probably regret it as soon as he was cogent. And then, he would probably regret it for the rest of his life. I couldn't let my friend make a mistake like that so although I hated to do it because of his delicate physiological condition, I had to get forceful.

149

I grabbed him by the shoulders and shook him once fairly hard, certainly hard enough to get his attention.

"Come on man! Ya gotta fuck'en do this shit! We didn't come all this FUCK'EN way for you to puss out! Now come on, be a FUCK'EN MAN!"

"Okay, okay," he said reluctantly.

It was settled. All we had to do was wait for the bulls. Only as it turned out, that wasn't all there was to it because what came rambling down the road next were not bulls at all. They were pigs. There was a scuttle behind us and Carl and I turned to see what was going on. We saw two cops, a couple of yards back, pushing and shoving the crowd forward. They held their batons with both hands and were using them as plows, drawling them back to their chest and then slamming them into the backs of any poor bastard who was in their fascist reach. The crowd shuffled forward to get away from them but had no place to go. Some people sought refuge in buildings and others hurried forward, to get out of the street.

Carl and I were intent on running with the bulls so we had no notions of leaving the street. We just kept walking forward to appease the cops, but apparently it wasn't fast enough for them because all of a sudden I got whacked in the middle of my back. The concussion almost made me lose my breath and I flew forward about six or eight feet. I knew right away what happened and became concerned about Carl. I stopped and turned around just in time to see Carl getting shoved with a baton. He went flying forward toward me, almost falling over. Fortunately, I managed to catch him before he did.

He's lucky that wasn't a bull.

Carl and I got shoved two more times each and I must admit, despite the purported sympathy for human rights in Spain, the Spanish pigs were every bit as abusive as any police I had ever seen in the United States.

After getting pushed with the batons and shuffling down the street a couple hundred yards, we found ourselves at an intersection with a side street veering off at an odd angle to our left. In front of us was a giant wooden gate that partially obstructed both streets. From what I had seen on TV, I knew the gate was going to block the course off whichever way it closed; but, I couldn't tell which way that was going to be. I had to decide which way to go and had to do it quickly. People were pushing Carl and me from behind and the police were still menacing us with their batons, a few steps back. I looked at Carl to see if he had any ideas.

"Which way?" I asked.

He just shrugged his shoulders.

"Alright, let's go left then," I said.

We went to the left and were pushed down the street a distance by the crowd. To be honest, at that point, I had no idea of what was happening and obviously Carl didn't either. The wooden gate swung closed behind us and then, absolute bedlam broke out.

We were standing by a group of about twenty Spanish guys who suddenly started chanting something that I wasn't able to pick up. I could tell by their faces and voices, though, that they were extremely agitated. While the chanting was going on, I noticed a couple of guys try to scale the gate. They just about made it over but were pushed down when they reached the top by cops. Then, a few more guys tried it and were also pushed down by the police. This seemed to infuriate the crowd. More people started climbing the gate and a bunch of others began slamming themselves into it, attempting to break it down. There were at least thirty people battering the gate and thirty more trying to climb over it.

I watched this for a few seconds then my attention was drawn behind me. There was a circle of about fifty young Spaniards who were probably high school age and a little older singing something. They had their arms around the shoulders of the guy next to them and were jumping up and down and swaying back and forth. I had no fucking clue what they were singing. While I was watching this, an arm hooked me around the shoulder and pulled me in.

I looked over to see who had me. It was a random Spanish guy. He looked at me and smiled. I smiled back and put one arm around his shoulder and one arm around Carl's. Then Carl and I joined in the jumping and swaying. It was pretty fun despite the fact that I didn't understand what it was all about.

We bounced around for a minute when without warning, a wave of screaming people slammed into us. My heart skipped a beat.

OH FUCK! THE BULLS!

Carl and I took off, racing down the street, but oddly the crowd abruptly stopped after we got about twenty yards. Carl and I looked at each other for some explanation.

False start. I reasoned and began to prepare myself for the bulls.

A few seconds later the same thing happened. There was some screaming and a wave of people rushed toward us. We sprinted with the mob about twenty yards and again abruptly stopped.

151

After the second time, I was determined to find out what was happening. I pulled Carl to the side of the road and stood with him, our backs pressed up against a building. The crowd scampered for a third time but we stayed put.

When the pack cleared, I could see what the situation was. There were about twenty guys throwing bottles and rocks at some cops down the street. They were doing a pretty good job keeping them back as well. I watched a guy pick a beer bottle up. He took a few running steps and chucked it in the air. The bottle landed harmlessly in front of a cop, littering the street with broken glass.

I was just about to tell Carl that we should get out of there, but when I turned he was no longer next to me. I looked around for him and noticed him in the middle of the road. He had a big chunk of concrete in his hand about the size of a softball.

Even though, he was only about six feet away, I had to scream for him to hear me over the ruckus of the mob.

"CARL! CARL! LET'S GET THE FUCK OUT OF HERE!"

He spun toward me and gave me a look of acknowledgment. Then, he turned back quickly toward the cops, drew his arm back and let the concrete fly. Fortunately, it didn't hit any cops. Unfortunately, it landed squarely in the back of another rioter's head, knocking him to the ground. Carl turned toward me again with a stupefied look. I chuckled a little despite the misfortune of the poor son of a bitch he knocked out. Carl shrugged his shoulders as if to say, "I don't give a fuck!" and came over to me.

We started to walk away from the battle line when we heard a thunderous sound echoing through the street that was so loud it eclipsed the clamor of the riotous rampage that surrounded us. Carl and I spun around to see what the noise was. There, marching arm and arm, down the street were nearly twenty cops armed with body armor, helmets, shields and batons. It looked like a scene from a Third Reich documentary. I got a hollow feeling, the type that can only be experienced in the grips of true terror. Those fuckers looked like they meant business and we had already seen from personal experience that the pigs were not shy about using their sticks. Rocks and bottles weren't going to slow those fucks down, that was for sure.

I didn't have to say anything to Carl. I didn't even have to look at him. We both took off down the street away from the riot police as fast as we could. It was clear that the pigs had won this round. Although, as I was running away, I noticed that some industrious bastard had managed to set several garbage dumpsters ablaze. This, I believe added quite a bit to the riot. I feel it elevated the situation from a mere disturbance to total pandemonium. I wish that I had thought of it.

Carl and I ran until we couldn't run anymore. We ran so far that when we stopped, we couldn't hear the riot anymore. We stood panting for several minutes trying to catch our breaths. Then, we sat down on the curb for a little quiet reflection.

That was the last day of the festival and therefore the last day for the running of the bulls. I was a little disappointed that we missed it although, in no small way being a part of a riot made up for it.

After all, what's the difference? Instead of running with the bulls, we ended up running from the pigs.

Vive la résistance!

The trip certainly did start on the right note. However, I hadn't gotten what I was looking for. I was no closer to understanding Madness and Insanity than I was before I left. I'm sure the answers were there, right in front of me. I just didn't know how to interpret them yet. It was going to take time. Fortunately, I had time. The trip was just beginning. I had weeks and thousands of miles to figure it out. I knew it wasn't going to be easy, but when Carl and I left Spain and headed to France, I was confident and resolute.

We arrived in Paris on my birthday. Carl and I were still sleeping when the train pulled into the station and the ticket collector had to wake us up. The seats we had weren't all that comfortable really; but, they were a whole lot better than sleeping outside like we did in Pamplona. In fact, the last night we were there an unseasonably cold, cold-front passed through and we spent the night wrapped in plastic grocery bags and newspapers. I curled myself tightly into the fetal position under this pile of debris; but, I still shivered throughout the whole night and didn't manage to sleep a wink. Compared to that, the train to Paris was fucking luxury.

For our stay in Paris, we booked a room that was close to the Louvre. I was looking forward to getting there and taking a shower. I hadn't washed myself since I left Manchester and I was already acutely aware of my odor. Chances were my smell wasn't going to get better by itself. I also needed to call my parents. I was running dangerously low on funds and that wasn't going to take care of itself either.

We spent the first part of the day seeing the usual sights. We took a tour of Norte Dame and spent several hours at the Louvre. We also went to the Eiffel Tower and walked down the Champs Elysées. It wasn't until late in the afternoon that we made it to the hostel.

After a shower and shave, I walked stoically down to the lobby to call my parents. I was going to hit them up for money once again. I wasn't looking forward to doing this at all because of all the trouble I knew it would end up causing. It was in reality much closer to extortion than it was to a request. After all, what choice did they have really? It wasn't like they were going to just say fuck off and leave me stranded and starving in the middle of Europe. No, that most certainly would not happen. Their love for me wouldn't allow it. However, there could be severe repercussions for so callously using their love against their pocketbook. These were intelligent people who would, no doubt realize that I had just strong-armed them. If they saw it for what it was, they might exclude me from future philanthropic acts. This was a very tough prospect to face; but, it was necessary. Desperate times call for desperate measures and all that.

I picked up the phone and dialed. It rang twice.

"Hello."

"Dad?"

"David! How are you?"

I could here music in the background and laughing. They must have been entertaining. My father sounded good-humored and excited to talk to me. I knew that that meant he had been drinking. He didn't drink that often but when he did, he became a different person. He became tolerable. It was one of the few times he and I got along. If you got a few drinks in him, he'd loosen right up. It was good Karma that I reached him in this condition. Fate was smiling on me.

"Ahh, I'm doing alright, dad. I'm doing well."

"Your mother said she tried to call you earlier but you didn't answer."

"Oh, ah…That's ahh…that's because I'm on a little vacation."

"A vacation?"

"Yeah, that's right, I'm, taking a little trip, you know to give my mind a break from the books. I've ah, I've been hitting them really hard lately, you know."

"Where are you at?"

"Ahh, actually dad, I'm in, ah…Paris, right now."

As soon as these mindless words drifted from my mouth, as true as they may have been, I realized that I should have lied. I also realized that like the previous time I asked him for money, I hadn't planned out what I was going to say beforehand.

"Paris? France?" he asked disdainfully. "Is that how you chose to spend your birthday money?"

"What birthday money?" I asked with confusion.

"The four hundred dollars, I put in your bank account yesterday for your birthday."

For your birthday, for your birthday, for your birthday… The words echoed in my head.

Of course!

It was my birthday and they had given me money like every other year. I should have known. What an amazing revelation this was. With all

155

the excitement with the robbery and the trip I had nearly forgotten. Four hundred dollars wasn't bad at all. Sure it wasn't enough to get me through the rest of the trip, but it meant I didn't have to ask for money right away. I had time to come up with a plan. I was off the hook for the time being.

***

After I got off the phone with my father I was in a good mood. I was mentally reinvigorated and rightly so. I had just brought myself back from the brink of poverty and destitution. I had pulled myself up by my bootstraps and I didn't have to use trickery of any kind. I felt empowered and vibrant. Although, I did realized I had actually done very little. All I did was to maintain life for three hundred and sixty five days. This, I will concede isn't the greatest of feats but it was, according to my parents, an achievement worthy enough to be rewarded by four hundred bucks.

With vim in my step and money in my pocket, Carl and I set out to celebrate my birthday. We went down to Champs Elysées and grabbed a bite to eat outside at a small café. After we ate, we strolled down to the Arch d'Triumph. This is, of course, a monument that attests to the great military conquests of the French under Napoleon, in the beginning part of the nineteenth century. It is a very beautiful and powerful monument. Upon first seeing it, I couldn't help wish the French would have had more military successes. That way they could have built other monuments as nice as that one. A monument showing a panzer division rumbling down the Champs Elysées doesn't quite make the artistic or nationalistic statement that one would like it to.

The sun was just starting to set when we got to the Arch. It was turning out to be a very pleasant midsummer evening. It was warm and calm with only a subtle breeze blowing. There were a lot of people out enjoying the evening, milling around and sitting at the café tables lining the sidewalks. Carl and I sat down on some bleachers that had been set out for a parade the pervious day, Bastille Day.

Carl and I were sitting on the bottom row of the bleachers, absorbing the whole Paris evening, when two girls came up and asked if one of us would take their picture. Even without hearing their accents I could tell they were American by their Asics shoes. The one who had the camera was short and a little heavy. She wasn't fat exactly; she was more like chubby or stout. Alright, she was fat. But, she had a cute face and a great personality. I, of course, am making this up completely. To be honest, I didn't pay much attention to her at all, and many details about her have escaped my memory, for example her name. I remember her name as being Camera Girl, because she was the one who had the camera, but she probably had a given name as well.

The other girl, though, was really cute in sort of an unassuming way. She had that girl next door quality and a killer smile that made my heart beat a little faster when I saw it. She was only wearing blue jeans and running shoes but she made them look sexy in an innocent way.

The two girls walked backward and stood in front of the monument. Carl took their picture and they came back to get their camera. I didn't take my eye off of the cute girl the whole time. While Camera Girl was getting the camera from Carl, I stuck up a conversation with the other girl.

"Hi," I said pretending to be a little shy.

She responded with a shy "hi" of her own and gave me a subtle smile. I could tell right away that the smile was sincere. I also knew that this kind of smile wasn't just a polite reaction to my salutation. It wasn't a reaction to anything. It was a reflection of a friendly, cordial personality.

I could already tell that I liked her. She had a friendly personality and she was nice looking.

Maybe she'll have sex with me!

The very idea titillated me, enough so that I had to take a few seconds to regain my composure.

"I'm David," I continued, pretending to be slightly more confident.

"I'm Dalya."

"Dalya. That's nice."

She smiled again.

I introduced her to Carl and she introduced me to Camera Girl and then Carl introduced himself to Camera Girl and just like that everyone was acquainted and getting along famously.

Dalya and I gravitated toward each other right away, so did Carl and Camera Girl. She and I stood around chit-chatting about where we were from and our schools and basic get to know you bullshit for about fifteen minutes. It was pretty easy talking to her so I decided to see if she wanted to hang out for awhile.

"Hey, ah, I don't know if you're doing anything now but it's my birthday and we were going to, you know, to get a drink or something. Do you...wanna come, or?"

"I don't know. It's just that ah——"

157

"Oh, that's alright; forget about it," I interrupted.

"No, it's just that it's pretty expensive to drink in the places around here, but maybe we could do something else?"

"You don't have to, I mean, if you don't want to."

"No, no, I do, it'll be fun!"

"Alright, so what, ah, what did you have in mind?"

"Well we could blaze one if you wanted to? We just came from Amsterdam and—"

"Blaze? I interrupted pretending to be shocked and offended. "You mean use marijuana?"

"No ah…ahh no…" Dalya babbled, trying to cover up what she said.

She was all tongue tied and awkward. It was very humorous to watch and I laughed.

"I'm just kidding," I said, smiling.

She realized right away that it was just a joke and playfully punched me on the arm and chest a few times.

"You made me feel bad!" she said, girlishly.

"It was a joke," I responded, still laughing.

"Yeah very funny," she said and punched me a few more times, lightheartedly.

When we were done laughing, I told her that we should ask Carl and Camera Girl what they wanted to do. They were sitting down on the bleacher talking surprisingly close to each other. I couldn't hear what they were talking about, but I suspect that Carl was telling her all about his tragic bus mishap. He was gingerly rubbing his gimp arm.

"Hey! You love birds what to go have a smoke?"

***

The four of us decided to go into the Tuileries Gardens to get high. It only took a few minutes to get there and I walked with Dalya the whole way. We were really hitting it off. The four of us went to the middle of the park and sat down in a place that was partially hidden by trees and shrubbery. It was dusk and the park seemed surreal in that light. The darkness prevented me from seeing the busy city that encompassed the park. It made it seem like we were in the middle of the countryside.

We sat in the grass. Camera Girl and Carl sat next to each other and Dalya sat next to me. Dalya took out a glass pipe and a bag from her jacket pocket.

"Smell this," she said, handing me the bag.

I took time to appreciate the potent smell of fresh buds and handed it back. She packed the bowl with an almost ritual fastidiousness.

After we smoked, we sat around in the grass talking. We shared stories for awhile and then tried to decide something to do next. Carl suggested that we go get some drinks. The girls wanted to head back down to Champs Elysées. I had a better idea.

"You know what we should do?" I asked, enthusiastically.

"What?" Dalya replied.

"We should go smoke a bowl, right under the fucking Eiffel Tower!"

Carl and the girls looked at me like I just had the best idea that had ever been had by anyone, ever.

Carl exclaimed, "Let's go!" and with that we were off for the nearest Metro station.

***

The grass was soft under the Eiffel Tower and nicely groomed. We sat down and Dalya packed another bowl. It had gotten cool, since the sun went down and I sat close to her to share our warmth. She passed the pipe to me. I took a hit, passed it on and put my arm around her. She gave me a smile. I wasn't really trying to make a move; it wasn't that at all. I just wanted to be close to her. As cliché as it sounds, Paris is a romantic place and something about it makes people want to be romantic. Hanging out with Carl wasn't satisfying this romantic urge. To be honest, I wished that Sunniva was with me. It would have been really sexy and romantic. But, she wasn't and Dalya was, so I was going to live an innocent fantasy, a fleeting romance in Paris with her. She snuggled closer to me.

There were several guys walking around trying to sell things like roses and blankets and wine to the various lovers walking through the park or sitting on the lawns, to enhance their Parisian experience. I asked one of the vendors if he had any beer. He said that he didn't but if we wanted some he'd go get it for us. When he came back, he had six lukewarm cans of Kronenbourg. I gladly paid him ten Euro for his efforts and passed out the beers. Although, it was warm the beer couldn't have tasted better. I was sipping it under the Eiffel Tower, on my birthday, with my best friend and I was cuddled up to a beautiful young woman who had me stoned out of my mind of premium Amsterdam greenery. It was the perfect setting. There was even someone playing the violin somewhere nearby. The music carried through the still night and gave the impression that it could be heard throughout the whole city.

"This is great," I said, "I couldn't think of a better way to spend my birthday than this."

Everyone nodded their heads in agreement. Dalya slipped her fingers through the hand that I had around her and I pulled her in a little tighter. I was close enough to smell her hair. It had a fruity aroma that wafted over to me. I took in a deep breath to absorb the fragrance. It made me feel at ease and my body relaxed.

"Hey!" said Carl, "We never sang you Happy Birthday."

"It's not too late," added Camera Girl.

Dalya passed me the pipe and I took another toke.

"Let's sing to him," she said.

"You don't have to do that..." I began but they had already started.

I leaned back until my shoulder blades hit the grass, bringing Dalya with me. She stayed above me propped up on her elbow and looked down at me while she and Carl and Camera Girl sang. I looked past Dalya's gaze, straight up at the Tower and watched the searchlight slowly canvassing the sky from its soaring reaches. I could hear the violin's song lofting through the city from somewhere in the distance. I listened to its melodic beckoning and felt the music drifting me up on a cloud of euphoria. The lights of the Eiffel Tower glistened and shimmered like I had tears in my eyes. The Tower has a nature and character that far exceeds its aesthetic limitations. It is somehow, despite its bulkiness and audacity, a beautiful, inspiring monument.

When they finished singing, Dalya said, "Now you need a birthday kiss."

She leaned down and gently pressed her slightly parted lips to mine, kissing me slowly. It was the type of kiss you give someone you are in love with, although it obviously wasn't love. It was the moment, the perfect Parisian moment we were experiencing. She gradually pulled her lips away and looped her fingers through mine again.

"Now you need a birthday kiss," repeated Carl jokingly.

"Shut up Carl. I don't see anyone kissing you," I replied, joking back.

"You're gunna be when I give you my birthday kiss."

"Funny."

"Get him!"

Carl and Camera Girl pounced on me. Carl grabbed one hand with his good arm and Camera Girl grabbed the other. I started to squirm but they sat on me, holding me down flat on my back. Then Dalya jumped on me too.

"Et tu Brute?"

She gave me a cheeky smile and pressed a sloppy wet kiss down on my forehead. Then Carl and Camera Girl joined in. They attacked me with dozens of sloppy wet kisses soaking my cheeks and forehead. I struggled to get away from their bombardment but I couldn't get free.

When we finally left the park that night, we crossed over a bridge. On our way over, we stopped midway. I looked down over the railing and saw the Eiffel Tower's reflection in the gentle, rippling waters of the Seine. I was holding Dalya's hand and Carl came up and put his arm around my shoulder.

"Happy birthday," he said.

"Happy birthday," said Camera Girl.

"Happy birthday," said Dalya suggestively.

Happy birthday, indeed.

***

Paris was a great time, the city was beautiful and Dalya and Camera Girl made it all that much better, but there really wasn't much Madness and Insanity. It didn't take us long however to get back on track. After we left Paris, we made our way to Reims to see the famous cathedral there. After Carl and I had a tour and took a few pictures, Carl decided that since we were in the Region of Champaign we ought to get a few bottles of bubbly, because as he reasoned, "It's probably cheap here."

We walked back to a little shop we had passed on the way to the Cathedral. It was a quaint, little market that was filled with old world charm. From the outside it looked like it had a nice selection of beer, wine, cigarettes, magazines and basic staples. The door of the shop was propped open with a tall three legged stool. On the stool, there was a squat, mentally retarded man of maybe twenty or so thumbing through a video game magazine.

When we entered, he looked up at us over the top of his magazine. His eyes were obscured and magnified by his thick, dark-brown grasses, which had slid down to the very tip of his nose. He took an innocent, inquisitive glance at us and then went back to his magazine.

161

As we entered, we saw an old man standing behind the cash register. He appeared to be around eighty years old. He also had big thick glasses, only his weren't brown they were black and round just like Mr. Magoo's. However, it was evident by the way he squinted at Carl and me when we walked in, the glasses were still not strong enough for him to see properly.

"Bonsoir," he said, shouting in the manner that old people with poor hearing sometimes do.

"Bonsoir," I responded loudly.

Carl and I went down an aisle of bread and canned goods, to the back of the store, where they had a refrigerated selection of Champaign. There must have been fifteen different kinds, but much to Carl's dismay they were all pretty expensive.

"Fuckers!" he said harshly under his breath. "I'm not paying that much for this shit!"

Then he mumbled something under his breath about appeasers and collaborators that I couldn't quite make out.

"Okay, let's go then," I responded indifferently and turned for the door.

"Wait a minute," Carl said grabbing the cuff of my jacket to stop me. "I said, 'I'm not paying that much.' I didn't say we weren't going to get some."

And just like that Carl opened the refrigerator door and started stuffing bottles of the most expensive Champaign into his bag. I stood behind him, pretending to look at potato chips, to block the clerks view, although the poor old bastard probably couldn't see anything anyway.

After Carl stuffed six bottles into his backpack, he whispered for me to go pay for some potato chips as a front and he would wait outside. I looked at his bag. The bottles were causing it to bulge. I was a little astonished that Carl had the balls to take so many. Not that I was worried. That old man was as blind as a bat and probably wouldn't see if we took the whole fucking store. It was just that it was ambitious. I liked the cut of Carl's jib.

We both walked to the front of the store. Carl veered toward the door and I went straight for the counter to pay for the potato chips. I was just about to put the chips on the counter, when I heard an extremely loud, high pitched shrill coming from the direction of the door.

"AHHHH, AHHHH, AHHHH, AHHHH!!!"

It sounded like a woman being axe murdered in some 'B' movie. It was fucking awful.

I spun around quickly to see what it was. To my dismay, I found it was the man-child, blocking the doorway and screaming his head off at Carl. It became immediately apparent to me that he must have somehow known that Carl was stealing and this was his reaction to it.

Oh fuck!

"RUN CARL!"

Carl broke for the door, but the man-child grabbed him tightly by the upper arms, right where he had the big bruise from Pamplona. Carl let out a scream of pain and surprise, which was, I feel, an appropriate response to the situation. Carl's cry of anguish, however, seemed to exacerbate matters. It frightened the retard and made him scream again, which led to a downward spiral of complete fucking chaos. Agitated, the retard started shaking Carl, applying even more pressure to his injury. This caused Carl to scream louder, which of course caused the retard to increase his volume.

I couldn't believe my eyes. The commotion was un-fucking-real. I just stood there awestruck, like a deer in headlights, watching my friend in the midst of a scuffle with a mentally handicapped person, where they were both screaming their lungs out at each other. My trance was finally broken when I heard the cashier's voice. I have no idea what he said, but it caused me to snap out of it. I ran over to Carl and tried to pull the mongoloid off of him. I got behind the retard and threw my arms around his chest. However, I couldn't budge him. He was too strong; he had been endowed with some type of special superhuman mongoloid power, which was intensified, no doubt, by his rage.

When I realized that pulling him off wasn't going to work I gave him a flurry of quick, hard jabs to the kidney. In retrospect, it wasn't very nice, but fuck this was war goddamn it! And it did have some effect. He let go of one of Carl's arms and reached back to protect the spot I was punching. When he did that, I grabbed his wrist with both hands and spun him around, like a professional wrestler gearing up to bounce him off the ropes. Only unlike in television wrestling, when I let go of him, he didn't bounce back. He sailed backwards into a display of wine, knocking it down with a huge POOHF, POOHF, POOHF of bottles exploding, as they hit the floor!

Carl and I ran toward the train station as fast as we could, we didn't even look back. The whole time I could hear those stupid bottles clanking together in Carl's backpack.

When we got to the train station we ran straight for the platforms to get the train leaving next. There was no doubt the authorities would be looking for us soon. Luckily, there was a train just about to depart from the station.

The conductor shouted, "En voitur!...all aboard!" and we plopped down into some seats, exhausted and breathless. My head pounded like thunder. I wanted to say something to Carl, I wanted to talk to him about what just transpired; but, I couldn't even manage a single word between breaths.

The train doors closed and we were headed for a placed called Longwy.

***

Longwy is tucked into the Northeastern corner Lorraine. It's just a few miles South of Belgium and West of Luxembourg. When we got there it was early evening. I wouldn't have minded to put a little more distance between myself and the fiasco we left behind in Reims; but, there weren't anymore trains leaving until morning. Reluctantly we wondered off to find a place to spend the night.

Walking around that evening in Longwy, Carl didn't seem himself, for quite awhile. He barely said anything and was walking slowly, unconfidently. I think the stress had been getting to him. He came to Europe for the vacation of a lifetime and since he arrived he'd been: involved in a larceny gone wrong, hit by a bus and was the victim of a *coup de main*, if you will, by a mentally retarded vigilante. It was certainly the vacation of a lifetime; but, probably not the one he expected. Sure enough he was a crazy motherfucker, but there are limits. You can mentally prepare yourself for many of Madness and Insanity's consequences like hangovers, arrest, VD, even death; but how can one be prepared for getting hit by a bus and being pummeled by a retard? It's just a lot to ask of someone.

I knew he would be okay though because after we settled into a little wooded spot across the street from a small chalet, he popped open one of the bottles of the Champaign he had worked so hard to procure. The cap exploded violently from the neck of the bottle and was followed by a stream of white bubbles that ran down the bottle and soaked his arm.

"Goddamn!" he said, with wide, excited eyes as he licked the drips of wine that trickled down the length of his arm and fell from the his finger tips.

The Champaign was just what Carl needed to lift his sprits. It tasted especially sweet, not only because of the trouble we had gone through getting it, but also they were eighty Euros a bottle. By the time we had finished the sixth one, Carl was not only himself again, he was in rare form.

"I'm hungry," he said, as a matter of fact.

"Yeah, me too, but we don't have anything to eat."

He stood up, half stretching, half looking around like he was about to do something.

"What are you gunna do?" I asked.

He gave me a mischievous look that was accentuated by the fractured moonlight that shone on his face through the trees. He wandered off for a few minutes without saying anything else and I wondered if I should worry.

He came back about twenty minutes later with his arms full of grapes that he had stolen freshly from the vine.

"Nice one! Where'd you get these?" I asked.

He didn't even bother to answer. His mouth was already stuffed with grapes. I took some and devoured them greedily, stuffing a handful in my mouth at a time. The grapes were firm and sweet, they were perfectly ripe. A couple of days earlier they would have been too soft and not as sweet. In a day or two they would've split open. Carl and I discussed this. We decided that that was the perfect condition for grapes. It was the exact perfect time to eat them.

And the perfect timing for the grapes led me to think that about timing in general. I thought that there must be a perfect time for everything or at least a best time. That trip, for example, was at a perfect time. It was a perfect time to understand Madness and Insanity. I was like the grape. A year or two before, I would have been too soft, too naive to come to any reasonable conclusion or understandings about anything especially the force that was dominating my world. But then, at that time, I was ripe, I was filled with the juices of inquiry. The danger was though that Madness and Insanity was everywhere, even in a sleepy little town like Reims. Things were getting a little hazardous and I knew it would only get more so. It had to. That was the only way to get my answer. It was the only way to understand the how and why.

When I couldn't possibly eat any more grapes, or drink anymore sparklingly wine, I lied back on the ground, shoving debris aside. I caressed my stomach as pregnant woman would do. My whole body was surrounded by empty bottles and the handfuls of grapes we hadn't manage to eat. My mind drifted sleepily and I thought about the next day and the rest of the trip. Soon, I passed out and slept soundly, until I was somewhat rudely awoken.

Just after daybreak, I heard a car driving by slowly. I opened my eyes and watched it creeping down the road. It stopped and then reversed until it was parallel with us. A middle-aged man got out of the car and shut the door loudly. I reached over and shook Carl's arm to wake him up. We both sat up and watched as the man come over to our makeshift camp. He said some shit to us in French. It didn't seem very threatening, not that either of us knew what the fuck he was saying. He did, however, seem really irritated, nonetheless.

"Look guy," I interrupted, "I'm sorry, but I don't speak French."

"I see," he replied in English rather condescendingly. "Are you British?"

"No, no man, were from America."

He let my statement register for a second, "American! Ahhha."

He said this like it was of great importance, like it was the reason why we were doing what we were doing, like it was an explanation.

I flashed Carl a 'what the fuck is that supposed to mean' look and he gave a quick shrug.

"What are you doing here?" continued the Frenchman.

Apparently, Carl didn't particular care for his tone because he replied in a tone of his own.

"We were sleeping," he said, only he put the emphasis on the "were" part, like the Frenchman was bothering him.

Carl's remark made the Frenchman turn up an eyebrow. This almost caused Carl to loose it. He started raising his eyebrow back at the Frenchman in a mocking way. Then he gave me one of those 'what the fuck is that supposed to mean' looks and I couldn't help laughing a little.

The Frenchman became irate at that point. "Ah yes! I see you think that it's funny, but this is MY PROPERTY!! And if you think that you can come over here, to MY COUNTRY and do whatever you want—"

"Take it easy, take it easy. I'm sorry. We didn't know this was your property," I interrupted to calm the situation down a little.

166

"What difference does that make? You knew it wasn't your property and that you had no right to be here."

To be fair, he had a good point.

"Hey, I said I was sorry, so forget about it."

"No, me forget. No. You Americans think that you can always do whatever you want—"

"Listen," I interrupted a second time, "we don't think anything. If you don't want us here then we'll fucking leave, no harm done."

"That's right. You will leave!"

"What did I just say? I said we were fucking leaving."

"WELL THEN LEAVE!!!"

"We're leaving. I already said that."

Carl and I stood up, dusted ourselves off and picked up our bags to go.

"What about this stuff?" the Frenchman asked pointing to the empty bottles, grapes and other debris that had accumulated from the night before.

"What stuff?" I asked, pretending to be innocent.

"The bottles!"

"The bottles?" I said, acting dumb.

I looked around like I didn't know what he was talking about. When I spotted them I said, "Oh! Those bottles there?" like I hadn't seen them before. "I don't think those are ours. I know that I didn't put them there…Did you Carl?"

Carl actually pretended to ponder the question. He even scratched his head for effect. "No, I think that they must have been there when we got here."

"YOU BETTER PICK UP THOSE BOTTLES!" screamed the Frenchman. His face turned a reddish hue.

"What did I just say? I just told you they're not from us!"

"Well! Who then is going to pick them up?"

"Well! Like you said it's your property; I guess that means you'll have to do it."

With that Carl and I walked away leaving the guy with the mess, which was actually pretty big especially given the sort duration of our stay. When we got to the end of the street we saw a police car turn the corner and go toward where we had just come from. I figured that there was a good chance that the Frenchman called them on Carl and me. We made double time to the train station and jumped on the first train. It seemed like every time we left a town we had to get out of it as quickly as possible. It was a bad sign but it was also good in a sense. I was looking for Madness and Insanity and I was certainly getting it.

"You know," Carl said as we relaxed into our seats. "They should have put that guy in charge of the resistance. Then they might have had a little more success."

I had to admit to myself he had a point.

Vive la résistance!

One for the Books

The train took us out of France and into Luxembourg. We hadn't planned on going there; it just worked out that way because that's where the train went. Not that we were bothered. We were beginning our third week of the trip and had been roving through Western Europe aimlessly anyway. Luxembourg seemed as good a place as anywhere else and it actually turned out to be pretty nice.

We only spent two days there, but managed to see a good portion of the capital. It seemed like one of those places from antiquity that was revered for its great wealth and dutiful, just governance. It seemed like the kind of place that maybe a poet or philosopher might have happened across and described in superlatives. In many ways, it captures a quintessential middle-Europe Xanadu feeling. It's prosperous, safe and isolated in the mountains. It is idyllic, in a sense. However, for me it had a feeling of being too pristine. And that, that sense of beginning immaculate, is actually, I believe, an underhanded tactic of Madness and Insanity to suck people in and drag them down. You can get a feeling that nothing happens in a place like that. You can get a false sense of security and let your guard down. Once you let your guard down that's it. It's all over. The next thing you know Madness and Insanity has swept you away and you're stark naked in a cave holding a prostitute captivate with a kitchen knife, screaming incoherent strings of expletives at her.

This apparently happened a few days before we got to Luxembourg City. Anyway, that's the story we got from the lady selling tickets to us at the entrance of the seventieth-century cave fortifications that surround the city. It could have been complete bullshit, but after what Carl and I had been through recently it seemed plausible. Regardless of the stories validity, I wasn't in the mood to chance anything. I didn't want the horrible breed of Madness and Insanity that the knife wielder got caught up in to snare us when we weren't looking. That was something I needed to be prepared for first. My encounters with Madness and Insanity had been steadily getting serious. Carl and I had been trying to push the limits, but after the events of Pamplona and Reims I realized that the limits were a lot further than I ever imagined. To really understand this force, to really understand Madness and Insanity, a real concerted effort had to be made and that was going to take some preparation. I needed money and drugs, for sure. And, we were going to need some rest, beforehand. The last weeks had taken a lot out of Carl and me already, both physically and emotionally. A few days or maybe a week of rest was what we needed. However, the money was first on my agenda. I was in dire straights. Paris had nearly tapped me out. Between the hostel and food and admission prices I had spent my birthday money. All that remained was enough for a little food and possibly a bag of weed but that was it. It was time to call my parents.

I got to the phone when I knew my mother was home and my father wasn't. It would be easier that way. My mom was more susceptible to my ploys and I had come up with a good one for this occasion. All I had to do was use her maternal instincts against her. Of course, this was a loathsome and shameful trick, but I didn't really have much of a choice.

"Hello"

"Mom?" I said, pretending to be despondent.

"David?"

"Yeah, mom. It's me."

"What's wrong?"

"Oh, nothing…"

"David, where are you?"

"I'm backpacking…didn't dad tell you?"

"Yes, he did. Is everything alright?"

"I guess so…I mean, I guess it was…until yesterday."

"What? What happened?"

"It's just that, I had to, ah…go to the hospital…I had umm…like a reaction or something."

"Jesus! Are you alright?"

"I'm alright now but…you know…the doctor said it was real touch and go there for awhile. It hurt really bad."

"Oh, Davey! But you're okay now?"

"Yeah."

"What was it a reaction to?"

What was it a reaction to? That's a good question.

"Ahhh…They didn't know. They said it was probably something I ate."

"That's awful! But, you are okay?"

"I'm fine physically but…"

"But?"

"It's just that I had to pay the doctor…and now I'm stuck here without any money."

"Oh, my God!"

"Yeah…I ah…I haven't eaten anything for almost two days." I ventured pushing the envelope a little further.

"Oh my God, Davey! Why didn't you call sooner?"

"I didn't want to worry you and…you know, you just gave me money for my birthday…I don't know what I'm going to do. I'm really hungry and I had to sleep on a park bench last night."

"Ohhh Davey, I'll give you money."

"Are you sure, mom?"

"Of course! You need to eat! This is serious."

"I know…I just, you know…I just didn't want to worry you."

"How much money do you need?"

"Quite a bit."

"That's okay; just tell me how much you need."

"Maybe…five or six hundred dollars."

"That's fine, Dave. You know you can always come to me."

"I know mom. You're the best."

"I'll go right now and put some cash in your checking account. That way you can go get something to eat."

"Thanks mom."

"You're welcome. Bye."

"Bye."

I felt bad about exploiting her motherly love, but the five or six hundred dollars made that feeling go away pretty quickly. Now that I had money, things were going to get good. Madness and Insanity would be at hand.

***

Carl and I spent the next five days resting and keeping a low profile. We bounced around the Belgian countryside sipping fine ales and smoking pot that we had gotten from an old hippie we met in Brugge. That time gave us the rest we needed. We recuperated and prepared for our next stage of the journey, unadulterated Madness and Insanity. The time for games was over. I could sense the truth was near.

We were going to begin stage two in Amsterdam. It seemed to me to be the only place for it. The last day and night of our rest was spent on the battlefield in Waterloo. That is, of course where Napoleon was dealt the major defeat that eventually led to the end of his ruthless attempted subjugation and conquest of the entire continent.

Twenty thousand men were estimated to have lost their lives on the battlefield that day and thousands more were wounded. It was a horrific scene. Bullets and cannon fodder sprayed the field ripping bodies in half. Arms, legs, fingers, intestine, heads and brains littered the area like carelessly disregarded refuse. The earth was flooded with soldier's blood, pooling inches deep in places. Injured men wept like children, calling for their mothers. Dying men screamed and begged of deliverance and mercy, while other men ran and climbed over their bleeding, near lifeless bodies, digging their heals into them eager and frantic to slaughter more, all in the name of a power lust and greed.

The day Carl and I were on it, the battlefield looked much as it would have in the seconds, minutes, days, decades and centuries before the battle happened. It continues to look as it did in 1815, once the piles of rotting corpses were carted off and hidden in the earth. It is a series of amber wheat fields and verdant farmland. Ironically, it is a place of bounty and nourishment.

Carl and I found a nice isolated place to spend our time there. We set up camp on the edge of a wheat field, near some trees. The day had been exceptionally warm and we weren't motivated to do much of anything. We basked in the August sun, drinking bottle after bottle of warm ale and smoking marijuana for hours. When the sun was well down and the ale finally ran out, I stared up at the stars alone. Carl had passed out long before that. There weren't any clouds and the sky beamed with starlight. The vast emptiness gave me a feeling of insignificance and doom. I laid down in the wheat. The stalks yielded to my weight and I sunk down in them. I was hidden from the world above, incorporated into the wheat.

It was eerie sleeping in a place like that, a field of carnage and pain, where so many had died. I closed my eyes and listened to the sounds around me. There were whispering screams in the night and a muted POP POP POP, a haunting crackle of gunfire echoing through the nakedness of the field.

I began to drift off to sleep and as I did I could sense the gray soldier-ghosts of the field gathering around. They ethereally encircled me with empty hands and ancient wounds. Standing with bowed heads and sad eyes, they looked down at my motionless, slumbering body and no doubt mistook me for one of their own.

Waterloo is a perfect example of the stupidity and futility of humankind. It shows us how the desires of a single man can betray logic and decency and lead to actions most can never and will never understand. How else but the betrayal of logic and decency could you explain what went on there? How else could you explain the presence of two grown men, on a quest for something they don't understand, sleeping in the middle of a wheat field?

***

All the travel guide books talk about how pot and other 'soft drugs' really aren't legal in Amsterdam. They say they fall into some weird legal conundrum where it's not exactly legal but the police can't do fuck all about it. The precise legal status made no difference to me. I didn't get wrapped up in all the jurisprudence nonsense. I just liked buying marijuana in bars and coffee shops.

Carl and I were quiet on the way there. It was, to risk sounding cliché, the calm before the storm. We sat in seats that faced each other, but gazed out the window in silent anticipation like soldiers moving into battle. As we entered the city, the train passed by a harbor filled with boats peacefully rocking in the water. The sun was shining brightly down. It reflected off the water and gave the harbor a warm and tranquil feeling. It reminded me of the harbors on the Eastern shores of Lake Michigan.

"Look at those boats man. I wish we had one of those boats," I said to Carl.

He shook his head in agreement, "That would be nice."

When we arrived at the station, I was a little surprised by the level of activity there. It was busier than any other train station of the same size we had seen. And not only was it busy, there were tons of fucking cops everywhere. At first, I thought that there must have been some kind of event or episode or something to that effect, but when I watched more closely I could tell they weren't doing any kind of investigation or making any arrests. They were just walking around, making their presence known. This was obviously a measure to prevent crime in the train station.

Amsterdam has quite the reputation for pick-pockets and bag snatchers. So in an effort to combat this image, the city put tons of pigs in the train station, which actually had a dramatic impact. Crime was lessened considerably. Unfortunately, this reduction can only be seen inside the train station. The rest of the city is still a good place to get ripped off or for that matter fall victim to more heinous crimes like organ harvesting. But, I guess that's all part of Amsterdam's charm. I didn't give a shit

173

though. I didn't go there to buy a kidney. I went there to get all fucked up.

When we left the train station, I was really taken aback by the number of derelicts around, mostly congregated in small groups. Granted it probably wasn't anywhere near the amount someplace like Detroit or Flint would have, but it certainly seemed like a lot for a socialized Western European country. With so many homeless people around, Carl and I decided that it probably wouldn't be safe to sleep rough in a place like that. Besides, as Carl put it, "All the good spots are probably already taken."

We didn't have to go far to find a place to stay. As we were standing around in front of the train station thinking about where to go next, a guy wearing jean shorts and a t-shirt came up to us with a couple of brochures.

"You guys looking for a place to stay?" he said with an accent that I wasn't able to place.

I looked at Carl and shrugged my shoulders.

"I guess so," Carl said undecidedly.

"Well here, look at this."

He handed us each a brochure, but I didn't bother to look at mine.

"I work for a place called the New Amsterdam and it's just around the corner—"

"What are you talk'en about? I thought the harbor is around the corner," I interrupted.

"Yes, the New Amsterdam is a boatel."

"A what?"

"A boatel."

"What the fuck is that?"

"It's like a hotel only on a boat. See?"

He pointed to the brochure in my hand. On the cover was a picture of a boat.

I turned to Carl. "What daya think? You wanna take a look?"

"Yeah, we can do that."

And that was that. Only moments earlier I was talking about a boat and now we were going to stay on one. It was good Karma.

The guy passing out brochures walked us to the boat. From the outside, it looked kind of majestic. It must have been a good thirty yards long and was painted a regal white. All the railings and windows, from bow to stern, glistened and shinned too. On the stern, painted in fancy black letters was the proud vessel's name, *The New Amsterdam*.

She wasn't quite as nice on the inside, however. In fact she was a piece of shit. The rooms were only big enough for a bunk-bed and a sink. The carpet was worn down to the sub-floor in spots and paint was pealing from the walls. But, it was relatively clean and it was on the harbor and it was cheap as fuck.

We took a room.

***

We dropped our bags off in our cabin and on our way off the boat ran into a couple of guys that were staying in the room next to us. They started a conversation with us and asked if we wanted to go up to the deck and have a smoke. Carl and I went up and had a quick smoke with them. After they left we sat around for a few minutes staring out into space.

"So what do you want to do now?" Carl asked.

"Don't know, what do you want to do?

"We can go to a couple of hash bars and then go look at the hookers."

It sounded like a pretty good plan to me; so, we set off to find a hash bar, which wasn't difficult at all to do. The first place we went into was a hole in the wall, but neither of us gave a fuck. The bar had a couple of miss-matched tables with a whole array of random chairs. It was hard to say if they were going for an eclectic look or if the place was just a complete shit hole. Regardless, even if they were going for the eclectic look they didn't do a very good job at it. Nor did they do a particularly nice job on the decor either. They had a couple of Jamaican flags and some posters of Bob Marley ornamenting the walls. And they weren't even nice posters. They were old and faded and had hundreds of tack holes in the corners. To be honest, the place sucked; but, we were already there and what did I care if they place looked like it came from a garage sale.

Carl and I went up to the bar. There were four people standing around behind it doing absolutely nothing. As we approached all the employees looked at each other to see who was going to have the misfortune of doing some actual work. Finally, a 'worker' (and I use that term very loosely) stepped forward. He was a short, chubby, redheaded guy with a sort of dumbfounded look about him.

175

"Do you want to see a menu?"

"Sure," I said.

He took out a menu and placed it on the counter. He flipped it over a couple of times to show us that it had items on both sides. I wasn't sure if he did this because it took him ages to figure the menu out himself the first time he looked at it or what. I was already familiar with how a menu worked so I caught on right away and so did Carl. But I didn't want to interrupt his routine. Who knows his 'work' might have been a source of pride to him. I just wanted until he was done to examine the menu. On one side it listed all the beers and spirits they sold. The other side, however, was the real *carte du jour*. On it was the selection of marijuana. I wasn't at all impressed with the appearance of the coffee shop but I was impressed by this. There were at least twelve different types of grass. They had names like Island Lady, Wonder Women, Swiss Miss, Shiva (the destroyer) and White Widow. I hadn't expected a selection like that at all. It was like a proper capitalist market for cannabis. There were choices and competition and they had different prices which were, no doubt, regulated by the almightily invisible hand of the market mechanisms. It was the first time in a long time that I thought capitalism might be a good idea.

We ordered five grams of White Widow and two Amstels. We sat at a table in the far corner. Carl rolled a fat spliff and fired it up. It was a strange feeling to smoke openly in public like that. It was difficult to get use to the idea of not having to be somewhat discreet about it. But then again, I had been conditioned for over twenty years that what I was doing was wrong and thus something which should be hidden. Overcoming that amount of conditioning takes some time. It was liberating in a sense though.

Carl and I sipped our beers and were considering whether or not to get another when something came to my attention. We had been there nearly an hour and they had been playing Bob Marley the whole time. At first, I thought they were just letting one CD play all the way through, but that wasn't the case. They had the shuffle mode going and all the CDs were of Bob Marley. It didn't appear they were about to change the selection any time soon.

Now, I've got nothing against Bob Marley; but, for fuck's sake, I don't want to sit and listen to him for hours on end. However, a lot of Bob Marley fans do it. They just sit there and let it play over and over incessantly. It's enough to drive an average person like myself or Carl fucking crazy. Which, it did. We finished our beers and left to find a place with more musical variety. Unfortunately, we didn't have much luck. Every other place we went had Bob Marley playing as well. It was like a non-stop Bob Marley fest everywhere we went. After the third Bob Marley playing hash bar, we couldn't take it any longer.

"Let's go check out the Red Light District," I suggested.

**

When we finally arrived in the Red Light District it was dark and we were drenched from the accumulation of the slow drizzle. The District seemed to have a lot of activity. There were hundreds of people walking around. They appeared to be mostly tourists and not surprisingly most of them were men. There were a few degenerate, perverted looking individuals there, but not as many as I imagined. Mostly, they were your average backpacker or tourist looking at the hookers in the store front windows and going into the porn shops more for the novelty of it than to fulfill some depraved sexual fantasy.

Carl and I walked down the street looking at the women posing for perspective clients in small store front windows. The legality of the situation certainly didn't make the whole prostitution business any less degrading and exploitative, but fuck some of them looked really good.

"What do you think?" I asked Carl. "You gunna get one?"

"Nahhh...What about you?"

"Nah, I'm not sure it's a good idea...you know...it's just that I might have some ethical and humanistic reservations about it...It just seems sort of exploitative, you know?

Carl indicated that he understood what I meant.

"Besides I don't have enough money for it anyway."

**

In Amsterdam, you get something that they don't really mention in the travel guides. When you walk down the crowded streets shabby looking street people come up to you and whisper, "Coke...Pills...Speed..." You get this a lot. It's a major enterprise there.

Now, obviously buying drugs from some random fuck on the street isn't particularly clever, but I really didn't have much of a choice. I was in Amsterdam and it wasn't like I knew anyone there who I could buy LSD from. And LSD was all part of the plan, all part of stage two. I decided to do the only thing I could do in that situation.

177

After we were done looking at the hookers, Carl and I walked down a busy cobblestone street and soon encountered someone whispering, "pills, coke, etc." He was a big, black man that had long, dreadlocked hair.

I wasn't exactly sure what the proper protocol for purchasing drugs from these guys was, so I just made eye contact with the dealer. Apparently, I wasn't too far off because he made a slight motion, a quick jerk of his head. I followed him to a side street. Carl stayed back a bit. That way he could observe the whole scene and make sure that nothing went wrong.

The dealer and I were the only two on the side street. Carl stayed on the other side of the corner from us. In a clear, deep voice thickened by an African accident the dealer asked, "What do you want?"

"You got any acid?" I asked, beginning to feel a bit of excitement from the whole thing.

He shook his head solemnly, "No, but I know who. Come, you follow me."

He turned and walked away. Although I hadn't established any sort of deep or consequential relationship with the man, he seemed to be on the level. So, I followed him. It wasn't long after my decision to follow this drug dealer to an, as yet, undisclosed location that Carl caught up to me.

"What's going on?" he asked. Anyway that's what's came out vocally. What he really meant was "Are you sure that we should be following this guy?" He didn't have to say that though because I knew he was thinking it. Those might not be his exact words; but, they more accurately represented the slightly bewildered expression on his face.

"He said to follow him," I replied in an artificially confident way.

"Where?"

"He didn't say; he just said to follow him."

"Is it safe?"

"How the fuck should I know…I guess so. He seems alright."

"What do you mean he seems alright?"

"I dunno. He just seems like he's alright."

It was hard to explain but my instincts felt like everything would be fine. Carl must have sensed that as well because he gave me a shrug of his shoulders and kept moving. We never left the main streets as we followed the dealer, staying a few feet back so as not to arouse any suspicion. For fifteen minutes we walked until we came to a plaza with brick sidewalks and a large, stone fountain that held no water. There was

178

a sparse collection of people spread throughout the square. The dealer scanned it painstakingly looking for someone in particular. They were not there however. I felt slightly irritated by this, having walked so far and getting my hopes up. The dealer wanted us to follow him to another place, but I told him there was no fucking way. I wasn't going anywhere. I couldn't take much more walking. I was already tired. Following this guy all around the city was making it worse.

Persistently, so as not to lose the sale the dealer suggested for us to wait there and he would come back with the acid. This seemed like a reasonable compromise. I agreed and he asked me how many hits I wanted. I told him that I wanted five, although really I would have liked to have more. I just didn't want to get ripped off. It wouldn't have been hard for that fuck to give me little pieces of paper with no acid on them. And if he did, I wouldn't know until I tried it. By that time he would be long gone. So, I calculated the risk. Five would be forty Euros and at the worst I would be out that, but if it was good I could always get more.

The dealer said he'd be back in fifteen minutes. Carl and I sat on a bench and waited for him to return. After about forty-five minutes he hadn't returned and we were tired of waiting for him.

"You think he's coming back?" I asked Carl.

"It's been almost an hour already."

"Yeah, fuck it," I said, agitated.

We stood up and started heading back to *The New Amsterdam*, ready to chalk the whole thing up to a learning experience. Just as we were leaving the plaza though, we saw our dealer walking toward us. We waited for him and as he approached, he said, "Where you going?"

"Fuck man, I didn't think you were coming back," I responded honestly.

"I tol ya I would be back, I am a man of my word."

Very noble.

"You got the acid?" I asked eagerly.

He pulled a little, clear plastic baggy, no larger than a business card from his coat pocket and handed it to me. I took a quick peek and saw there were five little pieces of orange paper inside it. I handed him the money and that was that.

Carl and I headed back to the boat. We did make one quick detour on our way back however. We stopped for a couple of shots of vodka and another spliff at a coffee shop. Of course, they were playing Bob Marley. It was completely out of hand. We hadn't even been there a full day and already I'd heard more Bob Marley than in the previous two

179

years of my life. Carl was frustrated by this as well. We made a decision right then and there. We could no longer subject ourselves to the never-ending barrage of Bob Marley. We had to leave the city and we were going to do it the next day. There were two things we wanted do first though, stock up on drugs and go to the van Gogh museum.

When we got back to *The New Amsterdam*, Carl and I headed straight for our cabin. We were tired from walking around all day and smoking weed and drinking. I boosted Carl up on the top bunk and sat myself in the lower. I took my wet shoes and socks off and laid on the bed. I felt nice not to have their cold irritation on my feet. For some reason their absence really put me at ease. I closed my eyes and rubbed my feet together, warming them.

I started to fall deeper and deeper, closer and closer toward sleep. As I did, a Bob Marley song popped in my head. I was too tried to try to get rid; but, I really didn't mind anyway. It might have been my exhaustion or all the marijuana I smoked during the day but I didn't find it annoying. Despite being bombarded by his music for hours, it was actually soothing in a way.

Emancipate yourselves from mental slavery
None but ourselves can free our minds…

I drifted off to sleep as the boat rocked in the small wakes of the harbor and Bob Marley's words resonated in my unconscious mind.

…We forward in this generation triumphantly
All I ever had is songs of freedom…

***

The first thing I did, when I woke up, was drop one of the acids I got the night before. I didn't want to waste any time. I offered one to Carl but he refused. He said he didn't like the idea of taking psychedelic drugs that were bought off the street. He had a point but I didn't have the luxury to decline. I still hadn't come to grips with Madness and Insanity and I was getting anxious. Admittedly, there might have been some danger associated with drugs from people you didn't know but it was a necessary evil. Anyway, I wasn't that worried. The dealer was a man of his word. He said so himself.

Carl and I checked out of *The New Amsterdam* and stored our backpacks in the lockers at the train station, not wanting the hassle of carrying them around all day. By the time I put my bag in the locker, I could already feel the acid starting to work. Of course, it came on slow,

180

but even that early on I could tell it was good quality. The beginning pulsations of the drug were intense, inflicting my vision and cognition.

A man of his word.

It took quite awhile for us to hike to the van Gogh but we managed to smoke a couple of spliffs on the way and that made the time pass more quickly. By the time we got there, I really didn't need to smoke another spliff. The acid was kicking in nearly full effect, especially with the aid of the cannabis. Objects were bending and flexing. Inorganic objects became organic. Colors of every shade and value intensified in front of me. They flamed and glowed. I was completely fucked up and I knew it. I had a stupid grin on my face that I couldn't get rid of much less cared about.

We waited in the ticket line for a few minutes. When we got to the cashier, Carl had to buy my ticket for me. I was too preoccupied watching light reflect off the Plexiglas the cashier was standing behind. I knew I was in a state and yet couldn't do anything about it. At that point, I was just walking through this world yet mentally in another.

"Let's go!" Carl said enthusiastically, waving our tickets. We had gone into several other art museums during our trip, but I knew that this one would be better. Not only was I more loopy going into it, Vincent was my favorite artist. And of course, the museum wasn't just named in his honor it had the largest collection of his work in the world. I was certain that it was going to be an experience. I just didn't know what kind until I got on the long escalator that leads to the main gallery.

I let Carl go first and then carefully edged myself on the first step. We slowly ascended to the top which looked to be miles away. With each second that passed, I strangely found myself becoming more and more anxious and excited. I was eager to see the master's works. The drugs were making the anxiousness worse. They made me feel like I had been waiting years to see the paintings although it had only been a few seconds. I waited and waited as the top slowly, painfully got nearer. Finally, when I felt I could no longer take the suspense, my head crested the landing and I could see a row of van Gogh's self-portraits. Just then I heard an unfamiliar, ghostly crackle of a voice.

"Hello David."

Who the fuck said that?

Carl was the only person in front of me and I knew it wasn't his voice. I turned around to see who it might have been, but no one was there.

What the fuck?

181

"I'm in front of you," the voice said as if it was reading my mind.
I got off the escalator and looked around.
Where are you?
"Over here," the voice answered.
"Where?" I asked aloud.
"On the wall."
I looked up at the self-portraits in front of me.
Couldn't be.
"It is," responded the voice earnestly.
"Vincent?"

Now, obviously this was only a drug induced hallucination, but at the time I found it quite moving and authentic. To be honest, I don't remember everything he said, but basically it was an invitation for me to discover the true essence of his work. Essentially, he (by way of the voice just made manifest) offered to guide me through the galleries and help me to see and interpret the paintings the way he saw and interpreted them. Of course, I had absolutely no problem with this. It was, after all, a wonderful opportunity.

Vincent didn't explain all of his pieces to me, only some of them. But each one he did, I relayed his words to Carl. He was however, unenthused. He didn't listen to me, refusing to accept the fact that Vincent was speaking to me. Carl, no doubt, saw me for what I was at the time, a senseless, raving drug addict. I didn't give a fuck, though. I had important things to say, van Gogh had important things to say and if Carl wasn't going to listen to them there was plenty of other fucks in the museum that would. At one point, I gave a rather spirited oration on a painting called Still Life with Red Cabbages and Onions. I was explaining its pornographic and satanic symbolism and had managed to interest a decent size crowd before a security guard intervened. It was one of those old-timers who was probably a retired cop or something. I gave him some lip and was about to explain the significance of what was happening to me but Carl pulled me away. He took me to another gallery on the lower level to get away from the guard. It was a relatively small gallery with dozens of sculptures or varying sizes and mediums.

At that point Vincent left me. I'm not sure why, but I assume it was because there weren't any of his paintings in that particular gallery. I was a little disappointed by this. However, my disappointment quickly gave way to distress.

All of a sudden, I became acutely aware of the statues surrounding me. An eerie, hallow feeling filled my body. I could feel my heart pounding in my chest like a jackhammer. The hairs on my arms and back of my neck rose up. I stood panicked and frozen. I sensed danger. I panned the room with my eyes only. I watched the various sculptures, waiting for them to make their move, waiting for the immanent attack. Although, they remained still, they were threatening me with animation. One was particularly menacing. It was a human figure clad in a dark hooded cloak. He was about ten feet high but had his head bowed down so I couldn't see his eyes. I knew he was the leader by his size and his relative position amongst the others. I remained perfectly still. I didn't want any of them to see me or if they did I wanted them to think that I was just another sculpture. I reasoned that they wouldn't attack if they thought I was one of them. I stayed motionless for a few seconds while I planned an escape.

"Pist, pist, Carl," I whispered, "don't fucking move…They can see you."

"What?"

"Shhh, don't talk. Just listen to me and do what I do. On the count of three we'll make our move."

"What?"

"One…Two…THREE!"

I sprinted toward a nearby emergency exit and crashed through the door. The alarm wailed as the door swung opened. I ran out the museum and down the block as fast as I could with Carl giving chase. I didn't stop until I had gotten several blocks away. It wasn't until then that I finally felt I had put a safe distance between us and them.

It was clear by the look Carl gave me, he never even realized the danger we had been in.

***

After the van Gogh, it was time to stock up and head out of Amsterdam. We went to a hash bar and bought twenty-five grams of pot. Admittedly, this was a lot but we had been smoking weed like it was going out of style. For several days, we had been continuously high or at least I had. Carl, I think was beginning to slow down. It wasn't really anything he said or did, but it was in his face. He had had enough. All the Madness and Insanity was wearing away at him, which made sense. He had been getting the worst of it. Not only had he been hit by a bus and assailed by a mentally retarded boy, he had also gotten attacked by fleas the night we spent in Waterloo. Since then he had walked around scratching himself like an animal. I think he was a little relieved that his flight back to the states was soon.

Although, Carl was slowing down, I was speeding up. I was in rare form. To be fair, the drugs and alcohol and late nights had taken a toll on me physically, but mentally I was alive with energy. The rest in Belgium had done me wonders and for the first time since the journey began I felt like I was getting at the heart of Madness and Insanity. I was going to keep pushing it, too, even after Carl was gone. I decided to head up North, just myself and an arsenal of drugs to meet Mikko in Finland. This was another reason for the abundance of marijuana. I knew the ride up there by was going to be boring and somehow being bored and crazed on drugs is a hundred times better than just being bored.

After we got the marijuana, we went into a little head shop that sold all sorts of things, not only pipes and paraphernalia but also an assortment of different pills. They had amphetamine pills, sex enhancement pills, erection enhancement pills, pills to help you sleep, some which help you stay awake, pills to get you laid, etc. They also had pot seeds and psychedelic mushrooms.

I went up to the counter. There was an old hippy wearing a tie-dye t-shirt standing behind it. It looked like he had been there since the sixties. He addressed me with an American accent.

"Yes please."

I eyed the mushrooms.

"Hey Carl!" I yelled across the store. "Should I get some mushrooms?"

"Sure," he answered indifferently.

"Give me three packs of mushrooms, please."

"What kind do you want?"

"Ah, I don't know...What do you recommend?"

"These are my favorite."

He pointed to a row of packages that were labeled, 'The Philosopher'.

The Philosopher!

"Alright give me three of those."

He handed them to me and I paid him.

I was just about to turn around when Carl called out from across the store, "Ask him how many to take."

"Eat half the package at first...then take a little more every couple hours after that," the cashier replied before I had the chance to ask.

184

I thanked him and took the bag.

When Carl and I were outside, I took all the drugs we had and put them in my jacket pocket. It was one of those sporty jackets that have a big pouch-pocket that zips across the torso. Since I rarely took the thing off, I had been putting everything important in there: my money, bankcard, train pass, passport, and of course the drugs. The way I figured it, even if my bag were stolen, I could function, still keep going with what I had in that jacket pocket. They were the bare necessities.

"Train station?" Carl asked after I finished zipping my jacket pocket.

"In a bit, but first I want to get some more acid."

"Fuck man. You don't need anymore drugs. Come on lets get out of here."

He was right, I didn't need anymore drugs. There was plenty, for sure. But, that was precisely the point. I was pushing the limits.

"It won't take long man…then we'll leave."

Carl conceded and we headed back to the area I bought the acid, the day before. I looked for the Man of His Word, but I didn't see him anywhere. Since he was nowhere to be found, I was forced to take my business elsewhere. I didn't want to but I really didn't have much of a choice. I was slightly apprehensive about going to someone else, but then I thought, *What's the worst that can happen?*

Carl and I strolled down the street and waited to hear the standard proposition. Then it came.

"Pills, coke…pills, coke."

As before, I made eye contact with the whisperer of these words. He was a short, skinny African immigrant. He was wearing a dirty, yellow jacket that made him look homeless. Although, one could tell by his beard and the aging of his face, he was well into his thirties, maybe even forty; his height and build made him look twelve or thirteen.

He walked to the street corner and I followed him. Carl stayed a few steps back to keep an eye out again.

"Jhew wan?"

I could barely decipher his words. His command of the English language was perhaps functional but limited and his voice was harsh, raspy, and pneumonic. It seemed to reflect the harsh, worn-out, beat-down lifestyle of a derelict.

"Two hits of acid."

"Wha?" he asked exposing a row of decaying teeth.

"Acid. Two." I gestured with my index and middle fingers.

185

"Was this?"

"Acid."

"Axid?"

"Yeah two."

"Twenty euro."

What's this fucko trying to pull?

It was evident that he was trying to take me for a ride. I decided to turn the tables on him and take that fuck for a ride.

"Man fuck that! Eight. I'll give you eight." I said determinedly.

"No, twenty for two," he replied forcefully. Interestingly, his English had improved.

"I just bought two for eight yesterday."

This, of course was a lie, but I said it for dramatic effect. This guys was driving a hard bargain.

"Impossible. You ask anybody, I sell two for twenty! Everybody sell two for twenty."

"Eight."

"Two for twenty. Ask anybody."

I looked over to Carl who was about ten feet away, "Two for eight, right?"

He nodded his head in agreement.

"No, two for twenty."

"Then fuck it. I don't what them."

I started to walk away, but he put his hand out in front of me. "Wait."

He walked over to another African that was standing nearby. The other man was tall and lanky and had the same shabby street dweller appearance as the man I had talked to. Although similar in untidiness, the difference in theirs heights made them look awkward standing next to each other. I saw the tall one slip the short one something. The short one put it in his coat pocket and walked back to me.

"Here," he said reaching in his pocket and placing two blue tablets in my hand.

I handed him eight euros, stuffed the tablets in my pants pocket and walked away. We got about five steps and the tall guy jogged up to us.

"How much you give him?" he asked in a threatening voice.

Fuck! A hustle! Fuck! Okay, okay…don't show fear…act tough…

I turned and looked him in the eye. He towered above me and had a shaky, unpredictable manner about him. I was little concerned.

186

"NONE A YER FUCK'EN BUSINESS!" I said with the most hostile voice I could summon.

"How much you give him?" he asked again, less aggressively.

"LOOK, if you want to know, you ask that fuck'en guy!" I replied pointing to the shorter dealer.

The tall one stopped to look back at the shorter one and Carl and I continued walking. We got a block or two further when we heard, "Wait! Wait!"

It was the little guy again. He was jogging up to us.

"You owe me! You owe me!" he yelled.

The tall dealer had disappeared so, I stopped to confront the little one.

"Fuck you. I'll already paid you!" I said assertively.

"No, you owe me more."

"Fuck off!"

I was hoping that would do the trick but it didn't. He continued to follow us and I became a little more distressed. My heart started pounding a mile a minute. It was especially unsettling because I was all fucked up on LSD and marijuana and didn't have full use of all my mental faculties and motor skills.

He jogged ahead of me and stopped, blocking my way.

"You owe me twelve! You want trouble?" he said threateningly.

I didn't respond although my mind raced with alarm and anxiety.

"You want trouble?" he repeated this time less convincingly.

Of course, I didn't want any trouble, but even being as fucked up as I was I knew that that fuck didn't want any trouble either. If something happened I was pretty sure the police or whoever would take my side. But, that didn't remove the possibility of me going to jail or the possibility of that crazy fuck sticking me in the ribs with a screwdriver or something.

Again, I didn't respond. I decided that ignoring him would be the best thing I could do. Carl and I just continued walking toward the train station and he continued to follow, demanding money. However, I noticed something with every step I took. As it became more evident that I wasn't going to give him anymore money, he became less aggressive and the amount allegedly owed starting decreasing. After I noticed this, I seriously considered kicking the shit out of him and ending it. I was feeling pretty confident and wiry after my go around with the mongoloid in Reims. But, I decided not to. I was so fucked from the drugs, I wasn't sure I could. Besides, I didn't know if he had some type of a weapon or not.

He followed us all the way to the train station, nearly a mile. When we crossed the threshold of the train station, it must have become painfully obvious I wasn't going to fork over anymore of my father's hard earned money. He must have been getting desperate. I headed through the grand foyer, toward the lockers where our bags were. Suddenly, I felt a harsh tug on my sleeve from behind. I knew it was the African and didn't hesitate. I spun around with my other arm, and clocked him squarely in the ear with a big sweeping hook. My fist landed hard and there was a loud popping sound. Instantly, he was hunched over, his knees to his chest, clutching his ear in obvious pain. While he was down, I managed to give him a good kick to the ribs. He retreated to the fetal position still cupping his injured ear. I was about to give him another when I began to hear gasps of shock and horror. I looked up and saw people scattering away from the altercation. This caused a big commotion. Someone started shouting across the foyer and two cops came running toward me. The African saw them too and ran for the door, one hand covering his ear and the other holding the side of his torso where I kicked him.

You want trouble, you fuck?

It's hard to explain my condition when the police got to me. Physically, I was wired, cat-like, but mentally I was in a fucking daze. The drugs and the emotional excitement of the fight wouldn't allow me think strait. Everything was a confusing blur of sounds and images, a montage of strange, incomprehensible stimuli. I felt mentally adrift like my thoughts were traveling murky waters.

"What was that all about?"

The voice sounded distant, dreamlike. It was coming from one of the cops. They were both the stereotypical, big, bone-crushing, grain-feed Dutch country boy type. They made me very nervous. They looked like they might have had a lackadaisical approach to judicial due processes. They looked like the kind of pigs who might just handle a situation like the one I found myself in, by taking me out back and beating some justice out of me.

I tried to answer, to give some response, but my words failed me. "UMMMMM…"

There was a disconnect between my brain and mouth, a failure in my synapses. I couldn't get a word out.

"EHHH AHHHH…" I stammered, gripping for articulation.

The other cop interjected, "What are you doing here?"

I couldn't think of what to say. I'd been questioned by police hundreds of times before; but, this was the first time I was completely unable to respond. I felt helpless, inept and the more I thought about it the worst it got.

Again, he repeated the question and waited for my answer.

"I'm...Ah...I'm ah..."

Say something!

"I'm looking for my locker. I'm leaving..." I finally spit out, feeling a sense of relief.

The two cops eyed me over. It was probably evident what had happened. They almost certainly saw some dumb tourist getting into a dispute with a drug dealer once a week. They were probably sick of dealing with stuff like that all the time.

"You are leaving the town?"

I nodded my head yes. The two cops looked at each other trying to decide what to do.

"The lockers are over there," one said, pointing to them.

What a relief that was. I thought I was going to be in big trouble. I walked away and headed toward the lockers. Carl caught up to me and walked down the corridor. As we turned a corner to get to our lockers, I quickly took the tablets out, stuffed them in my mouth, and swallowed them. I figured the cops would follow me and I didn't want to run the risk of being caught with them. I didn't have to worry about the cannabis or the mushrooms and I knew they would never find the other acid. I had hidden it too well. But, I didn't want them to run through my pockets and find that stuff, so down the hatch they went. I knew that I would be completely fucked once they started to work, but jail would have been much worse. Anyway, I wanted Madness and Insanity and I was getting that for fucking sure.

We got our backpacks and like I predicted, the pigs followed us. They tailed us all the way to the platforms. We decided to take the next train out of the station. It was bound for Maastricht.

"Run out of town, again," I said to myself, as Carl and I boarded the train. My life was becoming a cliché, a reoccurring theme of alienation and banishment.

Carl and I sat in seats next to each other. I wanted to talk about what just happened, I wanted to remark on how fucking nerve-racking it was and what a close call it had all been, but I just didn't have the energy. When the train departed, I started to calm down a little. I closed my eyes and tried to relax. While reflecting on the events what had just transpired, I had a strange thought.

I wonder why this acid was in tablets and not on paper like I got from the Man of His Word?

I shrugged this off and fell asleep, listening to the hum of the train as it sped toward Maastricht, wherever the fuck that was.

***

Carl woke me up just before we got to Maastricht. He shook my arm and said, "Come on man, we're almost there." He didn't say it very loud; but, I bolted upright, frightened. I didn't know where I was. I looked around franticly, panic-stricken. Something didn't feel right. I didn't feel right. My heart was pounding uncontrollably and my whole body was filled with a tingling sensation. I felt agitated, like I needed to do something; but, I wasn't quite sure what it was that I needed to do. I couldn't think straight. Strange, random, irrational thoughts raced through my head. I became fidgety and stood up. I gazed up and down the long aisle of the train. The whole car was shrouded in a white haze. Carefully, I assayed the people in my car to determine if I was in any danger. They were horrifying. All of them were distorted like mutants. They had huge, disproportionate features. Their heads and hands were twice the normal size. Their eyes were enormous as well and had empty stares.

Cretins…no, not cretins…Oh Fuck! Aliens!

"You're not gunna probe me, you fucks!" I said to myself.

I quickly sat down, slumping low, in my seat so they couldn't see me. However, I could only sit for a few seconds before a feverish twitching in my body forced me to my feet again. I felt too vulnerable, cowering in my chair. I needed to move, to stand up, to get in a defensive position. I put my hands up and out in front of my face like an old style pugilist and waited, but no one made a move. I kept my eyes moving however, darting them around the car with constant vigilance. Suddenly, I noticed a familiar face across the aisle from me.

It was the old lady I talked to on the bus in Pamplona. At first, I thought it must have been someone else but it wasn't. It was her and I could tell she recognized me too. She was looking straight at me and had a disappointed, solemn face. Next to her was the grocery trolley I had seen her with on the bus. I caught a glimpse of something in her hands. She was running her fingers over it. It was rosary beads.

190

"Doña? Usted esta aquí. Porqué?"

"I say ta be careful. I say is no'tin but trouble. Ya donna lis'en," she replied.

Her words were accusatory and I suddenly became defensive. I felt like she wanted me to justify what had happened. I felt like she wanted an explanation of what I was doing, an explanation of my quest for Madness and Insanity. I stared at her but couldn't explain. She sat there, rubbing her rosary beads, agitated and waiting. My inability to respond began to frustrate me.

"Porqué?" she asked in a whisper.

I still couldn't answer.

"Porqué?" she asked again. This time there was anger, derision in her voice.

I just looked at her, silently.

"Dime!" she demanded.

"I can't tell you," I said, timidly.

"Dime!"

I felt my frustration welling up inside me.

"I CAN'T TELL YOU GODDAMNIT!" I screamed at her. I was surprised by the harshness and volume of my voice but it felt good, almost orgasmic. It vented my frustration in one immediate burst. It felt so good in fact that I wanted to repeat it. However, when I opened my mouth, I realized she was no longer there. She had vanished. I was staring at an empty seat.

"David...dude...what the fuck...are you okay..." The words sounded distant like they were coming through a telephone receiver.

I cautiously turned my head to see who was talking. To my astonishment, it was Carl. I had forgotten about him until then.

"Are you okay?" he repeated. This time his voice was clear and direct.

Am I okay? I wondered.

To be honest, I didn't really know at the time. I had to give it some thought. I sat back down and looked at Carl intently as if he might have the answer. He just stared back at me expressionlessly. I started to take stock of myself. I examined my mental condition first. I didn't feel bad at all. I was a little anxious and confused but that was it. In fact, I felt quite euphoric and extremely lively. Next, I assayed my physical self. I wasn't doing badly in that department either, except for my hand. It felt sore. I looked down at it to examine it closely. The knuckles were bright red and swollen. I pumped it open and closed a few times. It hurt but wasn't broken.

But why? I pondered.

Then, it started trickling back to me, the cops…the fight…the African…the drugs.

THE DRUGS! The acid…but this doesn't feel like acid…but what then? Cocaine? Couldn't be. I feel good but not that good…Speed? Maybe, but what about the tingling?

Then it hit me. The tingling, that type of sensation could only come from one drug that I knew of, ecstasy. Ecstasy would account for both the euphoria and the tingling.

But, what about the hallucinations?

I can't really account for that. It might have been something in the ecstasy, or the LSD I had taken earlier or even the marijuana for that matter. Mostly likely it was a combination of all of them. My system was saturated with drugs and it was starting to affect me mentally. At least I knew it was the drugs doing this to me though. At least, I knew I had been hallucinating.

By the time the train came to a stop, I had managed to control the hallucinations; but, I was still extraordinarily energetic and fidgety. Carl and I piled off and stood on the platform. We looked out over the tracks, out into the night. It was raining hard and a chill wind was blowing. Judging by the puddles on the ground, it had been raining for some time. Obviously, we didn't have reservations for a hotel and I was in no mood to sleep out in the rain.

I looked up at the departure board to see if we could keep moving. There was one more train leaving that night. It was bound for Liege.

"You want to take that train to Liege?" I asked.

"Where's Liege?"

"I don't know…Belgium, I think."

"We need to get to Berlin, at some point. My flight home leaves from there in a few days."

"I know we need to go to Berlin, but that's not a choice. We can either stay here in the rain or we can go to Liege."

"Alright, let's go to Liege. I don't want to sleep in the rain."

"Sounds good. We can head for Berlin tomorrow."

We boarded the train to Liege and sat down. As soon as I did, I became restless again. I started racking my brain for something to keep me occupied. As anyone who has ever done ecstasy would no doubt

192

attest to, being stuck on a train while you are rolling is about the last place in the world you would want to be. It is a drug that demands activity and motion and a train is transportation that demands confinement and patience.

I thought about things I could do to satisfy the demands of the drugs.

"I want to drink!" I exclaimed.

Carl shook his head in commiseration. "Yeah…me too. But, there's no club car on this train."

I looked around. He was right. There were only three cars on the train. We were in the middle and I could see that the two others were passenger cars as well.

"You know…" I said. "We do have that peach liquor I bought in Luxembourg City…the stuff that I got for my father…"

I opened the bottle and took a long pull from it. There was a slight burning sensation as the alcohol rolled down my throat. I relished the warmth and libation of the liquid, letting my whole body ease and relax then passed the bottle to Carl.

By the time we got to Liege, I was completely fucked up. We had finished the booze and the ecstasy had fully kicked in. I could tell the liquor had worked its magic on Carl as well. He was starting to slur his words and he had a clumsy, drunken manner about him.

"Fuck man! It's still raining," I remarked as we grabbed our backpacks and stumbled off the train. "Let's see if there's another train going somewhere."

We walked over to the departure screen and I looked at the times. There was only one listed, 01:40. I looked at my watch. It was 1:39! I looked for the platform number.

"Platform seven!" I yelled, "Hurry!"

Carl and I raced, drunkenly through the station to platform seven. The controller was already blowing the whistle when we got there. He saw us running and held the train for a few seconds until we arrived. As we were getting into the train, Carl nudged me and pointed to a small yellow sign in the window.

Berlin.

We had boarded a midnight express to the destination of dreams. It had worked out perfectly. We needed to go to Berlin and that's where the train was taking us. We couldn't have planned it any better, not that we had planned anything. But apparently, you don't need to plan things when you have good Karma.

We went straight for the club car and sat down at the bar.

"Fucking hell!" I said to Carl, "That's fucking amazing. We catch the last train from Maastricht and it takes us here and we catch the last train out of here and it takes us to Berlin!"

Carl replied, "Ohhh man! That's one for the books!"

One for the books, indeed.

***

I drank two beers before Carl finished his first. The ecstasy was at full force and it made the beer taste exceptionally good. I swished it around my mouth, then let it roll down my throat feeling the bubbles from the carbonation tickle it with thousands of tiny explosions. It was an incredible sensation.

We had been drinking for a good hour or two when the bartender told us that he had to close the club car for the night. I didn't want to go. I was having fun drinking with Carl and talking about the crazy shit we had been getting into.

"Ah man! Don't make us go!" I pleaded.

"Sorry," replied the bartender apologetically.

"Can we at least get some bottles to take to our seats?"

"Sure. How many do you want?"

"Give me eight beers!"

He gave me a queer look and came back with six 700ml bottles of beer.

"That's all we have left."

I paid the bartender and Carl and I set out to find some empty seats. We made our way to the economy section, because our passes were only good for economy seats when I noticed an empty sleeper cabin. I stopped in front of it. Our tickets expressly forbid us from using these cabins but I didn't give a fuck.

"What do you think?"

I didn't have to ask. Carl was already through the door.

I found a light switch and turned it on. The cabin was small maybe seven feet by seven feet, but it had everything we needed. There were two beds, one to the left and one to the right. Straight ahead were a window and a little table with cup holders. It was cozy. I pulled the door closed providing us with complete privacy. Carl handed me a beer and I stood, drinking it while I looked out the window. I noticed that unlike most train windows, it opened. I went over and slid it open. Air rushed into our room, circulated through the cabin and was sucked out again like a vacuum. I looked at Carl.

"Are you thinking what I'm thinking?" I asked.

He gave me a serious look like he was really trying to read my mind, "That's hard to say...You're not gunna jump out that window are you?"

"No, why the hell would you think that?"

"I don't know. You've been acting funny since the van Gogh."

"Don't be fucking ridiculous. I'm not gunna jump out the window...I gunna throw you out!"

"Jesus Christ, David!"

"I'm just joking for fuck's sake. Calm down. What I was gunna say was that we could smoke a spliff in here, if we leave the window open. No one would even know."

"How do you know nobody will smell the smoke?"

"Because the wind will circulate the smoke right out the window."

"Are you sure?"

"Am I sure? Of course! It's science goddamn it!"

He couldn't argue with science.

In retrospect, I should have seen it coming. I should have seen things starting to get out of hand. But, I didn't because that's how Madness and Insanity works. Although, even if I did see it coming, I wouldn't have stopped. That was the whole idea of phase two, let things get completely out of hand, push the limits and all that. It had been constant Madness and Insanity in Amsterdam and it was about to carry on. Like the tendency is, one spliff turned into two and then three... For hours, we sat around smoking spliff after spliff and drinking beer, pausing only when the train passed through stations. We didn't want to drawl attention to ourselves so when this happened, we turned the light off, put the spliff out and sat down quietly.

We had just finished the last beer and smoked our fifth or sixth spliff when the train approached another station. Like before, we shut off the light and sat down. I put my head down on my pillow and looked up at the ceiling waiting for the train to start moving again so we could resume our party. Carl sat upright, looking out the window. The train was stopped for a little longer than it had done in other towns and I started to get bored. Just to make conversation, I asked Carl what he was looking at.

"Nothing," he replied indifferently, "there're just a couple security guards out there."

Security guards? I thought. *That's weird.*

In the weeks we'd been traveling, I hadn't seen one security guard at any train station. Curious, I sat up and looked out the window.

"Those aren't security guards, they're cops," I said and laid back down, waiting for the train to start moving.

A few seconds later, I heard the train doors open.

"Now what's happening?" I asked.

"The ticket collector is talking to the cops."

I looked out the window again. The ticket collector was standing with the police. He was smoking a cigarette and they appeared to be joking around.

Hurry up.

I laid back down and stared at the ceiling for another minute, then Carl said, "Hey, look at this."

I looked out the window and saw the two cops walking toward the train.

"Looks like they're getting on," I said.

I lost sight of them when they got close to the train; but, knew they had entered when I heard the train door again. Carl and I gave each other a slightly concerned look. We could hear them walking through the corridor. Their footsteps were loud like they were wearing heavy boots. I suddenly became very nervous. I was thinking about all the drugs I had stashed in my jacket pocket and the horrible consequences of getting caught with them. I listened to the footsteps moving down the corridor closer to our room. My heart raced even faster than the ecstasy was making it. I anticipated my arrest and waited silently for my captors to come. But, the foot steps stopped somewhere down the hall and there was a banging on someone else's cabin door. I was relieved that it wasn't our door; but, I knew I wasn't in the clear yet. I didn't know what those pigs wanted; but, I knew I wasn't safe until they were off the train.

I couldn't make out what was being said in the other cabin, although I could tell that the tone was serious. They spoke for a minute or two then I heard the cabin door shut. I hoped that that would be it and the cops would leave but it wasn't. The footsteps got closer to Carl and me and another door was banged on.

Maybe they just had the wrong cabin the first time?

Minutes later, that door was shut and yet another one knocked on. The cops were getting closer. A sense of imminent doom crashed

196

down on me. It was only a matter of time. Carl and I looked at each other. We knew what was coming. We knew they would be paying us a visit. We smiled and gave a little laugh about the situation. We were so high, we couldn't help it. We were going to be fucked and there was nothing we could do about it. They were coming into our cabin and we were trapped there, helpless prey. They were going to find the drugs and lock us up. It was going to be a big fucking, unpleasant, messy ordeal which we could do nothing about. All I could do was accept this calmly and stoically.

I did consider throwing the drugs out the window, but knew it was a bad idea. I wouldn't be able to throw them far and when the pigs got off the train, they would see them and bust us for sure.

I took my passport out and put it on the table so I wouldn't have to dig through my pocket with all the drugs to find it. Carl took his out too.

"What should we do?" whispered Carl.

The police were now next door and I considered his question thoroughly while trying to listen to what was being said in the adjacent cabin.

"Let's act like we're sleeping," I whispered back.

Obviously, it wasn't the greatest idea I ever had; but, it was the only thing I could think of doing at the time.

Suddenly, BOOM! BOOM! BOOM!

Our door was thrown open and the cabin became saturated by harsh, invasive light. Standing in the doorway were the two pigs. All I could see of them was their silhouettes. They looked like giants, towering above me.

"English or Deutsch?" one demanded.

"English," Carl and I replied, cooperatively, in stereo.

The cop who spoke entered the cabin. He surveyed the room and scrutinized Carl and me. My heart pounded in my chest, worse than before, and I began perspiring. Carl and I sat up in our beds and waited for the cop to say something. Finally, after several nerve-racking seconds he spoke.

"Vhere zo you come frum?"

I had to bit my lip not to laugh. There was a comical quality about his accent. It was like it had come from a really bad or ethnically insensitive movie or something. He sounded just like Colonel Klink from Hogan's Heroes.

"America," I responded, holding in my laughter.

197

I picked up my passport and offered it to him. He stepped forward to take it and accidentally kicking around a few of the empty beer bottles. He took my passport from me, but just looked at the outside cover and gave it back.

"An zo?" He asked Carl.

An zo, Hogan? I thought.

I had to stop myself from laughing again.

The cop looked at the cover of Carl's passport and handed it back. Then he looked at both of us.

"Do zo belung to each uther?"

Do we what?

"Pardon?" I asked. I wasn't sure that I understood what he had said.

"Do zo belung to each uther?" he repeated, only this time I understood. Carl got it too.

Do we belong to each other?

I looked over at Carl and gave him a 'what the fuck is that supposed to mean' look. Obviously, he was trying to ask if we were traveling together, but the wording was so fucked up we almost lost it. Marijuana makes you want to laugh anyway and that question was funny enough by itself. It took every ounce of self-control I had not to break out into laughter.

I managed to maintain my composure, which was a good thing. I don't think that Klink would have found it as amusing as I did.

"Yes, we're traveling together," I replied.

"I zee," he said nodding his head.

Then he stood silent for a few seconds. I could feel him studying us, waiting for us to fuck up. Those were long seconds and passed painfully slow. I didn't breathe the whole time. I knew this was the moment of truth. He was trying to decide if he was going to harass us more or if he was going to fuck off.

Fuck off! Please…Please just fuck off.

Suddenly, he spun around to his partner. His motions were quick and direct.

We're fucked!

But, I was wrong.

"Zats good enough," he said, "Letz go."

I couldn't believe it. They just left. They didn't search me. They didn't find the drugs and I wasn't going to jail. It must have been a miracle. It was certainly good Karma.

The pigs left the train, the miracle train, and a few minutes later, we were Berlin bound once again.

***

We didn't sleep at all on the train. I was still under the influence of the drugs when we got off, but it was mostly the beer and marijuana at that point. The LSD had completely worn off and there were just the occasional lingering shivers of the ecstasy remaining.

Carl and I caught a morning commuter bus to the Potsdamer Platz and went to a café for breakfast. It was busy at that time of the morning; but, Carl and I managed to find a table.

"What day is your flight?" I asked after we had finished our meals.

"Wednesday."

"Wednesday? Are you sure?"

He fished his ticket out of his backpack and checked to make sure.

"Yeah, Wednesday. Why?"

"Because, today's Tuesday."

"Today's Tuesday? No shit?"

"No shit."

Carl gave me a quizzical smile.

"It's a good thing we got that train last night," he said.

"Yeah. You would have been fucked…So what time is your flight?"

He looked at the ticket again.

"Six, forty-five."

"Tomorrow night?"

"No. in the A.M."

I thought about that reality for a while, but the starkness of being left alone and even missing Carl was too much for me to handle at the time. I pushed it out of my mind. I didn't want to spend the remaining time I had with Carl distressing. I wanted to make the most of it.

"Alright, since this is your last day, we should do what you want to do?"

"I guess I'd just like to take a look at the city. We could walk around and see the sights."

"You just want to walk around and checkout the city?"

"Yeah."

199

"Alright, we can do that…but, first we'll eat these."

I pulled out two of the packages of mushrooms from my jacket. Carl looked at them hesitantly.

"Oh, I don't know," he said, "I got to catch that flight early…"

"Don't worry. What's the worst that can happen?"

I handed him a package and he examined it thoughtfully.

"How many do we take?" he asked.

I recalled what the cashier had said. *Eat half the package…*

"The guy at the store said to eat the whole thing."

Madness and Insanity.

***

I was really surprised how quickly the mushrooms started working. Whatever the reason, a short walk to a place called the Sony Centre, which we had read about in our travel book, was all it took for them to kick in.

The Sony Centre is a collection of eight buildings that all share a giant atrium. The atrium is actually a separate structure that spans the tops of the buildings, allowing people to go between them without being exposed to the elements. It looks like a giant parachute falling from the sky, creating a vast public space underneath. When we entered, we were immediately consumed by the enormity of the parachute. There were easily hundreds of people in there, but compared to the size of the structure, it was like ants on a hillside.

The noise of the centre was very unsettling. There was a cacophony of voices like in a shopping mall only they lofted high into the sky and bounced back down as muffled echoes. It was a constant pulsating drone that weighed down on us from above with an oppressive energy which penetrated my ears like a liquid. It was so oppressive I felt like my head and shoulders were being pushed toward the ground.

Carl and I made our way to the middle and sat down at a cluster of picnic tables. Carl looked at me with big, catlike eyes. I could tell the drugs were working on him.

"We got to get out of here!" he said.

His words had an urgency about them that made him seem on the brink of panic. It was no doubt a reaction to the drugs.

"You don't want to go into any of the shops?" I replied calmly so as not to alarm him.

"No."

200

"Why not?"

"I can't take all this goddamn noise."

"It's loud but it's not that bad."

"It sounds like death!"

"It doesn't sound like death…It's the drugs man. They're fucking with your head."

"I don't care. I know it's the drugs; I don't like it. We need to go NOW!"

"Alright…Alright…Let's go find a park and roll a spliff. You can calm down and we can think of something to do."

We found a park about ten minutes away and sat on an isolated bench. I thought about just rolling one spliff, but then decided to roll enough for the whole day. I got the pot and tobacco out while Carl looked at the map.

Within a few minutes, I had rolled nine spliffs and turned to see Carl's progress with the map. He was clutching it tightly like a student in drivers training grasps the steering wheel. He was also staring at it quite intently.

"You see anything good?" I asked.

"I don't know."

"What do you mean you don't know?"

"I can't figure the map out."

"For fuck's sake."

"It's difficult."

"Give it here."

I snatched the map from his hands and looked at it. I could tell right away what Carl meant when he said it was difficult. The lines representing the streets ebbed and flowed like computer generated depictions of gamma rays. The letters composing the street names crowded into each other and formed shapeless blobs. Not only that, the map as well as everything else for that matter was obscured by a light pink tint. I wadded the map up and threw it on the ground.

"I can't read this man…" I said defeated, "It's fucking gibberish!"

"So what do you want to do?"

"Let's smoke a spliff and then just walk around. We're bound to run into something good."

We smoked two spliffs, left the park and soon found ourselves wandering around a commercial area. There were lots of retail stores on both sides of the street and we were stopping periodically to look in their windows. We had just looked in the window of a watchmaker when I noticed my shoe was untied. I bent down to tie it and when I came back up, Carl had disappeared again. Amazingly, I didn't panic, despite the events of Pamplona. I just went to look for him. Luckily, it didn't take long. I discovered him a little while later, down an alley. I thought it was strange that he would be in an alley; but, I thought that it was even stranger that he had a rusted length of pipe about the size of a baseball bat in his hand. He was swinging it with his good arm in what looked like an attempt to flog a concrete wall. He had an intent, almost angry look on his face. Seeing Carl with that pipe was a little unnerving. I wasn't sure what he was up to or what could possibly be going through his mind. The mushrooms might have really had him in an unpredictable state. I approached him slowly so as not to startle him. When I got near, he stopped swinging the pipe and looked at me.

"I can't break it," he said, evenly.

"What can't you break? The pipe?"

"No, the wall."

"Why the fuck do you want to break the wall?"

"I want a piece of it…I want to take it home for a souvenir."

"Why?"

"Why?"

"Yeah, why do you want that for a souvenir?"

"Why, because it's history!"

History?

"What the fuck are you talking about?"

"It's a major symbol of the twentieth-century."

"This place is?"

"Yes. Don't you know what it is?"

"Yeah, I know what it is. Do you?"

"Of course! It's the Berlin Wall."

The Berlin Wall?

"What? No it's not. It's not even a wall you jackass. It's a building. It's a goddamn delicatessen…You're beating the shit out of a delicatessen."

***

After that we continued to wander the streets of Berlin. We had absolutely no idea where we were or where we were going. He just walked. When we saw something to stop for, we stopped. When we wanted to smoke a spliff we smoked one, regardless of our location. The

202

mushrooms had us so fucked up we didn't give a fuck about anything, laws, cops, decency, traffic, gravity. We were simply ambling in our own world. We would start in one direction and then for no particular reason dart off in another. We walked out in front of traffic. We circled city blocks two or three times before moving on. We went in and out of stores with no intention of buying anything. We were meandering fortuitously like the fish I had seen in Sunniva's fish tank. It was actually a lot of fun.

We zigzagged the city centre this way for hours until we found ourselves in a big public park. We were actually trying to find our way out of it, when we ran across a beer garden that was seemingly hidden in the middle of the park. We decided to get a beer and rest our legs. I sat down on a picnic table and Carl went to get the drinks. Even though there were other people sitting near me, I sparked up another of the pre-rolled spliffs. They had slowly been diminishing so I rolled a few more while I waited for Carl, smoking.

He came back with two gigantic, ceramic beer steins and handed me one. The beer was cool, cooler than I expected. I drank it quickly, letting it refresh my throat. After a few drinks I noticed something strange and wondrous. Electric shock waves were flowing through my body. I could feel them start somewhere in my back, run up into my shoulders and exit through my fingertips. Then as the energy exited my body, I saw it arch and explode in pink and purple sparks.

Fuck man! I'm electric!

It was amazing. I had somehow become a live electrical wire. I had no idea how such a thing might have happened; but, the possibilities of such a power were limitless. I considered telling Carl about it, but he would never have believed me. It was just like the thing in the van Gogh. I couldn't just tell him, I had to show him. I had to shock him and then he would be convinced.

Whoa!

Another electric shiver jolted through my body and exploded from my finger. It happened so quickly that I realized I had to time it just right to send the current into Carl. I felt another one come on and readied my finger. I reached over and poked Carl on the forehead with my right index finger. Not surprisingly he gave me a strange look. I felt the energy go though me and out my finger but nothing happened to Carl.

"Mistimed it," I garbled under my breath.

Another one hit me and I tried to send the volt into Carl forehead. Again, nothing happened. I couldn't figure it out. I had seen the charge bursting from my fingers with my own eyes. I decided to give it another try and put my finger on Carl's forehead for the third time.

"What the fuck are you doing?" he yelled.

I tried to explain but couldn't. Reluctantly, I gave up and had another beer.

After my third drink, I had to urinate. I stood up to find a place to go. When I did, I realized how fucked I had become. The mushrooms and all the marijuana were starting to get on top of me. I felt completely numb and had lost my sense of proportion. I surveyed the area around the beer garden and spotted a nice place to take a leak. I headed toward a cluster of bushes and trees. Under my feet, the ground had somehow lost its solidity. I felt like I was walking on the bladder of a waterbed. I didn't sink in, but I could feel the liquid sway underneath. I began to loose balance from the motion of the liquid earth under me. I had to extend my arms out, like a surfer, to keep my balance.

I made it to the edge of the bushes and pushed my way through the foliage and into a clearing. I suddenly felt very isolated, but a solitary peace filled me by being there. Everything was a vibrant green like I had never seen in my life. I heard loud chirping and looked to see where it was coming from. There were dozens of birds flying around me. But, these weren't normal birds. They were cartoon birds, the kind that fly around people's heads when they get hit by something. It was incredible. Not only were there birds, there were also Technicolor, cartoon rabbits and other woodland creatures hopping and frolicking carelessly around. Everything was beautiful and copasetic. I felt an intense euphoria overcome me. I never knew such a place existed.

This must be where they filmed Sleeping Beauty.

I unzipped my pants and started peeing. The urine had the hiss of a waterfall as it poured to the ground. An astonishing amount of liquid vacated my body. It pooled at first but then became a large river. It must have been as big as the Detroit River. Fish were jumping from out of its depths and doing flips in the air. The sun glistened off their silver scales as they broke from the water and hit the air. I watched the fish and listened to the birds chirping as the river snaked a path. It continued to stretch before my eyes, growing longer and longer until it flowed far beyond the park, far beyond Berlin, beyond Germany and Europe into an arid desert. It brought water to a parched earth and vegetation started to grow on its banks, exploding from the ground like fireworks. Then, vast fields of marijuana began sprouting from the soil. They grew into adulthood and flowered bountiful buds, in seconds.

I gazed out over the marijuana fields in awe. I couldn't believe what I was seeing. As I stared out at them, I noticed a dark figure, way in the distance trekking through the field toward me. He was too far to make out at first; but, as he got closer and closer, I recognized the dark skin and dreadlocked hair. Nearer and nearer he came until he reached the edge of the field. He stopped and waited for me to speak. I didn't know what to say. How would anyone know what to say to the ghost of legend?

Finally, he spoke.

"Hey mon, why don't you like my music?"

"It's not that I don't like your music—" I began but was interrupted.

"Just listen to the words," he said plainly and disappeared in a cloud of smoke.

After he did, the river continued to grow again. It got bigger and bigger until it was no longer a river. It was a sea, flooding everything in my view, until there was nothing but ocean and sky. There was nothing out there, that is, expect for a tiny, black speck on the horizon.

It approached me at lighting speed. From a distance, I knew it was a bird and as it got closer I could hear its wail, increasing in volume as it advanced.

"aaaaaaaaaaaaaaaaaaaaaaaaaaaaaavvvvvvvvvvvvvvvvvvvvvvvvvvvvaaaaaaaaa aaaaaaaaaaaAAAAAAAAAAAVVVVVVVVVVVAAAAAAAAAAAAA **AAAAAAAAAAAAAAAAAVVVVVVVVVVVVVAAAAAAAAAAAAAA AAAAA**," It screamed.

Then, with a flash, the noise stopped and the bird was in front of me. It hovered three feet from me, just above my head. Its hawk eyes were glassed over and I could see my reflection in them. At first the bird did nothing, but then it opened its mouth like it was going to shriek again. I braced myself for the noise but it never came. In a gentle tone, barely auditable, it spoke a single word.

"Aava," she said and flew out of sight with one powerful flap of her wings.

Aava, I thought. It was the word Helli had taught me. I stood looking out over the water and pondered it. I didn't know what the bird had meant and wished it would come back to explain.

Carl found me in the clearing. I don't know how long I had been peeing when he came. I had been too entranced to even guess. I know it had to have been quite a while because when he got there I wasn't actually peeing anymore. I was just standing around with my dick in my hand. I zipped up and Carl led me back to the picnic table. As we made our way, I notice my shoes were soaking wet.

The Expanses of Aava

Somehow, we managed to get Carl to the airport and he caught his flight home. It felt strange not having him around anymore. We had been together day and night for nearly two months. I started missing him as soon as he was gone. Not only was he a sound companion, he had been keeping me, somehow, grounded to reality. This was not easy and I wasn't sure if I could do it myself. Since Amsterdam, I was constantly grappling with the effects of varying combinations of drugs and alcohol. To make matters worse, I was also suffering from a significant lack of sleep. These things had taken a toll on me. I was becoming a mental cripple. My reasoning and judgment were deficient and I had started to have difficulty telling the hallucinations from the shit that was actually there. Carl was my only point of reference. He was guiding me though life during some of the more intense episodes. Now, all of a sudden, he was gone and I had no one to help me. I was a vessel sailing the narrow, rocky banks of Madness and Insanity and I now had no beckon. I found myself standing alone in the Berlin airport with no one, nothing to keep me in line. This was a freighting proposition. I had no one except myself and I was all strung out. These were not ideal traveling conditions; still, I had to go on. My trip was nearing an end and I needed answers, answers I was fairly confident that would to be found further down the tracks and hidden in my persistent chemical delirium. I had a huge cache of drugs and miles of ground to cover.

It took me two days to get to Finland. I stayed awake for almost all of it, smoking spliffs in the train bathrooms, eating mushrooms and drinking little bottles of alcohol, I stole from a refreshment cart just before I got to Denmark. I swiped them when the attendant wasn't looking. I was actually a little surprised I didn't get caught because I had stolen so many. I got eighteen or nineteen, which was close to half what was on the cart. There was a whole assortment, vodka, gin, rum and even some twelve year scotch. I drank them warm and straight not wanting to dilute them, adulterate them in any way. They were my fuel and I didn't want to compromise that.

I really didn't want to steal them, but I didn't have much of a choice. Things were out of hand and I needed the booze to calm my nerves. Since it was a long trip, I needed plenty and I didn't have the money to buy them. My resources were starting to dwindle again. They weren't dangerously low; but, I still had to be responsible about it.

I rode a series of trains all the way up to Stockholm. I'm not sure how many or where the exchanges were. There was nothing that distinguished them from one another. I didn't talk to anyone or see anything memorable. I just sat next to the window staring out at the blurry landscape and sipped my warm gin and vodka from the bottle. The only time I left my seat was to lock myself in the john and get high. When a train stopped, I'd move through the stations mechanically letting Karma guild me to another. It was like that the entire distance from Berlin to Stockholm, however far that might be.

From Stockholm, I had to take a ferry across to Finland. It was actually more like a miniature Love Boat than it was a ferry. It was called the *Europa* and was an overnight vacation cruise ship that traversed the Baltic between my city of departure and Turku then back. The *Europa* had all the amenities. There were several restaurants, an indoor swimming pool, a bar and even gambling. I was lucky enough to get a sleeper cabin free because the ferry ticket was included on my Eurorail pass. The cabin was in the lowest deck and I had to share it with two other people but I didn't give a fuck. It didn't cost anything and it was nice to have a bed and some people to talk to.

I had two teenage Finnish guys for my cabin mates. They were only about sixteen, but they had a couple bottles of vodka and spoke English so I ate a few mushrooms from the pack I had left and partied with them until they passed out.

After they passed out, I didn't want to quit partying, even though, I hadn't really slept in nearly three days and it was almost four in the morning. I couldn't go to sleep. I felt like I would miss out on something. I decided to take the rest of the vodka, go up to the deck and smoke a spliff.

When I opened the door to the outer deck, I was struck by a brisk gust of wind that almost forced the door shut. The deck was eerily vacant at that time of the night and the wind and chill made me feel even lonelier than I was. I walked all the way back to the stern of the boat and stood next to the railing. I took a spliff I had rolled in the cabin and lit it. The taste of the smoke was warm and familiar. I smoked slowly while I looked overboard. The Baltic Sea was swishing beneath me as the *Europa* chugged toward Finland. I listened to the hum of the engine and watched the moon's light reflecting brightly in the wake we were leaving behind as we raced toward the other horizon. The moon was full and lit the sky, like a paper lantern. I could just make out the Western horizon in its glow. There was nothing to be seen but sea and sky.

Aava, I thought remembering my vision of the bird.

I finished my spliff and drank the vodka as I stared down at the sea. I was thinking about going to Finland and reflected on my trip thus far. Then, I looked out further, all the way to the horizon and thought about Manchester, about Sunniva and Solis and the rest of my friends and of course Madness and Insanity. I thought about them for a long time, until my eyes began to squint and I was able to see out even further, even closer to the horizon. I looked out as hard and as far as I could and pondered aava.

I was awoken in the morning by the sound of the ship's whistle. It split the tranquility of the morning air, as we approached port and thrust me awake with my heart pounding. At first, I had no idea where I was. I wasn't in my cabin, for sure, or any cabin for that matter. I could tell that much by the sound of the people walking past and the cry of the gulls. Above me the sun shone through a canvas tarp that looked like a tent and I realized where I was. I was in a lifeboat. I had slept there, for reasons that are unclear to me still to this day.

I was groggy when I lifted the boat cover off and stumbled when I was trying to climb back on the deck. Luckily, I fell in the right direction and nothing happen. It was a close call and scared the shit out of me, but Karma was on my side.

***

When I got to Turku, Mikko was waiting for me at the dock. He had gone home for the summer shortly after the break in, so we arranged for me to pay him a visit. I hadn't seen him since he left Manchester and I was glad to see him. I was tired of being alone and he was a good friend. We greeted each other with a hug and he took my backpack for me while we walked to his car.

I sat down in the passenger seat and put my seatbelt on. The irony of using my seatbelt after just doing everything I had done on that trip so far did not escape me. With the buckle fastened, I rolled a spliff on my lap. I didn't even think about doing it. By that point, it was an automatic motion. It was simply a habitual reaction like smoking cigarettes. When I finished rolling, I lit it, took a couple puffs and passed it to Mikko.

"So where are we going?" I asked.

"We're going to the chalet."

"The chalet?"

209

"Yeah, my parents have a little chalet on the sea, it's quite nice. My grandfather built it."

We turned off the highway and crept down a long winding dirt driveway. It snaked for nearly a mile through a pastoral landscape spotted with birch trees. Although we where only twenty-five minutes from Turku, we were miles from anywhere. The car pulled up to a modest two story villa with white siding and blue shutters.

The chalet had a simple country design that wasn't much different than the summer houses I would visit in Michigan. It was situated atop a bluff and overlooked the Baltic thirty or forty feet below. Curving their way down to the beach were wooden steps that provided access to the water. Next to the house, there was a cedar hut looking structure painted the same white as the house. It was almost oval in shape and had a thatched roof that looked like pubic hair.

"What's that?" I asked indicating the hut. "It looks like a vagina."

"It's the sauna. My grandfather built that as well."

"Why did he make it look like a vagina?"

"It doesn't."

Mikko took me inside the chalet and showed me around. It had a standard layout, a couple bedrooms, a living room, kitchen, etc. Mikko showed me the bathroom last.

"You can wash up in there." He said, "You look like shite."

I hadn't really thought about my appearance before he mentioned it; so after I shut the door, I went to the mirror to see how bad I looked. Mikko was right. I did look like shit. I hadn't showered in days or washed my clothes in weeks. My face was chapped and burned from being exposed to the sun and wind. My hair was shaggy and my beard had become scruffy and long. My fingernails were long as well and the undersides were caked with black dirt. The liquor and drugs had also made an impact on my looks. My eyes were starting to sink in and had dark circles around them. The whites were a dark red, bloodshot web. I touched my face and ran my fingers over my cheeks. I hardly recognized myself.

I got to clean up.

I opened the medicine cabinet and went though it to see what I could find that would help. I took out some eye drops, a disposable razor, shaving foam, hair scissors and nail clippers. I set them on the vanity in a neat row. I took the eye drops first and put them in, blinking several times to allow the cool saline to soothe my irritated eyes.

Next, I trimmed my beard with the scissors and shaved my neck, in steaming hot water. I decided to leave the beard. I liked the look and feel of the course facial hair. It made me feel rugged and primal.

After I shaved, I cut and cleaned my finger nails, brushed my teeth and got into the shower. I made the water as hot as I could take it. Steam poured up around me and flooded the bathroom, like a thick, hot cloud. I took meticulous care to clean the filth and soil from my body and hair.

When I got out of the shower, I felt reinvigorated, new. I felt like I did when I first got to Manchester.

I got out of the bathroom and borrowed one of Mikko's bathing suits. I threw all my clothes in the wash. I found the smell was especially fetid in comparison with the fragrance of the soap and deodorant that emanated from me.

I found Mikko outside. He was sunning himself on the deck and reading. When he heard me he peered over the top of the book.

"So what do you want to do today?" He asked.

A smile crossed my face and I raised my eyebrows at him. "You want to get fucked up?"

We took a cooler of beer, my stash of weed and the rest of the mushrooms down the steps to the beach. We ate the mushrooms right away and rolled up a stockpile of spliffs for the day and night head of us. I wanted to get right down to business. There was no sense wasting time. I knew what needed to be done. I knew Madness and Insanity must begin again.

I stuck a spliff between my lips and pressed down letting the moister from my mouth dampen it. I lit it up and took a deep puff, releasing it quickly. I could feel myself get high, immediately. Actually, I was only feeling myself getting higher. I hadn't not been high for a couple of weeks and no longer thought in terms of being high or not being high. I thought in terms of being either fucked up or only a little fucked up. Only a little fucked up had become my normal functioning state. Because of this, my mental faculties had started to become somewhat inadequate. With my mental faculties down, I was forced to rely on my instincts instead. I was actually a little surprised that they were so good. With the exception of nearly falling from the *Europa's* lifeboat to a tragic death, I was managing quite well.

Mikko and I laid our towels down on the sandy shore and sat up looking out to sea. The water was a dark blue and contrasted with the clear, azure of the sky. There was a gentle summer breeze coming in

211

from off the water, bringing with it a saltwater mist from the Baltic. I took another toke off the joint, this time letting the smoke sit long enough for me to feel it penetrate every fiber in my lungs before I slowly released it from my nose.

I passed the spliff to Mikko and thought about the perfection of that warm summer day. The water and the sky were clear and I heard the squawking of seagulls in the distance.

"You see that shit?" I asked.

"See what?"

"Out there," I said pointing out in front of me.

"What, out there?"

"Everything."

"What are you on about?"

"I mean when you look out there, do you see everything?"

"Of course."

"That's aava, right?"

"Yeah. Where did you hear of aava."

"From Helli. She told me about it. She said it was the most important thing in her life."

"Aava is?"

"That's what she said…But I don't really get it…I mean, I know it's supposed to be like the sensation of looking out to sea right? But, she said you couldn't like translate it into English correctly."

"No, I don't think you can."

"Well, what's the big deal about it, then?"

"It describes the feeling of openness that the sea offers. It's like a freedom."

"Yeah, but I still don't get it…I mean, when I look out to sea, mate, I don't really get that feeling of freedom. I get the feeling of openness but, more like, I feel very small. I feel my smallness in contrast to the vastness…to the vast, opened, exposure of everything."

"Yeah? I'm just the opposite. I feel very small when I'm on the water and look back at the shore."

"Why's that?"

"I'm not sure…I think it's because on shore there's societies and rules and that shite. So, I feel smaller looking at land because I'm confined by rules and regulations and norms."

"Yeah, but mate, there's rules in the water as well."

"There are…but not really. I mean, for the most part if you go out in a boat that's a distance offshore, no one can fuck with you. You just do whatever the fuck you want."

"But, you can do that on land as well."

"Fair enough, but you can't really do whatever the fuck you want. You can push the limits of acceptability but that's not the same thing. Take Solis for example. That guy doesn't give a fuck and he still conforms in some manner."

"Fair enough. You know, mate, that's what Madness and Insanity is all about. Doing whatever the fuck you want…like the night we were doing blow on the bus. That was complete Madness and Insanity."

"Yeah, but Madness and Insanity is only a response to the rules of society that we don't like. If there were no rules, then there wouldn't be any Madness and Insanity…Out there, mate, there are no rules or laws or society. No Madness and Insanity either…There's just aava."

***

When we left the beach, it was late afternoon. We spent a good portion of the day lying out in the sun smoking spliffs, drinking beer and tripping off the mushrooms. I had a good time. It was a nice relaxing day but, by that time, I was getting hungry.

"Fuck man. Let's go get some food!" I suggested after I had changed back into my now clean clothes.

"Sounds good mate…You know where we should go?" Mikko asked excitedly.

"Where?"

"Hesburger!"

"…What the fuck is Hesburger?"

"Ah, mate, that's right. You never had that. It's this Finnish place, like McDonalds only better."

"What do they got there, hamburgers and shit like that."

"Yeah, mate, they got hamburgers with special sauce and they got onion rings and chicken sandwiches and French fries. You want to go?"

"Fuck yeah, let's go!"

We dialed up a taxi and it took us to a Hesburger in Turku. It looked pretty much like every other fast food restaurant that I had ever been in. I was just about to bit into a Megaburger combo when I remembered that I had hidden away some acid from Amsterdam.

"Fuck man! I almost forgot. I scored some acid."

213

"Ah nice one, mate. Where did you get that?"

I told Mikko about getting the acid and what happened the second time, about the fight with the African, the police and all that. Then, I told him about Pamplona and Paris and fighting the retard and all the crazy shit that had happened to me and Carl. At first he didn't believe me; but, the sincerity in my tone must have convinced him.

"How did you get yourself involved in all that shite mate?"

"To be honest, I went looking for it."

"What do you mean, you went looking for it."

"Basically, I've been on a quest to come to some understanding about Madness and Insanity?"

"What does that mean?"

"Just what it sounds like, I've been trying to understand it. To see why it's always trying to trap me."

"Ah, mate, it doesn't trap you, you bring it upon yourself."

"No man, it's like a force of nature or something…I'm pretty sure of that."

"Is that right? And you figured this out on your quest for Madness and Insanity?"

"No. I already knew that."

"So what did you learn on your quest?"

"Nothing, yet."

"Nothing. Well what do you hope to learn?"

"I'm not exactly sure."

"You don't know?"

"Not really."

"How will you know if you find it?" he said jokingly.

"I'll just fuck'en know." I said becoming somewhat defensive. "Christ you sound like Sunniva…Just drop the fucking LSD and let me get back to my research."

I took two hits out of my jacket and gave him one. He put it in his mouth and I put my under my tongue.

After we ate, Mikko showed me the around the city centre. We saw a few points of interest, smoked a spliff behind a garbage dumpster and ducked into a small pub, for a drink. We sat at a table in the back corner. The bar was dark and smoky. It had some mirrored beer signs on the wall and dark brown lacquered tables and chairs. It looked like it could have been anywhere in the world.

There was a jukebox in the opposite corner from us. Two nice looking girls were pumping coins into the machine. They were both blond and had a typical Finnish look. They were tall, almost six feet and thin. One had slightly larger tits but both were highly attractive and dressed fashionably in tight blue jeans and denim jackets. I was just beginning to feel the first sensations of the acid rise up through my spine and neck when I noticed them. I looked at Mikko and could tell he was already in another world. He was gazing blankly at the wall behind me. I turned around to see what he was staring at. It was a poster of a woman in a swimsuit holding a bottle of WKD.

"What do you want to drink?" I asked.

He didn't respond and I couldn't be bothered to ask again. I just went up got us two beers from the bar. When I got back to the table, Mikko was still staring at the poster.

"You know, man, there're some real ones over there."

My voice snapped him out of his trance.

"What was that?"

"There're some chicks over there."

"Mate, I don't think that I could even talk to them. I'm really fucked right now."

"Nonsense! It's all in your head."

"I don't know-"

"Don't do this to me, man. It's early yet. The night is young; there is Madness and Insanity to be had tonight. I'm on a quest, remember."

"Fair enough, but if you want to meet those birds, then you have to talk to them."

I was just about to go to the jukebox and talk to the girls when I noticed them walking toward us. They sat at the table nearby.

"Hi." I said addressing them.

They looked at me and smiled. They seemed friendly and outgoing. I was encouraged by their smiles.

"You want to join us?" I asked returning their smiles.

"Sure." They replied affably, getting up from their table.

They sat down with us and I introduced myself and Mikko. Speaking with Americanized accents they introduced themselves as Johanna and Katja. By their pronunciation I thought that they might have had spent time in the US or maybe Canada.

We had a couple of drinks there and were having fun talking to the girls. They had actually been on exchange for the semester past in Ann Arbor and were relating some stories from Michigan. After awhile, the girls invited us to go with them to a club. They said it was going to have a live band and promised to be a good time. Mikko and I didn't have to discuss it. We all left the pub and started walking to the club. I could tell the girls were interested in us and we of course were interested in them. I was a little apprehensive about how it would be decided who was with who but it had actually worked out nice. Whether by design or Karma, Mikko and Katja sort of orbited toward each other and walked a few paces ahead of Johanna and me who were orbiting together.

I pulled out one of my pre-made spliffs and offered it to Johanna. She lit it up and took a few hits before passing it back to me.

"This is stuff is quite nice." She said.

"Yeah, I got it in Amsterdam."

"When were you in Amsterdam?"

"Just a few days ago."

"Why were you there?"

"I was looking for Madness and Insanity."

"You were doing what?"

"I was like, searching for Madness and Insanity."

"What does that mean?"

"It's complicated…but I'm on a sort of a quest…a spiritual quest if you will…for…like, fundamental answers to my life's condition."

"I'm not sure, I know quite what you mean."

"…Well, basically, I've just been getting all fucked up on drugs and seeing what happens…"

"And this will give you your life answers?"

"That's the whole idea."

"Well if you want to get all fucked up, like you say I have something for you."

She reached in her pant's pocket and pulled out a little sandwich baggy with some small white pills in it. She took two out, popped one in her mouth and handed me the other. I put it in my mouth and swallowed.

"Ecstasy?" I asked.

"Yeah, it's really good too."

"Thanks, nice one."

***

There was no line outside the club, so we walked right in. The club was long and narrow. In the front, near the door we entered from were some round tables and the bar. All the way in the back, there was a

216

stage set up a few feet off the ground with a large dance floor in front of it. A band was on the stage tuning up their instruments and getting ready to start playing.

"Should we get a table or..." I asked Johanna.

"No. I want to dance. Let's dance." She responded eagerly.

"Sounds good to me."

We asked Mikko and Katja if they wanted to dance; but, they said that they were going to sit down. Johanna and I left them to themselves and headed for the dance floor. There weren't many people on it but neither of us gave a fuck. We wanted to dance not be part of the crowd. The band had just begun playing a Bowie cover when we got there. We wasted no time, dancing like drug fiends as soon as we hit the floor. After a few songs, I was really digging the whole scene. The ecstasy was pumping through me and the LSD was too. The drugs were a good combination. They seemed to make the floor and walls pulsate and flutter, to the music. I felt like I was drifting a foot off the ground but somehow my movements seemed heavy and laborious. The colored stage lights flashed in front of my face like fireworks. The music thundered from every direction and rocked the insides of my body.

While I danced, I caught sporadic glimpses of Johanna. She had her head thrown back and swung her arms wildly as she spun in circles. It didn't appear that she even heard the music she was moving to. She looked riveted in ecstasy, both the drug and the emotion. Her movements were zealous, like she was performing a pagan rite or, like a pagan rite should be performed in her honor. She looked like an earth goddess, the earth goddess of beauty and ecstasy. I was filled with a pleasure of my own seeing her dance like that. I liked women who danced like that. Sunniva danced like that.

When the band's first set ended, Johanna and I each took another pill and then went to look for our friends. They were sitting at a table near the bar and had amassed a stack of empty shot glasses on the table. I could tell they were bombed. Johanna and I had a few drinks with them, until the band started playing again.

We went back to the dance floor and again started to dance, this time to a New Order cover. The second pill was already working and I was overcome by the effects of all the drugs and alcohol in my system. The music crackled and boomed though me and the lights cast colored confusion and disarray around the room. I tried to think straight but I couldn't. The lights were fracturing and bending like a kaleidoscope and all the shapes I could see were losing their form. It was too

217

overwhelming. I shut my eyes, danced faster and surrendered to the drugs. Suddenly, I felt a hand grip mine. I opened my eyes and looked down at it. Johanna had her fingers wrapped through mine. My eyes followed her arm up to her body and then up to her face. I was looking at her through the kaleidoscope. She had her head flung back in apparent ecstasy, like before. Her hair dangled in the air moving like water and shimmering like gold. It looked mystical or even divine. I reached out to touch it but the clusters scattered from my hand, eluding my touch. She let go of my hand and started spinning in circles. As she did, she faded in and out of my vision, as the room and floor and colored lights and bodies and instruments and vivid kaleidoscope colors conquered my sight, overlapping her and piling on top each other. I tried to focus on her, on her divine hair, but I could only see her obscurely, like she was an Impressionist painting or a memory. Then there was a flash of a strobe light and she was right in front of me only inches away. There was another flash and a noise, a dissonant cord on the guitar and Johanna was kissing me. Her hands were caressing my cheekbones and her fingers ran up into my hair. Her touch set eclectic energy through me, tingling in my organs and bones. I tried to concentrate on her face but I couldn't. All I saw were colored lights and flashes and dissolving images. I kissed her back and she pulled away. I caught a glimpse of her face but it was featureless. I tried to look again but she had disappeared in the kaleidoscope. I looked at the band and they had been consumed by the kaleidoscope as well but, the music continued from somewhere in the chaos of colors and splintered, undulating shapes.

Everything had become meaningless and bizarre. I realized then, how truly fucked I had become. The drugs had completely taken over. I was swept up in Madness and Insanity, but so far so that I couldn't even begin to ponder it. I was too fucked up to find my answers. All I could do was go with it, to keep my head above water.

Apparently, Mikko, Johanna and Katja were wrapped up in all the Madness and Insanity too, because when the club closed, we all piled into a taxi and went back to the chalet for more.

***

When we got back to the chalet, the party continued. Mikko mixed everyone some drinks and I loaded the disk changer and cranked the volume up as high as it would go. The Beastie Boys poured from the speakers, shaking the entire house. Mikko grabbed Katja and started dancing with her. They were clumsy from their drunkenness and had to lean on each other to support themselves. I sat down on the couch next to Johanna and watched them. Their bodies had a liquid quality about them. They looked like they were molten or rubber the way they moved and they left behind a trail of liquid color, like a comet's tail, when their positions changed.

I allowed my mind to drift and go further into the trip I was experiencing. Mikko and Katja's bodies disappeared and became nothing more than blobs of vibrant, flowing color. The warmth of Johanna's hand, massaging the back of my neck, brought me out of my reverie. I could feel the sensation resonate in every nerve in my body. I turned and looked at her. She had a reddish tint enshrouding her head like a halo.

"Are you there?" She said smiling, still in ecstasy.

I could feel the tiny vibrations of her words enter my ear and tingle in my head.

"Yeah…I was just…watching."

"Watching what?"

"Watching them dance…They look like they're melting."

Johanna gave a look that showed she had no idea what I was on about.

"Here," I said and took out the other two hits of LSD, "You'll see what I mean."

I put a hit on the tip of my index finger.

"Close your eyes," I whispered.

She shut her eyes and opened her mouth allowing the tip of her tongue to come out. I placed the hit on her tongue and felt her lips close around my finger. She took the other hit from my hand and put it on my tongue like I did to her. As it melted, I thought about how fucked I was and how much more I would soon be. The prospect had no effect on me whatsoever. I just accepted it as an inevitable fact of existence.

Johanna leaned back and relaxed on the couch. I put my head in her lap and she ran her fingers though my hair. We smoked a spliff, sipped our drinks and watched Mikko and Katja dance like beautiful fools.

"You know what we should do?" Johanna whispered as she stroked my head.

"What?" I replied dreamily.

"Let's go take a sauna."

When we walked outside, I was overcome by the sight of the sky. It was a *mêlée* of shooting stars and sparks and streaks of fire. The moon was consumed in crimson flames and there were blinding explosions of pure white light. I squinted to protect my eyes and stumbled sightlessly toward the sauna. I could hear the muffled sounds of the music hammering the night, from inside the house.

I opened the sauna door and could smell the cedar. I found the light switch and turned it on. Pink and purple and red, wavy lines streaked across the oval room. The benches bowed and undulated, in front of me. Johanna started the fire and the temperature rose quickly. We took our clothes off and sat on the wooden benches across from each other. I stared at Johanna breasts until steam filled the room and made it hard to see. Sweat covered my body in no time. Giant beads poured from me and emitted the smell of alcohol from deep inside my pores.

I was looking down at the tip of my nose waiting for a drop of sweat to fall from it when I heard a familiar sound. Although it was faint, I recognized it straight away. It was the screeching of the bird I heard in Berlin. It was a distance away but kept getting louder and louder as if it were getting closer and closer.

"Fuck! Do you hear it?" I asked.

"Hear what?" Johanna answered nonchalantly through the steam.

"The bird!"

"I don't hear anything."

"How can you not hear it? It's so clear."

"I don't hear anything."

"I have to go see it!" I said urgently.

My instincts told me that I had too.

"But, there's nothing out there." Johanna said, coming over to my bench, trying to settle me down.

"Yes there is. It's fucking close too."

"I think you're imaging it."

"I'm not. I know it's out there. I can hear it and I'm going to see. Stay here if you want."

I stood up but Johanna stayed where she was. I didn't bother to get dressed. I just flung open the door and jumped out. The chill of the sea air shocked me as I exited the sauna. I could hear the clarion call of the bird even better on the outside.

"AAAAAAAAAAAAAAAAAAAAAAAAAAAVVVVVVVVVVV
VAAAAAAAAAAAAAAAAAAAAAAAAAAAAVVVVVVVVVVVVVV
VVVVVVVVVAAAAAAAAAAAAAAAAAAAAAAAVVVVVVVVVVV
VVVVVVVVAAAAAAAAAA" it screamed; but, the cry was no longer

moving. It was coming from somewhere in the woods. I had to find that bird; every instinct I had told me so. I just knew that the bird had the answers I was looking for. I knew the bird was the key.

I headed toward its call barefoot and naked underneath the still exploding sky. I walked at first; but, the bird urged me faster and faster until I found myself running at full speed through the birch trees and shrubbery. Soon, I was deep in the forest and the burning sky was darkened into shadows by the sprawling limbs of the trees. I ran toward the cry trying to dodge the branches as they reached and clawed me. Some of them tangled me up and raked my body. I cried out in fear and pain. I could feel the warm trickle of blood from the scratches they inflicted. I followed the bird's beckon until I finally reached a clearing.

I saw the silhouette of the bird in the upper branches of a birch tree and was filled with joy and relief. I hunched over for a second to regain my breath then labouringly pulled myself up and stared at the bird. It cooed at me softly.

"Please," I began breathlessly, "please tell me."

The bird stopped cooing and looked down at me.

"What is it? What do you know?" I pleaded.

It opened its mouth like it was about to say something but flapped its wings instead. It hovered in the air for a second and flew slowly away as if requesting me to follow. I followed it, having to jog to keep up. We went through more forest and some open fields. It stayed just ahead of me tauntingly until we came to an isolated country lane. I stood in the middle of the road and the bird hovered just above me.

"Tell me!" I cried.

Again she opened her mouth and I waited for an answer. My whole being was consumed in anticipation. I longed for what I was about to learn. It was going to be the necessary fulfillment to my quest.

"I DON'T GIVE A FUCK!" The bird screamed down at me and with a powerful flap of her wings sped off into the night. It was going to fast and I was too exhausted to chase after. All I could do was watch as she disappeared into the night.

I collapsed, dejectedly on the pavement and just lied there until my breathing was normal again. I felt defeated and wanted to cry.

When I got up, I looked around and came to the painful realization that I had no idea where I was. I had been blindly following the bird and didn't know how to get back to Mikko's. I looked down both directions of the road but they were equally unfamiliar to me. I considered going back through the forest; but, I had no idea which direction to even start in. The prospect of trudging through the woods, naked and directionless was too frightening. I had to use the roads to find my way back to the chalet.

***

When I finally got back to the villa, the sun was just starting to shine through the trees. As I approached the house, I could hear the music inside, still blaring. I thought that everyone was still awake but they weren't in the living room. I peeked in the bedroom and saw Johanna and Katja asleep in the bed. The first morning light shone through the window and covered them like a shroud. They seemed to glow in the brightness. They looked so serene and beautiful. I shut their door and went to look for Mikko. I found him in the bathroom. He was curled up, in the fetal position, naked and shivering. The toilet and the floor next to him were covered in vomit. His clothes were scattered around the room also soaked in his sickness. There was a horrible odor coming from all the vomit.

I tried to lift him to his feet; but, he let out a sickly groan that told me it might be best to let him lie. I set him gently back on the floor and covered him with a blanket from the linen closet. I felt sorry for him because I knew what he had gone through. It was sort of a human devolution, a transformation into a more primitive beast brought on by too many drugs and too much alcohol. I knew that scenario very well. I had gone through it many times myself. It is a fulfillment of Manslov's hierarchy of needs, only in reverse. In Manslov's hierarchy basic needs are met first. After that, social needs are focused on. When you do too many drugs and have too much to drink just the opposite happens. At first you're outgoing. You're chatting with everyone and striving for social acceptance, but after a few drinks and a couple of spliffs, you lose interest in social acceptance. You start thinking about sex and that becomes your only need. This stage lasts quite awhile but at some point you have more drinks and do some more drugs and you can't even think about sex anymore. All you can think about is getting a pizza or some takeout. You start worrying about more basic human requirements like food and water. If you get more fucked up than that, so much so that you lose control of your faculties, you still somehow manage to meet the two most basic life needs. You keep breathing and curl yourself up in a ball to maintain bodily warmth. That's where Mikko was, so fucked up

222

that all he could do was act on the primal instincts to keep breathing and not freeze to death.

After I covered Mikko he uncurled himself and rolled onto his back. He stretched his arms out far to his sides and crossed his legs. There was a look of serenity on his sleeping face. The blanket seemed to make a big difference in his comfort.

I went back to the living room and shut off the music. The house became suddenly quiet and there was also a quieting in my head. I started thinking about chasing the bird through the woods and remembered how the branches scraped me as I ran. I examined my body and found hundreds of tiny wounds all over me. I ran my fingers over the scratches and dried blood as if I was searching for something.

The living room was one gigantic mess. It seems like the girls and Mikko had some party when I was out in the woods. I noticed my drink from the night before sitting on an end table. I picked it up and walked out the sliding glass doors that led to the deck. I finished my warm, watery vodka tonic with one swallow and set the glass down. The liquid felt good going down my parched throat. I could hear the waves crashing on the beach and decided to go look at the sea.

I stood at the edge of the bluff and looked down at the beach. I was reminded of the time I was in Greece and met Xia on that beach. It seemed so long ago, yet it was vivid in my memory. I remembered the vastness of the Aegean, the sexy curves of Xia body, talking about Camus…

I brought my head up and looked out into the vastness of the sea I now stood before. The sun had risen just above the trees. Its rays warmed my cold, nude body. I stared and stared out looking for nothing, until my mind became a complete blank. Then, an epiphany hit me. It didn't bowl me over but was more like a subtle revelation that came as a calm whisper inside my head.

Aava, I thought and was overcome by a strange euphoria. Mikko had been right. Out there, out to sea there were no rules and there wasn't any Madness and Insanity either. I realized then how truly beautiful that was. I had spent my whole trip searching for Madness and Insanity when I could have been looking for aava. This was a self-gratifying realization and I was struck with an overwhelming sensation to manifest it, an impulse the power of which I had never felt before.

I lowered my hand and started fondling myself franticly, tugging on my limp penis until it became hard. I closed my eyes and I felt the sea breeze on my face. The sun continued to shine down on me, heating my

223

back and shoulders. I no longer felt cold. I took a deep breath of salty air and masturbated rapidly to the sound of the waves below until I climaxed in immeasurable ecstasy, exploding my semen out into the expanses of aava.

***

A few days later, I took the *Europa* back to Stockholm, to catch my flight home to Manchester. I had been through so much and abused my body with so many chemicals, I was weary but complacent. I had run out of drugs the day before and was slowly allowing my mind and body to adjust to it. Sobriety seemed so strange to me. But, I found the lucidity of my thoughts refreshing. Everything seemed so much easier and less complicated.

I was happy to be going home. I wanted to see my friends and Sunniva again and to sleep in my own bed. The trip had, after all, been fruitful, a little dangerous, a little self-destructive, but fruitful nevertheless. Still, I was sad that my trip was drawing to an end. I would have to go back to classes and papers and deadlines and schedules. I had become accustomed to the freeness of a vagabond lifestyle. Not surprisingly, I really liked it. It was going to be hard to give that up.

When I got to my cabin, on the boat, I lied down on the bed to rest. I shut my eyes and felt the soft rocking of the vessel. When I woke up it was late in the evening. I got up and went to get something to eat. Afterwards, I decided to go into the bar and have a few drinks.

The bar was more like a small disco, with a DJ and a dance floor. I bought a beer and sat at a table at the back of the bar by myself. I took a drink of my beer and thought about taking Sunniva to Krö Bar when I got back to Manchester.

The DJ put on a song that I wasn't familiar with and I watched a group of thinly-clad teenaged girls go out on the dance floor.

I leaned back in my chair and sipped my beer. I felt the cool lager ease down my throat. In front of me were the dance floor and the girls dancing and the DJ and everything I could see. Behind me there was a window. Beyond that window was aava.

Anthony Squiers is a writer and literary critic. *Madness and Insanity* is his debut novel. Anthony is also pursuing a Ph.D. in political theory from Western Michigan University. His research is on the social/political thought of Bertolt Brecht. He lives in Portage, Michigan.